YONDER STANDS
YOUR
ORPHAN

YONDER STANDS YOUR ORPHAN

Barry Hannah

Atlantic Monthly Press
New York

Published simultaneously in Canada
Printed in the United States of America

FIRST EDITION

Library of Congress Cataloging-in-Publication Data
Hannah, Barry.
    Yonder Stands Your Orphan / Barry Hannah. — 1st ed.
        p.   cm.
    ISBN 0-87113-811-5
    1. Vicksburg (Miss.)—Fiction. 2. Murderers—Fiction. 3. Sheriffs—
Fiction. I. Title.
PS3558.A476 Y66 2001
813'.54—dc21   2001018846

Design by Laura Hammond Hough

Atlantic Monthly Press
841 Broadway
New York, NY 10003

01 02 03 04   10 9 8 7 6 5 4 3 2 1

Dedicated to

my wife, Susan,

and our

beloved captain, father, hero

Antel "Bud" Varas

(1917–1999)

YONDER STANDS
YOUR
ORPHAN

PROLOGUE

INSIDE AT THE WALNUT BAR LEANED THE DISAMBULATORY god of the lake. The man was both lazy and quick. Many sought him out.

You needed the luck, the stories, the bait, the clarity of the water, the barometric report.

The roadhouse was a mile from Eagle Lake, a plank box of one warped room a mile off the Vicksburg highway and up a piece of neglected gravel. It harked back to the fifties, when Vicksburg was wide open. Cecil and Robbie had been coming down from the Delta ever since the days of cotton prosperity. They remembered an era of state prohibition and the curious black-market tax and the Mulberry Street fleshpots. The river walk where bottles of cheap liquor and wine were sold in bathtubs, teenagers and policemen shopping side by side.

The lake was storied for bass and crappie, calf-size cats. Carp and six-foot saurian gar, and buffalo fish, which the poor ate fried in balls. Leon Jr. behind the bar knew all the fishing news. Spinners, plastic lizards, worms, jigs, live bait. What depth and what time of day. Leon Jr., whose father ran the roadhouse in the fifties, was no longer young himself, with a blond-gray stubble and sulking orange lips. He was neither happy nor sad from repeating the same stories. These narratives increased the cost of the liquor nearly twofold. All were aware of this. It was overpriced as if bootlegged, which it nearly was. The place was unlicensed, sometimes locked, sometimes open, depending on the whim of whatever sheriff at whatever season. Sheriff

Facetto, newly reelected, seemed to be allowing a month of Christmas.

The shelves behind the bar were bare unfinished pine, a few bottles of brown whiskey on them, not that many choices. Leon Jr. did have a rye and a single-malt scotch, sold in a shot glass and priced as liquid platinum. He had Jägermeister with its alleged opium. Some, meaning to fish, had fallen across the bar and slept the main part of business hours. Cold beer sat in a horizontal Coca-Cola watercooler, ancient, faded to pink and brown-speckled with rust. One large clear urn full of vinegar-brine eggs, a full carton of salt and a can of pepper beside it. No napkins. No chairs. No rest room except a deep path in the kudzu and gorse around back.

All this the parcels of its charm. Its absolute freedom from a woman's touch. An old-time titty-girl calendar on the bar side wall, perhaps from the beloved years of the Korean War, when it was daring. Miscellany of bar glasses with the imprint of loftier saloons, atmosphere of a careless desperation. A must-visit of the bass veterans, their sons, fishing sluts, grave trollers, for its promise of good luck and fine days on the water.

After all, some had died out there on the enormous lake, which would whitecap and roll dangerously in a gale. Some by lightning, some by heart attack, a few by suicide. Two game wardens blown nearly headless by a short twelve-gauge. And you never, never wanted the rare east wind to come on you. All at once nothing bit. Many men, black and white, vowed Satan was at work. For Christ was a fisherman and did not subtract from your allotted lifetime the days you spent on the water. Nobody spoke it, but Leon Jr. might be the version of Christ himself the Lord would give to the state of Mississippi.

Old globe of a gas pump out front. Sign of the old green dinosaur, Sinclair. God knows the actual gasoline it pumped nowadays. A screen door browning, worn blond at the handle, like a sacred stairway in Italy. One pool table to the rear, its felt used to almost gray as if violent football games had struggled over it forever. One stick in the corner, ulcered balls. Better a drunkard's napping berth than billiards. One man had a giant catfish fellate him there. He was not ashamed to return.

Leon Jr. was famous. He was the last to offer roaches for bait, kept in a cardboard palace and fed on his wife's cooking. Northwest corner out back.

Lately Leon Jr. had a newer cardboard box under the bar, a new wrinkle, videotapes stacked and unlabeled. He had been assured it was local talent, even though it was slick as Hollywood. What it did was open your eyes to the potential in this state. Peer about for talent.

This day Cecil and Robbie were at the bar talking seasons and waters, salad days, flush tented ballrooms on the levee, always the best bands. The Red Tops. The Tangents. Good old saxophone Charlie gone down in an overdose in New Orleans. They were three whiskeys in and almost weeping.

Now the villages from which they hailed were shut and dust-windowed. As if a neutron bomb had fallen on the towns. Only a ragged, sullen shifting of black folks back and forth from porch to porch, in their sections, on Saturday afternoons. Automobile wrecks up and down Highway 61 for little more reason than raw liftoff speed. Colonists in retreat from their Egypt, flat land uselessly rich still, its old profiteers scattered. Hunkering men turned to nagging barbershop hags, monologues about niggers, niggers and other niggers, beneath their talk a yearning for homicide, themselves included. Surrender to the old Shintoism where grandpas cruised in their Caddies, every stud one of them a kingfish.

Leon Jr. knew worse stories. Of men gone mad with religion and vicious with regret, mass conflagrations, graves. A camp for indigent orphans razed to the ground. He reached into the box next to his foot and brought up an unlabeled black videotape. Placed it on the walnut. "I got something new here, maybe up your alley, maybe not." Wiped the whiskey sweat from it. "You ain't the law or no deacons, are you?"

"Well hell no," said Robbie, older than Cecil and with sunspots. Four whiskeys in now, the two had almost forgot fishing, although their boat sat outside on its trailer fully suave and loaded as carefully as a space station.

"Fifty-five dollars. I'll throw in the sales tax."

"What show could be that good? Good hell, Leon. You got some new bass fool selling his miracle bait? It ain't even labeled."

"On purpose. It's some show. And I hear local talent."

"Local. You mean an appeal for some poor soul with no liver and no insurance," said Cecil, whose face got even redder.

"Boys, it's 'Teenage Lesbian Comedown.' That's why it ain't labeled. This here is professional stuff. Real slick and Technicolor. Either the law or my old lady caught it on me, wouldn't be nothing left of my free ass."

"You mean child pornography?"

"Well. You decide. There's titties. It's cultured. Violins. It starts them in big fur coats, mink or Asian-wolflike. You got some fine young nookie here, and it's like medical art, say. Don't have no secrets. Then a man come in, like they's ruler."

"You're changing, Leon," said Robbie. "Aren't you making living enough?"

"We're all changing," said Cecil. "Lots of us ain't making living enough. Give it here."

"You gonna buy it?"

"Sure. Who's the artist? Where do I get my money back if it's some dog or a fraud?"

"Now, that person has to remain unknown. But you ain't going to want your money back. Just don't invite the wife or the kids or the preacher over. This here is bachelor art. Still, one old boy told me he did invite the wife. Said it went just fine. There ain't no law, state nor federal, says what kind of home you got to have. That's why the good Lord made venetian blinds."

They walked out whiskey-righteous, and Robbie started the Jeep Grand Cherokee with officiousness, like a senator entering a filibuster. Then he spoke.

"I don't know. This place had a purity to it. Low-down but pure. I hate to see him join the common, I guess go modern, you might say."

"All those poor colorful folks we been watching all our lives and wishing they'd never change, Robbie. We thought they'd just grind it out and be our what, wallpaper. Pretty selfish, us old heads."

"You got a point there, pal."

"Nostalgia, shit, me too. I got it every second. Nothing new looks worth a shit to me. New houses seem like goddamn rest stops. We're dirty old men already, Robbie, face it. And even the dirt don't seem as tasty as it used to. Now the whiskey's talking, but I tell you. I'm willing to look at anything'll change my life before I blow this weary head off."

"Now, Cecil. Don't forget a big old she-bass snapping down a top-water plug. About sundown on your flat green water."

"I never meant there wasn't still a God, old son."

"Just wait'll God's back in the office. And Cecil, if she could stand this speckled old ass, I'm not averse to teenage love myself."

They both laughed. A sort of burned laughter.

ONE

THIS SUNDAY MORNING MAN MORTIMER AND MAX Raymond sat in the pews of the same church, a little white steepled one in a glen set among live oaks and three acres of clover. The jungle swamps encroached on and squared the glen, deep green to black. Loud birds and alligators groaning in their mating season roamed in songs from bayou to bayou. Some fish walked on land in this season.

Cars, just a few of them, sat on the pea gravel under the trees just outside the windows of ersatz stained glass colored like the wreckage of a kaleidoscope. Mortimer and Raymond knew each other then only by automobile. Mortimer favored a rotation of expensive foreign sport utility vehicles. Raymond drove the same old Lexus he had bought when he was a physician.

Raymond came to worship, and to repent, and he wanted a vision. Life heretofore had not instructed him. He had won his wife, a raven-curled, writhing singer of Latin jazz, in a ghastly way that wrecked him as a doctor. He was a dread-stuffed saxophonist in her band. Afraid of his own irony, his insincerity, his ambiguity. Now Raymond had come to repent. He loved Christ, but he yearned for a solid thing to witness, a vision undisputed, because his faith was by no means confirmed.

Man Mortimer was slightly drunk, a state unusual if not unprecedented for this quiet man, a gambler, a liaison for stolen cars and a runner of whores, including three Vicksburg housewives. He was small but substantial, with a big head of waved hair and hooded bedroom eyes. In high

9

school he was a dead ringer for Fabian but in recent years was verging toward the dead country star Conway Twitty. At forty-five he still retained his looks, and the women he sold kept a crush on him and liked his stares, which seemed to invite them into a dangerous ring of power. His charisma assured the women their lives were broad, deep and special, and that half the money in their adventures around the boudoirs of this poor county and in the lacier rooms of Vicksburg belonged to him. The law could not touch him because his bordello was spread in myriad chambers throughout the suburbs and even underpasses in giant, newish sport utility vehicles with flattened rear seats, good mattresses, sunroofs tinted by creamy smoke and fine stereo systems, the aphrodisiacs of new-car smell and White Diamond mist working side by side. These perfumes and compact discs were chosen by Edie, a gal Friday of his who otherwise worked as a blackjack dealer in the casino. His books on the car business were excellent, prepared by an accounting genius named Large Lloyd for his build and his hang, an ex-wrestler and permanent bouncer whose pride in his math and tax savvy was so wild it intimidated the auditors who had once looked into the business. Lloyd was a casino employee, chauffeur and gigolo. Man Mortimer owned three homes, and he gave parties, or mass appointments. He made a point of being nothing like Hugh Hefner, whom he despised for his philosophy and aesthetic pretensions. At Mortimer's parties there were no drugs, no guns, no liquor more than social.

The casino in Vicksburg was clean, even elegant, for these fly-specked counties, but its exits were full of ruined persons, many of them women. Edie and Large Lloyd could spot them and cheer them. Mortimer would appear in an exquisite sedan, as if happening in to end the night after some happy day with well-heeled Episcopals, and steer the women to their salvation. He knew the faces and the postures, and he never made the mistake of plying a busted gambler who was pious or gowned in unpurchasable pride. He couldn't afford noisemakers. On the other hand, he could take another kind of woman right off the arm of her escort, who was likely to be broke and puny too. For a man in such despair and trouble, the exit of his consort might seem merely another cloud in a black evening.

Mortimer had come to the church service in a spell of nostalgic spite. He wanted to see if the preachers were still as feeble and funny as they used to be when he was a kid.

The preacher was Egan, a reformed biker, gambler and drug addict, still with a ponytail, brown-gray, and a large black Maltese cross tattooed on his right cheek. A man immoderate in both callings, dissolute and sacred. He was preaching against the casino now, this nearby hell, a factory of thievery and broken hearts. He preached about hollow and slick men and slot-machine hags with no souls. The leering zombies schooled to rob the poor and sad in the name of fun. Worse than the liquor were the glamour and baying of Mammonites, who turned the soul into nothing but the arithmetic of want. His voice boomed out like Johnny Cash.

Then at the pulpit he tied off his arm with his necktie and injected a hypodermic into a great vein and plunged holy water into it, then withdrew the plunger, and they saw the pale blood in it. *This is what God gave us, not the green, gray dirty thing we call cash. Filthy lucre. Filthy, how the old scribe knew it.* Mortimer had to agree the man was good. A woman near him fainted and hit her head on the pew. None moved to comfort her, not her children, not her paramour in common-law union. Mortimer almost did, spying a piece of business, before he stopped himself.

Mortimer was a bit afraid of this loon high on his own rhetoric. The preacher looked at him and seemed to know him.

People used to have work, with their hands. But behold, the zombie of the empty, the Middleman, the parasite and usurer. God damns too the Usurer of the lost and confused man, especially his precious time, which is given to even the poor, so they might make a highway to paradise of it in their minds. Using your time, your animal want of sport and folly, and at the heinousest high percentage, oh fools, higher than the Carter administration. And you saw the crashed, blackened helicopters in the desert of the Holy Lands. You saw yourselves, paying those high mortgage notes! Handsome, smiling faces, the manicured hand out to clutch you in that old handshake with sick, sick ruin. And behind that hand with its rings and its Vaseline Intensive Care–lotioned palm and fingers, a heart deep cold and black as a well! I give you, brothers and sisters, evil passing for man. The bleached-blond son of Ham. But we know you. Solomon's robes can't hide you.

I see Little Las Vegas. Are you, sir, Elvis, Wayne Newton, Sinatra or the wolvine Michael Jackson, child eater? Those Las Vegas–greased and damned? Or are you only some shadow Lounge Punk, wanting to be big in lights? I know you, friend. I have been kin to you. Check your footwear and your belt buckle, Mr. Wannabe Caesar's Palace Puppy, oh you're sick all right. Do they call attention to themselves? Is your hair some kind of Goddamned Event?

Man Mortimer could not be dead positive whether the man was speaking directly to him. There were moans from others near by. But he would not look away from the preacher. He would drill him right back with his eyes. He allowed the fellow his moment. He had come to mock. Nostalgic, sporting, a bit tipsy. Now the man was way past that. He was good. He might probably be maimed. He might probably die. Mortimer had once killed, in a way. Without laying a hand on them. Not a little finger.

Max Raymond bowed his head, relishing the casino's condemnation, where people watched his wife onstage in her tiny dresses, her humid cleavage and thighs. He was her shill, he abetted her writhing with his horn. A jazz pimp, at worst. Her antiphonist.

Raymond heard the family beside him leaving after the service. A child asking, "Mama, who is Wayne Newton? Or Sinatra?"

"Old zombies with too much money," his brother said.

"Who is a good man?" asked the littler fellow.

"Your granddaddy. Billy Graham," his mother said.

"And Margaret Sanger," added the grandmother. "Was a good woman."

Ulrich lived alone at the lake but now, at Christmas, he was not lonely.

A bombardier out of England and over Germany for the Eighth Air Force, and a puttering aeronaut ever since, a tinkering veteran (though his only personal flight had been without an engine, some fifty yards during Hurricane Camille in 1969), he had thought science his whole life. But recently he had erupted in mourning over man's treatment of animals. And without gratitude to them either, a holocaust without a ceremony! Even primitive Laplanders gave solemn thanks to the animals for their own survival. He could not bear Napoleon's millions of dead horses. Nor could he forgive himself for the random horror he had visited on horses, mules, cows, deer and smaller creatures during the war.

He had no people, only a son back in Minnesota. He had been solitary a long time, and now another was present in his cottage. Death itself, which had a voice, which called to him not in English but he could hear it clearly, calling, saying, *It is not long, you can feel me, you know it. You've had plenty of time, plenty. And God knows, your wides of space, over Germany, France, back to England. You killed others before you even had a train of thought. You always wanted to go over and shake hands with those you bombed in the Eighth Air Force, but you chickened out, Captain Hypocrite. Besides, how were you going to shake hands with a horse or dog or kitten or lamb, those sad ones who never got to look up and hide, just stood there and had your hell all over them. As if nature itself didn't eat them up enough.*

Oh you're fat at the long table, stuffed with time, friends, your flat stupid brainstorms. Not long. You're going to shake hands with every dead thing. You recall you were a captain, a flyboy, an assassin's instrument barely beyond pubic. You could neither write a good check nor imagine any bill beyond a twenty. You had never had a decent woman's bare breasts against you. All you had was your dog and your model planes and good eyes and baseball. You weren't shit, and then your Minnesota yokel's ass made its wings and you commenced gloating over your own worth.

I almost got your blowhard ass again in that hurricane. You knew I was close, as close as your window with those handsome live oaks with their drapes of Spanish moss your retired old stuffed ass had bought into, flat nasty sand and the smell of dead mullet outside the window, that was me.

Well now you're fat, stubby, your spine packed down by gravity. Got emphysema, struggle about fifty yards without a blackout. I'm in the room, you can walk to me easy. Go ahead, light up another one, might as well make it an old Camel straight like you really want, and hack and hawk a spell, walk right into

These Old Arms. You know me, flyboy to aluminum walker, you've known me. It's always Veterans' Day over here.

For Christmas he mailed his son's family in Minnesota a Southern Gourmet Feast, a crate of tangerines and dry-iced jumbo rock shrimp. The son was back at the old farm with a gorgeous and pleasant Swedish wife and blond children, elfin beauties. They loved Ulrich and believed him to be a dear eccentric. Benignly senile, deafened to communication with any but the nearest friends, who whispered in his ear. They were unaware he was a fool who disastrously misconstrued aeronautical possibilities in his dreams of "personal flight." Which is to say, a minimalist backpack and propeller raised above the buttocks of the pilot by titanium struts and powered by a camshaft spun by a featherlight nuclear pack almost invented by a renegade physicist and airport bum in Huntsville, Alabama, with whom Ulrich was in correspondence. There were problems of torque in free fall and necessary wingspan and even of where to place the rudder. Reversing the prop for braking also brought the complication of chewing up the legs, ass and spine of the pilot.

This much had in fact transpired in Huntsville as Ulrich and the inventor looked not so much upward but more at tree level. The half of the pioneer aeronaut that remained brought a staggering lawsuit against the inventor and his philosophical adviser, Earl L. Ulrich of Redwood, MS. Though he lived, correctly, at Eagle Lake.

Ulrich had not told his son or his pals about this litigation, which he, the inventor and the aeronaut were just after settling in an anteroom of the courthouse where the Alabama magistrate declared all three rampant idiots who owed the scientific community an apology and a pledge to vacate themselves from his jurisdiction—a jurisdiction that now included all continental airspace into which they might in future hurl a human fuselage—forever. Ulrich rose and began an excursus in rebuttal, citing correctable errors quite obvious to them now, as if this project were steaming full ahead despite the judge, as the sad wretch with his artificial rectum and main colon gawked on from his wheelchair, until Ulrich's own lawyer hauled him away, then simply deserted him in a nasty alley near the courthouse. Cold, scrawny dogs drank coffee from Ulrich's large Styrofoam cup, and he knelt, weeping in sympathy for them.

He had not told his son he had the emphysema either, or that he continued to smoke seven long ones a day, against the expostulations of his doctor and the crowd who gathered at the pier. His son believed him to be happy, lucky, if misdressed, and a fine old geezer cheered by others of his kidney, who kept an eye on him that he should want for nothing. In fact he was poor, pitied and increasingly avoided. Some feared he was headed for a breakdown, many were concerned that he might be giving a speech and just die on them.

On Christmas Eve afternoon Ulrich waited in front of the paint and body shop for the boys in the Redwood garage to hammer out a dent in the door panel of his dear old woody wagon, a Ford he boasted he might sell for a little fortune on the West Coast. He had had wonderful trips and thoughts in this car. He waited and smoked, holding on to his walker with one hand, enjoying the nippy air. He dreamed of Minnesota, where the breathing would be easier. He thought of freezing at twenty thousand feet in a flak-holed and strafed B-17, damned near a flying colander, the .50-caliber shell casings rolling back and forth on the floor beside the head of the waist gunner behind him. Until they landed, he had imagined the boy was vomiting bullets the whole time. It might be that a small madness lodged with him then. Flakked, then strafed, by the first of the German jets in the war. Who was he to live, who was he to have madness, even to speak of madness, after the others dead who would give anything to be melancholy just once again? He was old, but he had no wisdom. Age bore him no rich fruit or gain, only the stare of inconsolable amazement.

    Ulrich watched while an odd vehicle came on toward him. A teenager in camouflage, speckled by acne in the face, rode an all-terrain cart across the front of which was tied a slain deer, its tongue out. The butt of a deer rifle rose from the frame in a hard scabbard behind his seat, handy to his reach. As the boy motored into the driveway of the shop, Ulrich saw the sparse and nasty whiskers around his mouth. A country girl came out of the garage, a high-schooler, with a body worker in overalls, greasy. The body worker held a rubber hammer. The boy on the cart was taken with himself. The deer flung over the hood, head and antlers down, the pink tongue out. Already the boy was spitting and acting as if this was not such an extraordinary deed. A killer with a sneer and a fine machine, that was about it. He spat. He could not help it, he was a stud with his booty.

    Ulrich trembled in a sudden revelation. The deer's full unearthly beauty. The punk who had turned it into trash. He was not poor, he was not hungry. He had driven miles to show it off. His bleeding trophy over the oily pavement.

    "Young man! I sense a wrong here." Ulrich left the walker and was soon at the seated boy, hands around his throat. Squeezing and squeezing to kill him. Choke the punk out of him. The boy could do nothing but claw and moo.

    The boy reached back for the butt of his rifle. Nobody had sprung to his aid. Ulrich released one hand and yanked out the rifle before the boy could get an angle on it. The boy was very hurt in the throat and his face was only now unbluing. He gasped. A rag doll, he fell to the concrete.

"This is a thirty-thirty all right, and a fine one. You strutting little shit. All this fine equipment. So much. Here, let me—"

Ulrich beat on the vehicle violently with the gun. Its hood, its lights, its rear rack. The telescope sight flew off, then smaller pieces, and finally the stock split, and Ulrich flung the ruined weapon off into the hard weeds in a yard next to the garage. Next thing, he mounted the vehicle and drove off, over the leg of the hunter. He roared out on the main highway awhile and made a turn for the lake, where they lost sight of him. He took the vehicle into the black deeps of the swampland, where only dogs or another ATV could pursue.

The hunter was in a condition beyond amazement. But he muttered, a sort of squall. "Crazy. Who *is* he?"

"That man is old, he's really old," said the body man, Ronny. "Man, that was some goofy-ass piece of work. He's off driving your ATV into them swamps, Percy."

"I ain't believing."

"He's done left his old woody wagon right here."

The girl had been giggling but trying to maintain her mascara and explosive dye job, newly teased, so you witnessed a kind of intermediate chemotherapy effect of the skull.

"What the hell you laughing at?" yelled Percy, holding his throat.

"Lookit there. He left his *walker*," she said.

"Damn. The man can't hardly breathe. This is one old sonofabitch who changed his life in fifteen seconds," said Ronny.

"I'll change him," croaked Percy. He spat.

"No you won't," said the girl. She had gotten sad. "You go hunt out that old man, one on one, I bet he'd walk out of them woods with your balls in his hand."

"Who the hell you think you are, Marcine?"

"Sick of this country is what. And all you puffed-up little dicks in it. All 'cause your daddies were too cheap to buy a good rubber."

"That's enough out of you now, Marcine," said the body man, lifting the rubber hammer as if he might do something with it.

"I'm sick of my name and I'm sick of my hair and sick of pickups and guns and y'all raising dogs to kick and people calling deer sonsofbitches and wanting me to settle down with them in some goddamn trailer home to breed more like them and—"

"Well, Big Missy Marcine. If you think you so wasted here, why don't you move on up to Vicksburg and sell what you got. I know the man can help you." The body man thought she was his.

"It'd be a step up," she said.

"And don't let the door hit your butt when you leave."

"That's original."

"Did anybody notice I'm hurt and robbed?" whined Percy, still sprawled on the concrete.

At the end of the doxology, Egan stood, a sinner. In his sweat he was miserable for his own former self as a drug mule. A methedrine bagman, a pavement thug. He himself had driven Mortimer's car years ago, although he had no idea whose car it was. He sensed something heavy and odorous in the trunk, but he was not paid to smell or reason. He was sent to get the thing below water in a twenty-foot pool of bayou at the rear of his uncle's land. A busted route of saplings and clipped post oaks was all there was for a path. He let it, a 1948 Chevrolet, below the chilly water, Missouri tag sinking, purple, at last. "Show me." Then he strolled back, sopping wet, to his chain-smoking uncle's house, careful to shout hello because the man kept a .22 Magnum rifle at his lodge. God knows what for, except for those who would poach or harm his many dogs and cats.

Egan's uncle was a decrepit Irish ex-priest, sent to minister to Mississippi, which the diocese described as a third-world country, forty years ago. The poverty of blacks, whites, the paucity of Catholics. But slowly he had turned landowner. His name was Carolus Robert Feeney, but he had long since gone by Carl Bob. He bought a lodge near Eagle Lake and made his peace with the lord of the coons, lynx, bobcat, armadillo and the rolling vinery of the lower Delta jungle. Now he was a pantheist and fairly profane in this faith.

His nephew Egan still loved him and appeared at odd times to make repairs to the lodge. In these chores he had found scriptures in the house and converted to Protestant ecumenism although railed at by his uncle, who now despised all churches.

Feeney loved Egan too. He nursed him through the jitters of several whiskey and methedrine collapses. The old man knew nothing of the underwater Chevrolet, as Egan knew nothing of its story. Neither Large Lloyd nor Edie, Mortimer's right hands, had any idea where it rested.

Scores of corpses rested below the lakes, oxbows, river ways and bayous of these parts, not counting the skeletons of Grant's infantry. The country was built to hide those dead by foul deed, it sucked at them. Back to the flood of

1927, lynchings, gun and knife duels were common stories here. Muddy water made a fine lost tomb.

It was just seven years ago Egan had been the driver who felt silent forms in the car seats beside him wanting to scream and party. When the car went under, he loved even the sweat on his brow. Done. The Christian antiapotheosis. *Now,* he said, *let's really get wasted, brother monkeys. Mister Me, I be dead.*

Two days later a deputation arrived at the body shop in Redwood. Dr. Harvard and Melanie Wooten in the front seat of her station wagon. The culprit Ulrich in the back, hangdog. Behind them they towed the ATV, dinged up and muddy. It was not Ulrich's only misadventure with a local machine. Two years ago he had bought a used Jet Ski and had gone airborne with it on the other side of the cove. Went out of the lake and pile-drove into blackberry bushes and wild vicious yucca plants. The steering column had driven his scrotum upwards into some unprepared cavity, and the yucca spears had entered his thighs and stomach very deeply before he rolled off into the lesser crucifixion of blackberry thorns. He could not recall what he was trying to prove. Perhaps atonement for the maimed pilot in Huntsville. Or all of his life after the war.

Melanie came out to the body man, Ronny, who was waiting with the same rubber hammer, and with Percy and Marcine too. They had squabbled but returned because there was nowhere else in Redwood to gather. Marcine was much taken with Melanie, who was elegant and lovely, but in a natural way that would have suited any outfit. Marcine was not aware there were any women in this county, young or older, like Melanie. And the older woman did work her charm, as the dignified Harvard leaned on the car hood smoking a pipe, her ally.

Melanie explained that Ulrich was very sorry, he was a sick old fellow with rare convictions. He had brought money to take care of the broken vehicle and the rifle. He had little money left. She felt he had been punished. Now he needed his woody and his walker back. The body man stood aside as if there was no more discussion, Percy took the money, and Ulrich struggled from the rear seat offering his hand but looking at the pavement. Percy agreed. He did not even ask about the deer, had forgotten it.

"Thank you ever so much," Melanie said as the body man handed over the keys to Ulrich. "You are very human and forgiving." She smiled at Marcine. "And lovely." Marcine had tamer, modest hair now, and wore only lipstick, mid-heeled white shoes.

They drove away in the two cars, and Marcine watched, a startled worship still on her face.

Next afternoon, she pouted, then went to the home of Ronny the body man's aunt, who worked for this man in Vicksburg at a kind of car agency. The aunt dressed well and seemed to have no worries, had a thirty-five-inch Sanyo television with Direct Digital TV system and a brick house.

"What is the name of the man you work for in Vicksburg, Bertha?"

"The man is *Man*."

"What?"

"His name is Man Mortimer. Hard, but a teddy bear. If you know him."

"You look to be doing fine."

"Oh, they is opportunities up there. If you get in, all you have to do is one main deal."

"What's that?"

"Forget everything. You going to rise, you gonna love forgetting you ever had a memory. I recommend it. You know there's no world with that pissant nephew of mine. You'll remember every day till when you cut your own heart out with a knife."

"I heard that."

When her husband Wootie died, Melanie stayed on the lake in their rambling vacation house. She was seventy-one years old and wished she were a poet. But she was too direct for that, her senses too good, her memory too precise, and she couldn't drink much.

She loved the egrets, the cranes, the herons, and in the evening the bullfrogs singing around the cove in their squat ardor. She was a pretty old woman, and her husband, a college president, had been very grateful. Theirs was a kind marriage without much fever, and in his sixties Wootie began falling in love with boy students and writing them letters. He was fired. This did not confuse Melanie's esteem for him. She stuck with him until he died in this house on the lake where he had fled in terminal depression. They had friends among the old men who spent their days on the pier.

She was an artisan who blew glass animals in a rear part of the house and sold them at the bait house in the crossroads of the lake and Vicksburg highways. She had living money and did not need to do this, but she had never honestly known the world of men and intended to have contact with it. The women she had known were trivial and glum academic wives. Without hate she withdrew from them. She also cheered the old at the Onward nursing home and gave away her animals there. She organized speakers and entertainments for them. She would sometimes visit the casino in Vicksburg all alone, not to gamble but because she rel-

ished the musicians. Men thought she was in her late forties, most likely, and some wondered if her elegance indicated a high-class prostitute of some sort. But she had a poise
about her that kept them polite and even a little scared,
because they assumed she must be connected to a powerful
man not of these parts.

She watched from her windows. She watched for
men like a teenager. She watched for wildlife like a child.
One day she saw an eagle fishing. Another day she saw an
armadillo mother playing with her children.

She liked a big-stomached black fellow who sat on a
white lard bucket fishing a lesser inlet of the big cove with a
cane pole. He was quiet until a fish was on, and then she
would hear him talking to it. Sometimes he whooped as if
rolling down the aisle in a church. He was engaged. Otherwise he ate his boiled meat, rat cheese and saltines with a
cold tall can of beer from the ice of his other lard bucket,
then slept whole half hours on top of the lard bucket in the
shade of the willows and cypresses.

This man was a veteran of Korea and Vietnam.
Melanie had seen him in Redwood one Veterans' Day. His
name was John Roman, and he was proud of the Indian in
his blood and adored his wife, Bernice, who looked even
more Indian than he did. On his last tour he was shot three
times, twice through the shoulder and once through the
mouth, in a cane field at twilight. He was heavy even then
and bore it well. He listened to Chet Baker on the tape deck
over and over when he was in the hospital. He belonged to
the world of smoky old jazz clubs and wanted fervently to
return to it. He loved how this white man held his tones with
an old sincerity, even when he was lacking teeth. He felt allied
to Baker because now he too had missing teeth from the
gunshot through his jaw. "My Funny Valentine." Never

enough of that. He was planning to sing like that himself when he got back to Bernice in Mississippi. He would struggle for the tone as the injured Chet Baker did. He sang with a whistle from the side of his mouth. He went to San Diego, Houston, New Orleans, then Jackson, Mississippi, where she waited in the airport.

She put her finger in the dimple where his cheek had sunk to the gap. "What you gonna do now, old soldier?"

"Wear out my ass. Wear sandals." White was on top of his hair.

He wasn't just coming home. He was making a home, and his ass was going to be nailed to it. They bought a Walter home on stilts near a pleasant green bayou a hundred yards from the reservoir road. The home was made to collapse about the time he and Bernice died together. Passersby could barely imagine the exquisite joy inside this meek home. John Roman himself could hardly believe his pleasure when he touched the front doorknob of this, his own settlement.

Melanie watched him and wondered why he had fought. For this home?

Last week a rain had come on suddenly and so white that her mind reflected to another rain in Caw, Texas, in the thirties, when she was a child. She was on the esplanade in front of the hardware store waiting for her father, a cattleman and well digger, inside. She was abruptly frightened by a white rain out of earthquake thunder, a rain of such density she could not discern buildings across the street. She looked five minutes into a writhing blanket of it and believed she saw forms go over, arms of darker frantic air. She had not seen a rain like this since, until last week on the cove when she was watching the heavy black man fishing from his bucket. She could not make him out in the downpour and thought it was because he was not there, was someplace dry. Yet when the rain dispersed, the man still sat holding his cane pole in the mist. He was drenched and he was singing. His motorbike lay in a puddle, knocked over by the storm.

It was a feat how he balanced his buckets and pole on the skinny machine. Big sandaled feet banked on either peg like underwings. The fish were in wire baskets saddled across the fender behind him.

She wanted to be his friend but was not sure how to go about it.

When you take someone for a friend, you feel you owe him something, she decided. You have owed him far back into unconscious time and will spend the rest of your days giving to him. The man brought tears to her eyes. White hair and wearing overalls, unconscious of her. She watched him pour Stanback powder into a Pepsi one afternoon. Then he drank it down in one draft. She wondered if he was a saint. If he had served a larger power without whimpering these years while she had served almost nothing but civility. Her parties among the chattering phlegmatists of the campus. Driven from fecklessness to symbols. *And yourself,* she thought in her nainsook, *you want him to be Uncle Remus goes to war, then the old happy fishing patriot. Who am I, old as he is and more? I might be an advanced case of local poet. A trivial and obvious woman, alone.* She wrote nothing.

Melanie had not seen many white men having fun or even smiling in Caw, a town thickly grim even by Texas depression standards. Most were Christian, but their music was dirges and they would rather nod than talk. Once musicians came to town in a dusty Airstream trailer towed by a Mercury. They did not mean to stop here, but they had no money for gas to move on westward, perhaps to Auburn, where one of them had an aunt of substance. They set up in the street and began to play.

One of them was a Negro who played trombone, a man of some girth like the present John Roman. He was not young but still had the face of a boy in his jowls. He wore spectacles. Nobody had seen anything like this. The man was from Galveston, dark as French coffee. Four men gathered around the front of the band, peering directly at the chubby Negro. Melanie was uncertain whether they intended to harm the dark man or were mesmerized by him. They were unschooled in an audience's relationship to a band, these weathered white men in gabardine pants or overalls and each with a felt George Raft hat the color of lead with sunspots and sweat lines on the crown. They stood right in the faces of the reed players on their folding chairs, planted almost in the band itself.

The sun made perfect high noon. This was no time to hear jazz, this Tuesday. Nor was any a good day in this part of Texas, she supposed, staring at John Roman asleep on his lard bucket.

The Negro trombonist might have been playing for his life. He set his horn and face, that face of a happy boy in rims of flesh, and never closed his eyes, as she saw other horn men do in later days. She knew one of the white men was a Baptist preacher who'd once ordered an unrepentant man's death as he sat drunk and cursing in bedroom slippers with his sex loose under a vomitous white shirt. One of the assassins his brother.

In the street before the one-room school, students of all heights stood at the window for a sight of the band. The bandsmen were unaware of interrupting school, and Melanie did not know whether the white men cared. The band kept playing, an open suitcase on the ground before them where folks might toss coins, but three tunes and none had dropped a penny. Urchins stood behind the legs of the men. The black man began getting happier and happier in the face around the big mouthpiece. He was the soloist often, with only bass fiddle and drums and tinkling piano nursing the silences.

Grown children now stood behind the others, and a little Chinese-Cajun man in a straw hat with an ethereal crown carried a bucket of water to the survivors of the music. A carpenter began nailing and sawing on planks across saw-horses at the hardware door four buildings northward. The hammer popped squarely like shots. The carpenter was good, off in his own dream. Then the Negro began to shuffle and dance during the trumpet solo. The dust rose around his polished brogans, his brown ankles went pigeon-toed and duck-footed, without hosiery.

The bell of the trombone seemed to Melanie like a cave for an elf city. The man worked the plunger with violence and trembling. He danced and danced and then played with the rest toward the end and they desisted.

The carpenter was walking rapidly to the band, urging himself through the crowd. He held a hinged-lid trunk clean-squared, nail heads sunk smoothly, an artifact of instant cabinetry. He knelt to remove the open suitcase and lock it. Then he put the trunk in its place, drawing the lid back. "So as not to get your luggage dirty," he said to the bandleader, whose hands had left his accordion as if to prevent blows on his person.

Then the rain of coins into the box began. The weathered men backed away. The spectacled boy in the face of the fat black man had never stopped smiling. Melanie dropped in her dime. She understood the man had saved his own life and her eyes grew wet in love for him. His music, the boy in the man's face, his peril.

Returned to our world, the next day she saw an eagle eating a gar carcass where John Roman had sat.

Wootie had been nearly a saint until the last, she thought. Goodness would wear you down too, God knows. You needed to see a bit of hell now and then. That and great joy. Would she ever have them? It seemed goodness was eroding her now, driving her into something flat and simple-headed.

At the bottom of her lawn was the pier. Old men gathered there, working on a sort of great cruising porch, a pleasure barge, under the supervision of Dr. Harvard. Dr. Harvard loved Melanie with a dreadful love, although she did not know it. His own wife, Nita, had cancer, so this pleasure craft could not be for her. He said it was for them all, for mild adventures up the enormous reservoir and for good philosophy and conversation, but it was really for Melanie. He was white-haired with a face unlined, four years older than Melanie. They were pretty old people and seemed matched and destined for a couple. Although there was the wife, taking her time to pass on, and Harvard, an ex-surgeon heavy with honors and thick with dignity, who could not declare himself. He wore his honors lightly, but the love of Melanie was like a tow chain locked around his neck.

Among the other old was Sidney Farté, with his shingles and bitterness, in starched shirts so stiff they seemed to make the little man into a kite, whispering with curses, bouncing in agony from one breeze to the next. Ulrich carried on with his new emphysema. He wore floral shirts and had cut down to five enormous Benson & Hedges cigarettes a day. Tall Pete Wren and his dog, Son, remained the only earnest fishermen of the pier crowd. Wren a master bluegill fisherman with fly rod and a Wake Island prevaricator who

had borrowed the biography of his cousin and written a letter from a Private Martin Lewis testifying to his captain's
heroism. The local VFA gave a ceremony in Vicksburg with
great belated reverence until the actual hero Wren was rolled
in, sad but not angry at the cousin he had not seen in years.
Pete Wren was a colonel who had made his rank in the
Oregon National Guard.

Melanie had seen the old man weeping for loneliness
in the middle of the pier crowd one afternoon. This emotion
did not surprise her, and she drove with Wren to get him a
dog from the Vicksburg pound. Now, with Son, a furred brat
needing all kinds of attention, Wren seemed better. Though
the dog, an Australian cattle dog, was a neurotic bother who
would dive underwater to retrieve a fishing lure. Sometimes
Lewis and his bride, Moore, only seventy, came to paint or
sand. They were both in chemo, but active and inseparable.
Moore was always overdressed, like a creature of ancient television housewifery. She wore heels and a pearl necklace when
she shopped in Vicksburg. She retained these habiliments
when naked and mounted by old Lewis, and this fact somehow got out to the rest, but the couple were unashamed in
this scandal. In fact, honored by it.

When Ulrich was told of the scandal, he blinked and
seemed pained, showing teeth in a yanked smile of incom-
prehension. It was feared he was headed for a breakdown.
Ulrich watched the dog Son constantly, always near tearbreak.

Among these denizens Melanie moved. Lean, clean
beige skin, bowed lips. An elegance on loan from the cinema, they thought. She was frank, to the point, with a high
brow under pulled-back white hair, a visage of permanent
gravity. The men almost quit their lies when she appeared,
and this disgusted Sidney Farté, who felt it squeezed him
into a church pew. It had been the same with the near-saint

Wooten, her dead husband, such a clean little statesman who had rebuilt the cove pier and given it handsome rails. Sidney felt censored around him and was overjoyed to hear, after Wooten's death, that he had begun running queer in his last days at the Methodist college.

Sidney's old papa, Pepper, ran the bait store and was even nastier than Sidney, who waited on him to die. Sidney suspected both of them were born without a heart, but this did not alarm him. He had been in a position to improve himself and leave these counties for happier parts, but he had turned down each chance out of spite.

After a month's visit, his nephew from Yale had told him he was a poisonous old coot who ought to be ashamed of himself. This floored Sidney for a week, but when he arose again, it was to enjoy this legend. He had been at it for seventy-eight years. Four years ago, when his wife died, he stood, dry in his eyes, blaming her for the cold rain over the hole but loving the fact the burying minister was a Korean Baptist who would have horrified her. Her form of dementia the last years was suspecting that Koreans were taking over all the acting parts on television.

During the actual Korean War, Sidney had volunteered to kill Koreans, having never known they were a possible race. The army turned him down for premature belligerency. Nevertheless, Sidney lied that he slaughtered gooks of all stripes over there and this was what had changed him. Not the guilt but the present absence of such happiness. Melanie, who wanted to know about men and war, looked through him with piercing gray eyes. He could hardly stand her presence. Oh, he wanted to sodomize her and puke on her back, but he certainly didn't respect her.

Even to Melanie herself it wasn't clear why she stayed here by the lake. Wooten's old boat hung by ropes in the carport next to her station wagon. She could live where they delivered drugs and groceries. She could live in a house next to Eudora Welty, the grande dame of American letters, over in Jackson, the capital city, if she wanted. They would say what a striking woman in the aisles of the Jitney-Jungle, and she could return to a home of bleached, ivied brick, three stories. But the land of wealthy widows and elderly divorcées was not hers anymore, and she feared it.

In Vicksburg, on the asphalt, the deflected minions of want walked, those who lived to care for and feed their cars, and she watched them outside Big Mart. And the sad philosophic fishermen who lived to drag slabby beauties from the water, that dream of long seconds, so they told her. About the same happy contest as sexual intercourse, as she recalled it, though these episodes sank deeper into a blurred well every day. She loved the men and their lostness on the water. Their rituals with lines and rods and reels and lures. The worship they put into it. How they beleaguered themselves with gear and lore, like solemn children or fools. She had spent too much time being unfoolish, as if that were the calling of her generation. As you would ask somebody the point of their lives and they would answer: *horses*.

TWO

NEAR THE BAD RESTAURANT A MILE AROUND THE LAKE lived the ex-doctor Max Raymond with his wife, Mimi Suarez, the Coyote. She was a good deal younger. They performed Latin jazz with their band at the casino in Vicksburg. The Coyote was Cuban, the singer. She had shining black ringleted hair, very fetching to men and to Melanie too, who adored watching her. She swayed and waved her arms, a torso in a storm of mutiny, the legs beneath her another riot trying to run away from her underwear. And the sheen of sweat under the lights. She was made for tiny dresses and flashbulbs under her face. But this was not the best. Her voice was. Men and women stared at her mouth when she began her singing, startled as if by a ghost flying from her lips. A review had once compared her to Celia Cruz.

But her husband, nearby with his saxophone, the one who enjoyed her pleasures, was a sullen middle-aged creature and seemed to stand knee-deep in unseen wreckage. You could imagine him her jailer. His playing was vengeful, abstract, learned at some academy of the fluently depressed. He played against her, mocking or blaming her for her gifts. He had his fans too, but they were ugly people, sneering bumpkin punks and those who had always had the wrong hair. He seemed driven into low postures by her beauty, clawing at a pole to rise, spit, curse and hurl imprecations at her. During his solos, the rest of the band, men, would look up into the rafters as if incredulous about this tax on joy. His few smirking fans wished he would bitch-slap this

Coyote woman once they were home. Because she was so
fine, fine, and beyond. Bring her back to heel.

But although he held her responsible for some of his
grief, Raymond was gentle to Mimi Suarez in their big decrepit cabin on the lake. He was a sort of Christian, but he
despised striving, waited for visions. And was a poet. The
Bible and whiskey on his desk, read randomly, drunk grimly.
At one time he had thought Mimi Suarez would save him
from all lost time. Her fire and rapture and flesh. But time
had quit forgiving him and begun running short. He knew
his poetry was not good, like his life, but he waited through
the weak words for a vision and an act, as you would pan
for gold by ten thousand wasted motions. He could get higher,
higher to God, by his saxophone, an instrument resuscitated
from his high school days when it was only a hole to hide
his miserable head in. He needed music, the Coyote and
God. And he needed to live close to evil. Mimi Suarez was
unaware of this last need.

She did know that Raymond, as the attending physician, briefly, of her violent ex-boyfriend Malcolm, had
destroyed the man by urging on his wish to commit suicide,
a thing he would announce after beating her. Malcolm became the patient, the weak one needing help, while she sat
in the waiting room, black and blue and cracked in the ribs.

Raymond saw her and wanted her. Both he and
Malcolm were high on drugs, but Raymond's drug was
cleaner, Demerol straight from the hospital. He was certain
he had identified intransigent evil in Malcolm. He dared him
to be a man of his word and sent him off with several pre-
scriptions. Malcolm succeeded only in giving himself a
stroke. He lay now or stumbled, unable to remember nouns,
no longer a songwriter, watched loosely by his old gang, who
demanded a hearing on Max Raymond as a medical doctor.

Raymond resigned the profession without much re-
morse and took Mimi Suarez to live with him at a lesser
house in Memphis. She too had been threatened by the old
gang. Raymond joined the Latin band she sang with by first
managing it and buying new horns and electronic refine-
ments, then stepping into Malcolm's old spot on saxophone.
They rode the trend for Latin and were very prosperous, as
bar bands went. Now they played the long casino job. Because Raymond knew the casino was evil. It meant nothing
for a Christian visionary to live among the good and the
comfortable, he thought. He wanted no cloistered virtue.

But he began seeing his splendid wife as the cause
of his despondency, which increased until he played his way
out of it. He felt unmanned by their lovemaking. It was all
right when it was a big sin, but now that it was a smaller one
undertaken with regularity, he felt weakened. He was both
voyeur and actor when he took her, in all her spread beauty,
but the part of voyeur was increasing and he knew he was a
filthy old haint, as far from Christ as a rich man. He could
have lived better with the memory of Malcolm dead, but as
a stroke victim who might wander in through a door in
Raymond's head at any time, slobbering and gesturing, the
guilt he inflicted was infernal, with no finality.

So far Raymond remained a hero to Mimi Suarez.
Before Malcolm beat her, mainly for being beautiful and
healthy and a drag on his addictions, she was attuned to the
old precept of the Indian. Life was a river, not a ladder, not
a set of steps. She knew something was wrong, but she was
unconscious to living with a dead man, which Raymond in
his current state nearly was. She knew many musicians
looked reamed and dried and skull-faced, but she did not
know that many of them, although mistaken for the living
by their audiences, *were* actually dead. Ghouls howling for

egress from their tombs. Pale, his black hair drawn straight back, deep startled blue eyes, Raymond was an older spirit gone into mind, a figure of desperate romance to her still. He hurt for things, and she pitied him as you might a deaf and dumb orphan around Christmastime.

He had chosen the very lake house, which he threatened to buy, for its late history of chaos. The landlord had told about these people proudly. He was in ownership of a rare legend. It was a poor county except around the huge lake and could not even afford much local color. Three years ago its tenants were middle-aged, a proclaimed witch and her sissy husband. The witch had been discovered leading a coven of teenage boys in turning over ancient tombstones in local cemeteries. She had plied the boys with oral sex at midnight. The authorities found the matter too stupid and nasty to prosecute. The youth were from good families the witch woman lived squarely among, in a grid of Eisenhower-era brick homes. Her husband stuck by her, and she meant to corrupt another bourgeois suburb in Shreveport when they left the lake house.

The next lodger was an embezzler who had drunk strychnine while the law pounded on the door. The enormous man, with his hound's eyes, survived, but only as a shrunken wraith in draping skin at a federal pen in Missouri. He had betrayed hundreds of Baptist alumni at the school where he was president, many of whom still prayed for him and were shocked by his transformation. Heretofore he had been taken for brilliant and righteous. But years ago he had lost a teenage daughter, and the more generous said this must be when he turned against God and man. Many of his fellows remained confused, even when they reviled him. He had run with harlots in faraway cities, he had stolen two million dollars, he had become a scholar of hidden offshore accounts. One dear friend said that when he looked in his own bathroom mirror, he saw the wrath of evil just behind his own regular features. This friend was the man who brought the law to the door. He was devoted to the embezzler and thought him the best man he ever knew. He felt a Judas when he turned in his friend. Many spoke of broken hearts, but this man was an actual case.

Two weeks after the arrest, this man, ex–football coach at the college and a fisherman to whom every second on the water was dear, every bass, crappie, bluegill hoisted dripping from the lake, the effluvia of marine oil and gasoline at dawn, the shuddering motor, the skate across the glassy reds at evening. This man returned to the cabin, spent one night there, went out early in his boat and died. They found the boat making circles in the water a mile out. His body, the sixty-four-year-old body of a once second-team all-American guard, finally dead from an attack on the heart. A chorus of moans back at the little college, and agreement. They had never watched a sadder man. A man who perished from belief in a soul brother.

Then two springs ago, the landlord told Raymond, the realtors he was using, a married couple, moved themselves into this place on its small hill, with its vine-wrapped fence, its bee-loud honeysuckle, dwarf magnolias and the palmettos farther into the dark of the riverine bayous behind. At night you could hear the bull gators, *hunka hunka*, and the bullfrogs. Throats of bleating tin. At dusk, against this forest night, you saw a crane take flight, big as a spread greyhound and purest white.

The couple, Gene and Penny Ten Hoor, were no longer enthralled with each other, but they had a long fishing partnership. Penny sometimes dove from their boat to swim in the green-black lake. The water was still chilly from

Tennessee streamlets into the Yazoo and Big Black, which fed the lake. She was in perfect shape and could stay underwater long distances.

In their slick boat, berthed at the eastern landing, was a cell phone. They were very prosperous in real estate, and they bought and sold lots in the pleasant venues remaining around the lake. Only local poverty stood in the way of a vaster development. It was a fishing, not a sports, lake. Bass fishermen do not as a rule care where they stay. Neither do they have much money left over after the outlay on the boat, trailer and tackle. They have brought their home with them.

The couple had dreamed once of an empire of condominiums at Eagle Lake, but that had stopped. Three times they had been threatened by angry callers. In this state live men and women nostalgic by age eleven. For things rambling, wooden, rain-worn, wood-smoked, slightly decrepit. The heft of dirty nickels. They flee to lakes from hateful pavements, concrete and glass. They are certain the great wars were fought for cheap fishing licenses.

More than by the telephoners, the couple had been stopped by the death of their young son in a school-bus accident. The lad was smashed, tossed. They had done nothing but fish since they lost him. Bass, crappie and bluegills. They favored the fly rod, an Episcopalian method in these parts. They fished too for catfish at night with a lantern on their boat. Monsters lay deep in this lake, so strong they could move their boat around like a sea fish when they were on. Gene and Penny frowned all the while now, as if trying to read a book in a foreign language. The book of rising each morning and for what? They hardly looked at each other. They returned to the huge cottage worn and sunburned.

When they ate at the awful restaurant, which some of the old fellows from the cove frequented, they were perfect consumers of its fare. They cared nothing for what they ate and barely noticed it. The old men thought it remarkable that the two of them had settled into this speechless apathy at so young an age, when two of the old fellows had waited decades to earn this pleasure from their own wives.

Sidney loved it. "They chanced to look at the other one and they'd kill the bastard, seems like. My word, it stirs the memory."

Unbeknownst to the other, each had saved up the tranquilizers prescribed for them in their grief over their lost son. They did not begin taking them until the second week in the house, in a lull of energy for fishing. She complained that both the fish and the water smelled like birth, and then they came back to the cabin on the lip of the swamp, which smelled like birth and diapers, itself. Then the restaurant, where the bathroom was the same. But they could not quit going to these places. They began leaving clusters of fish, uncleaned, ignored, around the house. They were barely eating. They began drinking vodka with Gatorade.

After four days in this haze, she saw him lying naked and fat on the bed asleep and cut his member with a fillet knife. He bled a great deal and needed stitches, but they went nowhere. He rocked with a towel in his lap and they talked it over and he forgave her. The next day they went fishing together.

At suppertime she called him to the kitchen, where it was dark. The rest of the house was dim, two bare bulbs somewhere. She stood at the doorjamb with a finger to her lips for him to be quiet. He stood by her awhile, and she said, "He's there, eating." She meant their son. He blinked, and he did see something in the chair at the table. "He needs all his nourishment. So long now without eating," she said. When she left for sleep, he walked to the chair and found the shape to be a tree limb she had brought in from the back and placed there. He cried but embraced the limb.

Then she began calling the ground evil, she could feel the evil in it right through her boat shoes. She felt men fighting, women struggling, animals fleeing. The groans of it shook her feet. They launched their boat on the water, but they drove it, a very nice cedarwood classic, very slowly, like old people with no purpose in an automobile. They never changed clothes anymore except to sleep naked.

They left the lake now and then, driving a Saab, again at the speed of elderly people in bad weather. The woman could not stand the voices that came in the window if they went any faster. They went to a cash machine in Vicksburg and withdrew thousands of dollars. The money was piled or scattered all over the house and they paid no attention to it. Apparently it was intended as *getaway* money, but they never left. They continued to fish and leave the fish about. Big catfish too, from the lantern fishing. They were pros. They answered neither the phone in the house nor the one in the boat. The phones kept ringing.

In the second week they bought tools in Vicksburg. Every movement was very slow now. If they heard the hammering from the restaurant across the meadow, the denizens might have wondered why anybody would put such effort into rental property. The husband began nailing everything he owned to the walls. Pants, belts, underwear and his fishing tackle, plug by plug. Nailed right through the breast of Lucky Thirteen, Dive-bomber, plastic worms.

Then he nailed up the fish, what grip he could find on what had rotted from the first week. He nailed up her clothing, panties and even Tampax. Then he slept, with the unnailed piles of tackle and money around him. He had begun nailing the money, but there was a lot. Pictures of his real estate office, photos of desirable lots. Big red Seconals and other pills scattered across the throw rugs.

The swamp got louder. The crane flew and brought a great shadow past the windows. The limb stayed where it was in their chair in the kitchen.

He was asleep on the bathroom tiles when she stabbed him again, this time in the thigh, just missing his testicles. He had never healed properly from the first assault, and this wound was deep. He heard her in the kitchen talking to the limb. The knife still hung in his thigh while he hit her across the back of the head with the flat of a shovel. Then he nailed her foot to the wall in the living room while she was unconscious, and then one of her hands.

He hammered a six-inch rafter spike through the meat of his left heel and was trying to do the same for his left hand when he either passed out or went to sleep. Both of them were full of Dilaudid, a narcotic used in recovery from lung and heart surgeries and sold at huge prices on the streets.

The phone kept ringing deep into the night. The sullen restaurateur was not stirred by their screams, but they brought Sidney Farté, Pete Wren and Dr. Harvard to the house. Then the odor, when they got in the viney yard. Under the hollering, the singer Aaron Neville crooned from the jambox, "Don't Fall Apart on Me Tonight," heaving out his grace notes to soprano. But way over that the hollers, now husky female and then croaking male. They were out of drugs, drink, mobility. The old men almost did not go in. An aggressive mirage when they opened the front door. But soon Harvard knelt and did what he could, and somebody telephoned.

Along with the ambulance came the new sheriff of the county. It was their first look at him. He was young for the job and had a master's in criminology from a school in Mexico. He seemed to be borrowing a southern accent for the benefit of the locals, and they thought him a bit too confident, not as impressed by this event as he should be. When the awe wore off, Sidney Farté felt all warm and lucky to have chanced on this crucifixion.

Months later but unrecovered, mildly brain-damaged, Penny preferred charges and sued her husband. He countercharged. They limped into court eighteen months later in Jackson. So much was revealed that each side retired and the gallery went away in disgust, horror and pity. Sated. In the middle of the litigation, the Ten Hoors fell back in love.

Or, at any rate, in their wreckage they had found the uncontrollable pity that calls itself love. They wept and fell together. Their new vows did not stop here. Across the lake was a deserted barracks and barn and fifty acres contained by a broken fence of storm wire, a former quarters for a football and majorette summer camp, and this maimed and devoted couple began to convert the camp into a resort for orphans. They kept four horses and a pleasure barge, with fields for softball, archery, volleyball and badminton, horseshoes. They built a hall for movie nights. Catastrophe had brought their earnestness together. Sworn to give something back, they fell more deeply in love. A few weeks back the first orphans had come.

The ex-doctor Max Raymond practiced his saxophone, tuned to this house of chaos and horror. It was spring, or starting to be, and he felt the ghosts passing and then struggling down the green alleys of the deeps in the swamp behind them. His wife sometimes sang, perhaps for the animals and birds, alone on the back stoop. Her voice was pure, lush and sweet, unconscious of ugly history.

Raymond was fishing from the other side of the pier from the old men at work on their own barge when another came over from the orphans' camp across the lake, twin Evinrudes putting behind, children at the rails. White, black, Vietnamese, Mexican. But they were all speaking like immigrants who knew only a few phrases of obscenity in English. The wife was at the stern trying to lead these children in song. They ignored her. Nevertheless, Penny kept smiling radiantly. Gene was at the wheel, also smiling with a sort of witless beatitude. The couple were still sallow and drawn from their calamity, no longer handsome but invested by their great pity. The children around them made rutting motions and blew noises on their arms. A small one urinated on the deck. All the while, many others were yelling filth. Reviling the dignity of this geriatric gallery on the pier. But the husband steered as if all was in hand and each child adorable. The wife kept leading the song. A vision beyond comment until they left and trolled southward to the dam.

Raymond thought of Malcolm, the rival he had destroyed. Did he look like the couple did now? Lunatic, pale, slumped. The idiotic hope in their faces. "I'm happy there's a lake between us and that," said Wren.

It looked like something, well, unlicensed. "My first look at them since they were hauled off in the ambulance," said Dr. Harvard. "Poor people. Crippled. Thinking they're doing good."

"You seen everything that's wrong with this fucking U.S.A. aboard that scow," said Sidney. He had a deep chest cold and had been enjoying heaving up phlegm and spitting the gouts into the water, going for distance.

Two of the orphans were well-figured girls, maybe fourteen, both smoking cigarettes, their faces already set hard, their eyes already gone whoring, leers ready. Each of the old recalled them in his own way. Glittering eyes of a lizard. Troubled homes, troubled streets. A foreign perfume in these dreams. Old men eaten alive. A mindless revival of unspoken sins. Death by arousal.

Raymond watched their faces. Then he looked up the yard at Melanie coming down the hill, bringing cold beers to them. Sweetness and light, he thought. She was amazing. A face and body kept lineless by virtue, self-sacrifice.

Ulrich had been quiet, painting on deck varnish. Now he spoke. "We don't love each other as much as we used to. You can see the uncertain looks, the calculations, the dismissals. People are not even in the present moment. Everybody's been futurized. You look in those eyes and see they're not home, they're some hours ahead at least. I hate to go into Vicksburg anymore. Anywhere, really. It's all like meeting people who have just departed. Old men and women don't look wise anymore. They are just aged children. And who gets the highest pay? Actors. Paid to mimic life because there is no life. You look at everybody and maybe they're a little sad, some of 'em. They're all homesick for when they were real." Ulrich began painting again as the others tried to guess what could have prompted this.

"Did you see them orphans?" asked Sidney.

"Orphans?" asked Ulrich. "Who isn't an orphan, I ask you?"

Sidney had a living father who he wished were dead. Pepper Farté hated almost everything that moved. To buy something in his bait house was like pulling goods from the hands of a vicious hermit. When Sidney himself entered the store, the older man became livid, angry at the custom that demanded you acknowledge your son. Sidney was going to correct Ulrich, but then he recalled these matters and merely sneered.

"When you're crazy like me, the brain keeps you warm. I haven't had a long-sleeve shirt on all year," Ulrich reflected.

"Shortness of air to the head is what explains you," said Sidney.

"I wonder who is helping that poor couple with the orphans," said Melanie. She handed a beer to Ulrich. "I don't think you should be breathing paint in your condition, Mr. Ulrich." She patted his shoulder. Ulrich painted on. She smiled.

Harvard watched Melanie in reverence.

I could love this woman too, thought Raymond. *Like a Madonna. Maybe she is all the vision I'll ever get. How can you have a faith without a vision now and then?*

The woman has been graceful so long, kind so long.

A vision cannot be indefinite, an apparition. No, you go down the road and you see something there, dense and none other like it. Those of us who want visions can't have them, maybe. They are given to old fools like Ulrich. I love him too. A better man than I am. Raymond thought this and then had a bluegill on. *But what of the other night when I became so glad all of a sudden and for no reason that there was an Ireland, and that the natives of its villages were going about their ways, to and fro, from stone cottages and green rocky hills. I had an ecstasy thinking that. What was that?*

Melanie walked with her small ice chest back up the pier and continued around the cove on an unknown journey. Her walking made no sense until she rounded the inlet with its thick lily pads, then went on to the point where the black man John Roman sat on his bucket fishing. It began to rain a little. The figures over there were small, but the man watched as she handed the fisherman a cold beer. He took it. The rain sparkled over the bent willows above the two.

Fairly soon, as it began to rain thickly, the pier crowd beheld this woman on the back of Roman's motorbike, clutching his stomach, as he rode them out of the trees and up the long rise to her house. Small figures, they entered her kitchen together.

"Lookee. She's steppin' out on you, Harvard," said Sidney with a wide sneer. "She been wantin' it, but she can't wait forever, eh, eh."

This man of great dignity and honors, the man I should have been, Raymond thought, watching Harvard again, pole-axed by love and this old guttersnipe Sidney. His eloquent white hair flattened out and dripping, eyes stupid. Like a bum with a ruined wig.

Down in the south corner of the lake, Mortimer watched the absurd floor and roof on pontoons move toward him. Two adults and crammed with children. He did not like children. But he became suddenly alert when he noticed the two fourteen-year-old girls leaning on the rail his way. They both smoked in the sullen manner of the hopeless. One was already bosomy. The other had fine bare shoulders. Just budding upper frame, but muscled long legs. Then he stared at the adults. They had loony smiles, but there was something depleted about them both. They must be church people, he decided. That stupid hope on their faces. That trust that they were always on the Lord's stage, pulled by the strings of a larger design. Looking for a cross. Maybe these brats themselves. He heard a few curses shouted his way, but the adult couple seemed oblivious. Speakers of another tongue.

He knelt here at the boat ramp with chipped granite boulders banked close to it, red sand to either side. It was his first time at the lake, he had come to take a boat from a man deeply in debt to him. The man had wanted to fish one last time in it. He was waiting. The girls were the first exciting thing he'd seen in weeks.

At this juncture he had no plans to hurt people around the lake. He did not like bodies of water much, had never seen the ocean. He was indifferent to trees. Soil was hateful to him, as was the odor of fish. But like many another man forty-five years in age, he wanted his youth back.

He wanted to have pals, sports, high school girls. This need had rushed on him lately. He lived in three houses, but he had no home. He did not like the hearth, smells from the kitchen, an old friend for a wife, small talk. It all seemed a vicious closet to him. He moved, he took, he was admired. But he had developed a taste for young and younger flesh. This was thrilling and meant high money. Men and women in this nation were changing, and he intended to charge them for it.

Religion had neither formed nor harmed him. Neither had his parents in southern Missouri. But he despised the weakness of the church, and of his parents, whom he had gulled. He was a pretty boy born of hawk-nosed people. It was a curse to have these looks and no talent. Long, lank. Hooded eyes, sensual lips that sang no tune. Still, he quit the football team because of what it did to his hair, claiming a back ailment that had exempted him from manual labor since age fourteen. There are thousands of men of this condition, most of them sorry and shiftless, defeated at the start. Many are compulsives and snarling fools, emeritus at twenty.

His parents doted on him. The pew in the church also hurt his back, he said. But he would go with them now and then, a martyr. Because already he liked to mock the sheepish Methodist minister, to whom the world was a terror from which he led his little flock in long, constant retreat.

The hymns of this church were like the moan of doomed animals to his ears.

Mortimer's parents were both unassertive postmen. They had no other children but kept a chicken yard in the back, which mortified him. He was often in the house alone, indisposed to school, to the wretched town, where almost everybody walked with a sag. A neighbor boy showed him a pornographic picture when he was fifteen, and the bone-deep thrill of seeing that woman in her happy pain had never left him, had never diminished. He looked for it behind every curtain of culture, of law.

His likeness to Fabian had attracted many girls, then women, often several at once. They loved his brooding, his shy muttering, his brute eyes. He seemed all hooded by his brows even when he had nothing on his mind. The thick wavy hair was eloquent for him. These were girls of lesser elegance, lesser clothes, lesser cuteness, but nice enough.

At home one evening he screamed out suddenly that he didn't have a fine car or any money, and he knew that the two of them, his parents, were hiding it for themselves. He promised he would never attend their funerals. There would be no grown son to honor them when they passed. He frightened his mother and father. They gave him a nice car and money. When he got enough, he left them. There was other money too, from the three girls who left with him, one of them a student teacher from a nearby college. She was his first conquest of the better sort, the scioness of a middling-wealthy owner of a department store. She had good legs, spectacles, grammar. He spent some years doing manual labor but cushioned by women, who gave him money. Then around thirty he found his calling, as most do.

He did not know the term *gigolo*. Something about him canceled scruples in women. He didn't know what that was either but accepted it as a birthright. For reasons he didn't ponder, he did not love but found the language of love came fluid to him. He never even had the puppy kind of love. He was jaded before he had a crush. He was a pimp before he comprehended what a pimp was. It was just that women liked him, especially the marginal breeds. They shed all natural jealousies, even pride, for him. They broke open on him. They went with other men and gave him half the money.

His name was Man Mortimer. Death by sea or by mother. He was horrified of progeny. Nothing was busy or brooding enough to follow him.

Seven years ago the girl from his early days, a store owner's daughter, had come to him with a child six years old she claimed was his. She was on hard times, drugged, worn, emaciated. She thought the son would bring him back to her. He denied fatherhood.

They were at an old gravel bed outside St. Louis. She walked back to his car where the boy was waiting and shot him in the forehead. Mortimer was not aware she had a pistol. Now she sat in the car beside the body of the child. The night silent, hot, the moon white somewhere. Mortimer's expensive loafers on the gravel. He always needed expensive shoes and boots. He stood looking in the foggy windshield at the woman behind it until she raised the pistol and shot herself in the temple. He looked away, and for a long while he watched lightning reveal shivering bushes in the field next to him. He couldn't be sure this was not a dream. Even while he dragged them both to the trunk.

A thin highway dog lurked at the edge of the trunk light. Skeletal but with full paps. She smelled the blood, thrust out her muzzle, wanting to eat but fearing him. He took pity on her and intended to use the pistol on her. With this thought he assured himself he was a right man. But she ran off into a dark field of sedge.

He drove southward with his burdens, hating that his shoes were scuffed from labor. These sordid details, these fluids. He could never forgive her. She had shown him hell.

"She just wanted me to watch, is all," he said aloud. "It was already done when she got here. She wanted to ruin me. Well."

He felt no pain outside this nasty theater of his mind. But he felt a surge of power. A tougher man seemed to drive the car now. He gathered himself into this new form. He took some pride in the force of his withdrawal from women. He had driven some into lesbianism. Or supposed he had. He had barely laid a hand on any of them. He believed in the mind.

Acquaintances in Vicksburg would help him bury his old history.

He wondered vaguely, and not for the first time, whether his departure had destroyed his mother. *A person like me don't come along every day*, he thought. *You just got to watch yourself. Don't ever mistake that I'm like you.*

It was only when his looks started to go, at age forty-three, that he became hungry for all the life he had missed. Something had made him grow up too fast, and he cursed that thing now. He fled from one of his three houses to the other, the next house always a getaway from the last. The people he knew were made curious by his changes this last year. With them he seemed to be doing some imitation of warmth, friendship, trust. Childish, stilted gestures, as if studied from some old book on stagecraft. They had no idea what he had on his mind.

When the man who owed him the boat at last came up, Mortimer told him to stay in it. He wanted driving somewhere.

"You see that pontoon barge way out there? I want you to follow it, see where they get off it."

"Those children? Them is orphans from the new camp."

"Orphans? Well. Let's see where they land. I might could help them."

The man was surprised. Then he looked at Mortimer's feet. "Careful. Them ain't no boat shoes. They like for selling cars in."

"Just drive it. If you can stay quiet, you might be earning this boat back."

The man was very warm to this idea. Parting with the boat was breaking his heart. He should have stuck with it and fishing. A simple soul who don't ask much more than God's waters. But no, he had to get off into gambling, borrowing and the night sweats.

The adult couple were weary, the same idiot glassy beams in their faces as they watched the children disembark to the pier. They seemed unconnected to the children individually but joined to their collective oversoul. Only about six of the children were tame. They peered at Mortimer and his pilot coming up in the boat, but he could not be sure they quite perceived him. The huge smiles were already on them when he came, and they seemed only a little puzzled.

"I saw you across the lake." Mortimer pointed. "A voice said to me, 'Now what can I do to help out?' And it not even Christmas. I said, 'I bet these good folks could use a hand.'"

"A hand?" the husband said.

"Myself, I had no mother or daddy either. I know where you're coming from."

With their great smiles, they seemed unequipped to deny him. Like they had already assented when he was on the way over. Both of them nodded. Mortimer knew they were damaged, and this fact pleased him. He felt to be their senior officer the minute he set foot on the pier, looking for where those two girls could have got off to. They were over to the side, watching him, sullen, too old for this camp, their legs jammed to the grass in a stance both defiant and beckoning. Street-corner women.

Mortimer found out he had much in common with the male adult. Their pain. As Mortimer walked up the pier to the lawn with the couple, the man in the boat whispered, "I heard a voice out there too. It said, 'Freddy, watch out. You driving up some nasty river with this shark.'"

THREE

DEE ALLISON HELD HER BRA AND PANTIES IN ONE HAND AND watched the reflection of herself in the blank television screen. She wanted to see if she still had powers, and she was satisfied, looking directly at her breasts, stomach, the lush dark curls of her pubic hair.

She was only thirty-six. Her husband was a memory since the birth of her baby girl, but she understood not being here. She was almost not here herself. Nor anywhere. At least he sent money. He was doing well. She didn't care what he did or where he was. She was just about exactly what she looked like, a phlegmatic starlet, made lazy by her rolling daydreams. But cheerful. Life had not beaten her. She was glad.

Each one has his master, and Mortimer had at last met a woman who moved him in all ways. Who could be visited but never occupied. He gave her money, a car, a television she rarely watched, drugs she threw away, drink she barely uncapped. She never asked for anything and was indifferent to her station in life, that of a nurse and single mother of four, in a sagging house on the scrub side of the lake not far from the new orphans' camp. He met her needs for animal passion, but he knew another man could furnish her just as well. Dee was heedless of the fact that he was very special, or that she was.

He told her dreadful tales about his business. The whores, the sharking, extortion, the ruined lounge rats who ran to do his will. With her, he had quit his laconic muttering. He had gone full-bore to revelations, which startled him.

57

There was a desperate poet suddenly grafted onto him. She barely responded.

She might writhe with him in bestial greed, but otherwise she seemed the nun of apathy. She was wearing him out both ways. Having her and not having her so quickly.

The truth was, she had her daydreams and did not live much outside them. Television bored her, but she sat wishing musical scores and images onto its blank screen. She worked at the Onward Rest Home, called Almost There by wags in the county, and many remarked that she was too bright and lovely to stop there. She was not trash, she was clean and dressed well. Her four children lived with her. Two boys, a near man of twenty, and Emma, a baby girl with the disposition of an angel and startling beauty, often baby-sat by a nearby Mennonite couple when she was out on the town. She paid little attention to her home and let her children run wild.

She did not know where the dreams came from, but she sometimes imagined men exploding into flame, and then the surrounding buildings, sometimes as she stared at them. Perhaps it was their strutting confidence that they belonged and were needed by their place. Women also drew her anger. The ones too assured, too comfortable with this world. Going down the road in their cars and thinking everybody waited for them like dogs, tongues all out and fawning. Her imagination was the Old Testament, although she had never read it and had no god.

In her nurse's outfit, white stockings, white shoes, she was a form of wreckage too. When she walked away from the old men at Onward, they witnessed the struggle of her rumpcheeks in the skirt and they knew hurt, even terror, and vast pity for themselves. She did not patronize them, never called them *sweetheart* or *boyfriend,* these convicts of time.

She did not mean to harm them. They were all right, they were reality, they knew their place, deaf and aiming monologues out the window and across the river at Louisiana. The democracy of the pained, the fearful, the unheard. She was gentle and content to be the young beauty among them. On whom they fastened the dopey old fogs of their desire.

They knew full well they stood no chance with her, even had their health and worried fortunes caught her attention. She had her man, in fact two of them, the Mortimer one and the sixty-year-old one who some days quietly drove her away in a restored battleship-gray Chevrolet Bel-Air from the fifties with its Antique tag. He was a recessive man, gentle, and loved that Dee shared his bliss over the oldies from the tinny radio speaker. He had added the FM band just for her. Frank Booth was his name. He wanted old-time dates, with courting and the moon, and especially the voices of Patsy Cline and Connie Francis. And the heartbreaking teen-angel ballads with God and the chapels in them. Things had not prospered for him in his earlier years, and he wanted the softness and the victory of them now, although he was by no means a failure. He had a jewelry business in Edwards just off Highway 20. He did not want to just coo and sigh either, no, he wanted full, half-clothed intercourse with Dee on a lonesome road with high orange moons up there, and her brassiere off and her priceless white stockings. Lover's Lane. He was sworn to this, he was sworn to stolen pleasure, so that God would barely know in the act's hot brevity what might have transpired. Yes he was strange, but Dee liked the manners and cherished the nights, odd as they were. They made her feel young too. The man Frank, he asked permission to expend himself inside her. Asked permission. I'd be hurt if you didn't, she'd say.

★   ★   ★

Not until the evening they happened to sit together and cross napkins in a bar of the casino and became single-malt neighbors did they know of the other's existence. It was a meal of crawfish lightly battered and with Chinese red pepper covering the best New York strips from Nebraska. They were having a tankard of Irish tea. This evening had begun early and rather lonesome and they could not quit drinking. Frank Booth seemed a man of more world than these parts required. He spoke of fine jewelry from his store in Edwards. Mortimer did not know jewelry except in relation to the necks and wrists and ankles of happier sluts, although he had once met up in Water Valley the poor man in a wooden shop who was compelled to make Elvis Presley's Tupelo space clothes and rings and belts and studded capes for his Las Vegas patheticon. He told this to Booth.

Mortimer had never heard of single-malt scotch. No real drinker, he did not understand what improvement *single* could be over more. He had been to California twice to talk to Larry Flynt the pornographer. In his opulent antiqued office, Flynt had expressed himself that a woman was the prettiest picture God allowed on this black earth. Mortimer's man had stolen Flynt's Lexus SUV and his secretary's Infiniti SUV. Flynt was an atheist and democrat who was scared stupid by snake handlers in Kentucky when he was a tiny lad. Woman, the most exquisite vision in nature, he said. It was odd there was also a Venice, California, with slimy moats or what all in it too. Sea slugs, for God's sake. He did not walk to the ocean.

Mortimer and Booth became large in self-congratulations. It was early spring. They discussed life's good old goodness. Then they gave their names. Then they talked about their fine hot women. Both women would lie a little, but that was somehow even more zesty. You had to say that for these days, they were living. They had it made, it might not get any better. Mortimer in sympathy imagined this gentle soul Booth with some pliant granny of a girlfriend he thought was a rich find.

He noticed the fellow was, well, a tad effeminate. That was fine. All types. This great U.S.A. open for business, to even old guys, twenty-four / seven. He cheered Booth and cheered his own Conway Twitty–faced self. Booth was a navy veteran, no damned sissy anyway. It was the malt, though, had to be, when Booth told him he was a SEAL in peacetime. His man Lloyd was a SEAL, and Mortimer exercised the courtesy of not mentioning this to the silvery-haired old dreamer. Booth told him his mission was to train violent assault dogs to swim underwater toward Japanese drift-net fishermen, the voracious everything-killing nets fifty miles wide in the Gulf of Mexico. Mortimer did not blink. He was just on the brink of handing the keys of his Lincoln Navigator over to his pal to use a week. Let him dream even bigger.

Then the name Dee Allison came up. The same nurse over at Almost There nursing home. Onward, rather.

"I'm proud to pick such a blossom off that tree, given my years," Booth said. "I must have something left, because that is one satisfied thirty-six-year-old minx."

His new pal blinked and got sober.

"You say Dee Allison? Then we both owe her something, Frank. Come on out here to the carport and let's chat on it."

He pointed to the Mississippi River when they were outdoors, wide and powerful. Just an old barge road now, with its memories. The Siege of Vicksburg, Gibraltar of the West, 1864. The flood of 1927. Lanterns on the levee. Oyster barrels from New Orleans and Texas grapefruit up for

Christmas plantationers. Mortimer did not know the dates. He did not like history or time.

They sat in the behemoth Navigator, large as some fighting machines in Desert Storm.

"Dee Allison should be floating dead down that water right now," he said to Booth. "We both guessed we got all of her. We gave her everything. All we had was another cheat. I love her, Frank, if I've ever had love. But she just grabbed for the leavings, likely just for spite of us both. I cannot believe you trained underwater dogs, old man. But I believe you came in my woman, unless this is a prank."

"No it isn't. I forgot your name."

"Man's my name. Man Mortimer. Means death by sea."

"Well this is a shock, with Dee."

"Just think on this a minute."

They talked about the sickening whirlpools down in that river. The Civil War dead in their sniper pits, still yearning for a clean head shot on Sherman or Grant. They agreed one expert Navy SEAL sniper could have won the war that month. When slavery would have perished as an institution. It was common wisdom that the South would have given the slaves their freedom the instant they kicked the North's ass, but that the slaves would have chosen to remain. This thought had brought tears to the eyes of many, many old southern frauds, some of whom still *owned* retarded black men as slaves, retainers, hostelries, cooks, deer dressers. The South was so good. Why was this never discussed? Someone should make an objective documentary, but you couldn't have it now, all this correctness.

"Was it correct when Dee Allison took your cock in her mouth?" Mortimer all of a sudden asked.

Frank Booth did not hate Dee Allison, but he was a bit afraid for her now. "You aren't talking hurting her, are you, truly?"

Mortimer said no, no, probably not. Booth was festering on his nerves. "You old queer. You ain't no navy man, just a jeweler, you lying son of a bitch."

A stiletto knife, which he used for a letter opener though mail was rare for him, was tucked in the sun visor, the handle above his right hand. It was a cultural item like from Sicily. It was the first time Mortimer had taken up any deadly weapon.

He rammed the stiletto into Frank Booth's left side. This was the side of the liver, he thought he recalled from a movie. The liver brought quick death. He did not expect it to go in so smoothly. Booth, he thought, was suddenly a cadaver, promptly delivered out of the night. Wet ghoul. Mortimer was up to the hilt in him. He heard the song "Mack the Knife" in his head. European-like, a jazz killing, so here it was. Or leaving him bad-off wounded.

Booth was effeminate, but he had been an actual lieutenant. He had known contact with heavy metal. He had swum underwater ten feet with a knife in his teeth and a Rottweiler right beside him in a scuba mask with a tank on its back, for two miles. He withdrew the knife from his side and then rammed it right back to its owner, his fingers slipping on the blood of the hilt. His mind was on his own nameless grief, but he was not destroyed. He knew full well where the liver was and he was in it, he thought.

Man Mortimer's belt buckle had bumped the point to a side. The stiletto faced down straight through his root and went then into one testicle, searching the underloin with its needle point. He left it there awhile, did Booth, then jerked it back and returned it to the crease of the velvet sun visor where it lived, now bloody but not all that much.

Mortimer bawled, then whined. He whimpered. He called to his mother without remembering her first name. Emmie? Lumpkin was his daddy, no use here. He couldn't see her or hear her.

The last sting to the groin was the worst pain now, beyond the balm of any mother, any history, any face.

Booth thought, *I split his cock. I didn't need the liver, didn't want it. He's going insane and I can't listen. I hated the navy.*

Then he let himself down from the huge Navigator, joining a saner planet although garish with lights. Orange, mustard, puce. This paramilitary scout stuff with these people. Like they needed another reason to keep one another's hands on their dick and their women, he thought clearly, but Mortimer's pain terrified him. Except for the blood in his jacket pocket, Booth was almost strolling away, down the casino esplanade. He called back, "I won't be seeing you or your woman again. But I'll have the law and my own gun so far up your ass if you come close to me, you'll want to forget this."

Again Mortimer was convinced this was a dream. Dee, double-tongued. She would laugh now. He cried in a hard sob. Over his middle age, his former life. Smooth, purposeful, prosperous, sane, on the downward slope. Oh Mother, Mother. He needed to put his head above his sunroof and scream. Call somebody. *Edie? Lloyd! Bertha! I got too high. Mother can't see me now.*

For God's sake, what is a man with no dick!?

You go to the emergency room now, Vicksburg, and all the porky and black-root dye jobs going Assembly of God on you at the glass windows, already waiting on you for the paperwork with a Chevrolet dealership cheap-ass ball-point on a chain. *I ain't got any Blue Cross Blue Shield, never had any, never been to that Warren General Hospital but twice when Edie had the Valium problem and wrecked my Mercedes SUV.*

The bitch Dee. Giving it up to the old navy nancy. Now she'll pay. She'll be vomiting my trinkets back to me and signing every one in blood. Them rotten kids'll pay too. They never took a kind look at me.

He walked into the concert side of the casino. Even maimed, he was drawn here. The hot Latin music, now slower, the relaxed crowd. Classier. Softness of just folks and glasses and the slowly turning woman onstage, the Coyote. She glistened from a Spanish picture book. It was a family scene. Nobody was hustling, nobody screaming for minutes or colors or change or keno or slots. He wanted to rest here. The Cuban woman sang nearly too well. He wetted up. Tears, blood, pants humidity. *What you call the sweat that runs down the crack in your sister-in-law's ass. Relative humidity.* The husband saxophonist managed a pleasant reprisal to the misty Cuban ballads his wife sang. She was not just loins and squalling voice box. Were Cubans a race? Nice folks then. Could she sing while cunnilingusing new little Marcine, who'd never even thought of a woman that way? He could just see it: *Cinema Marcineté: New Love.* The Coyote, whoa what a moment, in the Now, baby, in her flimsy skirt and strappy take-me-now pumps. Hugh Hefner should be stuffed and cornholed, right here, tonight. Chicago-ass Rodin in some pageant hailing his revolution, set a river on fire in the shape of Raquel Welch.

Larry Flynt was more Mortimer's style. Office in a black skyscraper in Los Angeles. The man assured him that none of his women were forced—no heroin or cocaine or poverty necessary for a real party girl. Throughout known history, a constant line stood at his door, clamoring to advocate themselves by public acts of eroticism. It was always fresh like a new colony shipwrecked on a far island. The women were like those busty Ph.D. women in rocket-ship movies. Present for no clear reason. Otherwise, they had boyfriends and lesbian lovers who respected their power.

This wisdom pleased Mortimer, especially as he pictured his fleet of SUVs circling down the counties even to Natchez, New Orleans; over to Jackson and Little Rock. These flush homes on the best tires, holding any number of men and women in them. The smoked windows behind which would be revealed to what state trooper or hamlet rubberneck no drugs, no weapons, little cash, the sweetest pop ballad of the minute licking the stereo four ways. An urban chauffeur like Lloyd, locked in his seat belt beside Edie, who could talk chocolate into your ears.

Think of the tiny beginnings from that old white hearse and limo rental in Cape Girardeau. A mom-and-pop affair. Five girls. He could get tearful about it. Somebody should've taken a picture. They couldn't afford a Polaroid.

But now, as a eunuch, what was he to them? Girls smiled over at him. Foxes. Those shoulders, those greedy eyes. Here was Dee, sitting at a long table. Dee was surprised to see him sit down at the table, hunched, hushed. The lying whore saw nothing but mirth. She must be drunk, chattering with Melanie Wooten. He knew Dee envied Melanie her natural style and charity, her clothes and carriage.

The only mistake he'd made was loving this woman.

Before he made his appeal for help and all would change at the table, yes they would love to hustle around as Samaritans, pushing each other out of the way to help, he could watch a bit longer. The Latin music was soft, the singer pliant, sumptuous. You wished she'd sing that way for you.

Her husband now a voice of restraint and muted refrain in answer to her. But he looked like a thin prisoner of disgust.

Mortimer continued the casting in his head for a video. *You'd take away the oldest here. Not Mrs. Wooten. She still has something that shocks you, that ageless grace, could be the wise elder madam. You couldn't do with the colored veteran John Roman, though. He's got a fine name, but you got no appeal with an older black hero. This man looks like he'd sing "Old Man River," anyway.*

It's a family dream here. What men and some women pay for, dreams nobody else talks about. You ain't got your odors, your armpits stink. Everything smells like a new car and roses. No birth control, no AIDS, no sad sermonettes the next day, no apology, no forgiveness. Nobody gets hurt. You get nasty, but nobody needs to kill or rob for it. This is my country.

Mortimer wanted to sing. He hurt so much and he knew it had only begun to grab him, but he wanted to sing. "This is *my* country," he began. "Land of the free that I love or something." The Coyote had quit singing entirely and they heard this patriotism, absurd, maybe drunken, around the table. He was nobody's friend here. But he knew things, felt them. He knew he had been born without a talent for love. He was not ashamed.

You take for starters those orphan girls with their light little neck chains, then you see chains just a little bigger around their wrists, ankles, down their crease. Fairyland bondage, like. Mrs. Wooten and Dee come over to them to explain about being women, easing off their garments, dropping their own, cheerful! Then Large Lloyd enters to prove it to both ladies while the girls watch. Edie in something red and wearing long earrings, and she bathes Lloyd with her tongue. Because she is an older woman too, maybe a widow in the middle of being a mature love acrobat when her husband fell off a barge, and she's been innocently storing all this up.

*The girls keep being astounded. Dee Allison will then sat-
isfy three men at once and then laugh as they shrink out of her.
Mrs. Wooten and the silver-haired black woman, Roman's wife,
cheering them on with some old island sex lore.*

*They take their own pleasure, otherwise it's all queered.
The whole thing is about female power, the man is just a friend to
it. That's why the pope and the hair evangelists hate it. It's about
Onan, careless with his seed. It's against populating the grimy
little flybit species except for them as can appreciate time and flesh
and imagination. It's about your high school play and sport and
it don't speak to nothing but itself. You can't tell me who's harmed
by it. The Internet is okay, but you develop there a lonely murderous kind of nerd who wears a raincoat in his own den, stepping out into the ether thinking it's real, realer than Mom, who
he's hammered to death because she wasn't some Power Ranger
with tits who makes waffles every day.*

*These people ain't the ones to get me to the hospital,
though. Bad choice. Whoa Lloyd, whoa Edie! Come here, get us
on out here down the road to Warren General. I've done excited
myself. That wasn't the way to go.* He rose gingerly and picked
his way through to the casino, still patient as a new night
watchman, as if he'd never coursed these alleys between the
dings and the screaming, the magenta, teal and garnet rugs.
Glorified bus station crying havoc. The blackjackers, the
seven-uppers and roulette bayers who would have worked
the state carnivals in other days, with their Chesterfield
growls, women and men.

He began to cry to himself. The pain. Amid the plu-
rality of pawnshop loiterers, lumpen proles. Like his father's
name, Lumpkin. Mortimer gambled, but he never liked it
here, even when he won. Too many times he saw the revenants
of his parents, yanking on the slot arms in wet-mouthed hope-

lessness. Like outpatients. The fine family locked and loaded to force once more the steely arm of chance.

Mississippians were good folks. They gave more in charity than any in the nation. Their hospitality seemed to be state law, and some white folks and black had quite a lot of dough now. Despite their rear-march structures in schools, religion, teenage pregnancy, money and tooth decay, the state was receiving an influx of black families. In flight from the cold North, which had revealed its soul after a century of moral high ground as a paved jungle issuing forth a life nasty, brutish and short. They resettled all the old counties, yet the Delta, richer in soil than the Valley Nile, was poor and home to casinos since the early nineties.

But in these poor counties there was other charity, in the form of suicide, often by cop. The lost soul saying, "I cease bothering, sweep me out." The river awaited nearby, as much death as life. Several hanged themselves in prison, in drunk tanks. One man slit his wrists in a Dumpster behind a Hardee's because the food was so bad and its black and white teenage staff did little but carry on a race war over its microphones. He left a note to this effect.

Then there was just the sorriness. Was it modern times? A Jackson policeman named McJordan shot two small pet dogs within two weeks. One was loose on its owner's land. The other fifteen-pounder, yapping in the policeman's driveway, he claimed was threatening his wife. Did he mean to announce that he was such scum that he must be annihilated by any dog-loving rifleman in this state? McJordan was found to be within the law. He was back on the force, armed. Even Mortimer wondered if the cop was something newborn from science, and Mortimer had no feeling for dogs. Large

Lloyd vowed to destroy McJordan, but he was intellectual and was taking his time planning the torture.

"What? What?" Mortimer suddenly shouted above all the noise, the croupiers, the money changers. He had been dreaming, was losing blood.

Just then Mortimer saw Egan the minister in the aisles and was about to pronounce him a hypocrite to his face until he saw the fellow's mission. Egan was in motorcycle boots, the keys to many churches and their basements on a ring at his belt. He was handing out business cards. Stared at Mortimer as he gave him one.

"You said in your sermon you know me. But Reverend, I think it's me that knows *you*." It dawned on Mortimer, seeing Egan up close, that this boy had driven the car with the woman and her boy in the trunk. He did not know where it was driven, didn't want to know, but he loved to feel the kudzu, the cane, the palmettos, the lesser Amazon bracken, the pestholes, the bayous and the creekbeds and oxbows all around him here these seven years. To know her and her infanticide would stay in undergrowth, underwater or, surviving that, would have been eaten by good time and its best friend, decay. He decided right then that the schoolteacher in the trunk must have been a dyke.

He understood he was sane too for not hugging nature and mostly spitting at it, wishing more of it was a rug and smelled like new cars. He was satisfied that he had never caught a largemouth bass or even thrown at one. Just the way they said Elvis was proud of never writing a song.

"No, I know *you*!" said Egan very loudly. Mortimer was not aware of others in the casino.

"Egan my holiness," he erupted as if with a thought roaring straight out of his gonads, lost in hurt. "There are near a million coyotes in this state. What the hell's *happen-*

ing?" All this stuff with eyes was crawling around the bodies in the trunk. Or it might be in the ocean. This boy Egan, the good shepherd. Once beat up women.

"You're wicked all the way through," Egan said. "Another day I'd already have jacked up a switchblade to your throat and you'd be forgetting you look like Conway Twitty."

Mortimer understood from his own grimmer days that it was not good to beat up women you thought weakened by speed and heroin. He understood this the afternoon he hit an almost giant girl with superb legs, messed up on everything. He'd never heard of some of the chemicals, and this girl beat him mercilessly. She was pure girl but could look done for when really she had another whole tank left.

"It's Fabian, Fabian, boy," he rallied.

"You might of once looked like Fabian. Not no more."

This assertion made Mortimer angry. But then he felt sick over the whole night, and small. Very weak, with the pain of monsters. Maybe he was in adrenaline shock. His legs sought a ladder of escape where there was none.

He read the card in his hand quickly.

IF YOU ARE HERE YOU ARE IN TROUBLE
MANY HAVE DIED HERE, LOST FROM BOTH MOTHER
AND CHRIST OUR LORD JESUS.
THIS IS HELL, FRIEND.
LET ME TAKE YOU TOWARD A HAPPY WORLD.

The Byron Egan Ministries
In front of you as you stand.

Mortimer was filled with sorrow and pity, for this boy and for himself.

"I believe," said Egan, "you are hurt, my man." Gold teeth, the brown but graying ponytail. The black tattoo of the cross on his cheek.

"I *am* hurt, Egan. Would you take me to Warren General Hospital? Would you?"

"I came for no other purpose."

Egan, not young anymore either, set a stack of his cards on the roulette table behind him.

They walked out and rose into Mortimer's behemoth Lincoln Navigator. Egan drove. Mortimer saw by the dash light that his car was very bloody on the seats, the carpet, even the visor where Booth had put the stiletto back. He asked Egan if he'd like him to put on a religious station. Egan said no. When he worked with evil, he worked with evil.

"Brother Egan." Man Mortimer rethought this. "Little Cousin Egan, Byron Egan. I never had the time to be good. You understand me? Something pushed me. I never liked it, but something always pushed me. Like Elvis, Twitty, George Jones. I feel uglier than Jones right now. But let me tell you. You ever write any songs or a book?"

"No, friend. I don't believe in it."

"Believe? Well you wouldn't, I guess. I just say to you, for me I'm happy I never wrote a song or any book. I did the world the grace of keeping my no-talent mouth shut and my fingers quiet."

"The first good thing I know about you, whore trader that used to be Fabian. Books are a very mortal sin. Books are not wrote by the Christly. I got no idea why a writer of a book should have respect. Or even get the time of day, unless he's a prophet. It's a sign of our present-day hell. Books, think about it, the writer of a book does envy, sloth, gluttony, lust, larceny, greed or what? Oh, vanity. He don't miss a single one of them. He is a Peeping Tom, an onanist, a busybody, and he's faking humility every one of God's minutes. Especially those Christian ones that write about lawyers or accountants killing each other."

"That's a sermon's sermon, boy. Well done. Drive on, my good man, drive on."

FOUR

DEE ALLISON'S SONS ISAAC AND JACOB WERE NINE AND TEN, but they already wanted a car, and they planned to take some orphans from the camp on a ride within the year. The car appeared one afternoon in June standing dry out of a former deep bayou that disappeared in a sinkhole. The earth opens and water goes downward in five or six seconds and you have a hole where a pond was, or a service station. Florida, because of its vast underground riverine passages, is first in sinkholes, but in other states wet over long periods you will hear of trailer homes, and a few times fishermen blandly working a pool, suddenly disappearing and the soil gray as lunar earth within the week.

The Allison boys had found the car all bare in the hole yesterday, on the back edge of the insane Irish ex-priest's land, with one of the priest's dogs messing around it in high anxiety. The car seemed to be a vintage something none of them had seen in person, but it was a ton and a half of rust mange in a coupe shape when they found it. They very much wanted this for their teenage car, the boys, and their older brother, Sponce, who did not confess it. You had the sense you could chip it out like a hunk of ocher marble and release a beauty within.

Isaac and Jacob did not care who they stole from, and they were also used to obtaining things just by guileless asking. But Carl Bob Feeney was an unbound hermit anxious to fire on trespassers. He loved his Irishness, had always been lonesome, and he compared himself to the expatriate atheist writer Samuel Beckett. He was given to patrolling the woods, as at this moment, with a .22 Magnum rifle, along with his dogs. There were eight of them, pound dogs ill used by deer hunters who'd run them for a season and then deserted them. When Feeney found them, they were feral and starved and had battled coyotes much more sophisticated and swift. Now they were merely loud and always in trouble. Not so much treeing creatures or baying at the moon or pursuing trespassers as rediscovering one another, beasts they seemed never to have encountered on this baseball field–size domain before, and beginning blind fights all over again. Most dogs do not have much recall or shame about recent hostilities. These dogs appeared not to recall other dogs as a possibility.

Today the boys had brought Sponce and his friend Harold Laird, who had such a sick crush on their mother. He fixed engines, but his main vocation was waiting for her to turn up from work in Mortimer's gift, the Range Rover, used and hunter green, and emerge from it in her white stockings and wary boredom. Harold could fix anything to run, like Ulrich's lost Jet Ski, given a strong limb and a chain and another working vehicle. He would show them the ropes once the thing was started. He owned a rugged high-horsepower ATV that they all sat on now, soberly driving short distances with a good muffler so Feeney wouldn't hear them.

The ex-priest's ears were not that good, anyway, from alcohol and heavy-metal music. Soundgarden, Motorhead, AC/DC, Black Sabbath, Marilyn Manson, the forgotten Irish rappers House of Pain. He may have stolen from the collection plate to buy the vast stereo system of 150-wattage that he and his nephew Egan thoroughly enjoyed.

The late seventies and eighties brought on the music of the homicidal charge, a home war after the lost war of Vietnam. This is the land of Visigoths, Picts, Celts, Zulus,

Huns, Indians, Scots, Vikings and Tripoli corsairs, with many substrata of Mongols, *banditos* and racial marines in a polyglot of fierce challenges. The ex-priest himself had been chaplain to the marines in Korea and still believed them the toughest armed force in the history of the world. What other kind of music was inevitable for these people? The armed services know it is classical and employ it freely. And civilians, dressed in the GI-black T-shirt with something nasty printed on it, hair long behind, short at the sides, greasy blue jeans and jackboots tougher than anything they might wear them to do, which is mostly listening to heavy metal and imagining a horde assault against dance majors and carrying off their willing women on their shoulders. The little boys joined the ex-priest in this enthusiasm unknowingly. Harold had gotten them small T-shirts to match their long hair behind. One shirt read: *There's Shit in My Ear Were You Saying Something?* The other on the nine-year-old said: *If You Ain't a Hemorrhoid Get Off My Ass*. These shirts were made for car drivers.

The problem of claim on the car might not be a problem. Who owned a sinkhole below the land after all? But less clear was whether the car was on Feeney's land or the disused grounds of the orphans' camp. They did not intend to ask the couple who owned and ran the camp. This fragile team stayed on Mars, it seemed to the boys, and discipline was so loose that they had seen many an orphan in Redwood and even Bovina when Harold took the family out to eat. They smoked and purchased naked muscle-women magazines, but most of them were nice enough, good playmates. They liked heavy metal too.

The ultimate goal of most heavy-metal rockers is to catch a sensitive wretch such as Michael Stipe of REM alone in a cow pasture and drive over him in a raid of motorcycles and war Rottweilers. The priest was quiet, however, like Beckett, and organized Gothic invasions of the Vatican itself in his mind when the hard stuff was on. He was in the woods with his rifle now, and he did not know what his dog was into. He could swear he heard bursts of grumbling heavy metal in the woods down to the east. He walked slowly, smoking Players one after the other, hungover on Colt 45 malt liquor, a can of which was cold in his pocket for the moment of necessity.

The boys went straight to work. They were going to ask the priest about the car but decided not to, because nobody knew quite how seriously to take the .22 Magnum. Feeney had shot nothing yet but a yard jockey he had stolen down the lake, from the lawn of white people he detested.

His nephew Egan had tried to take the gun away from him, but he would have had to take on a whole fresh paranoia, a job close to sweeping out a large hospital. Egan would lecture the old man patiently. Except for the idea of his trespassed land, his uncle remained still an ethical Christian without want or hope for material. Even his alcoholism could be moderate, leaving the juice alone three straight days with no real sickness. Egan held up his prized old switchblade with the Mexican flag colors one afternoon and offered to throw it as far out in the woods as he could if his uncle would throw that rifle the same. There was still much goth in Egan, he knew it. He did not think Christian heavy metal was possible, only heavy metal, but it might be the music of Christ's deepest anger with the whip against the money changers in the temple. The next trip to the lodge, he saw the old man had brought the rifle back in and had a whole new box of shells for it, polishing them, as no sane rifleman ever did. Some of the dogs were going unfed, they urinated and excreted in the hallways.

Egan was worried sick about the sanitation and even more about the fellow shooting an orphan or some other child around the land. Somebody just fishing for crappie in the grotto pond, one of the prettiest natural-spring pools he'd ever seen, where Christ Jesus might have knelt in his loneliness for solace from the ailing masses and baffled disciples. Egan was going to have to put his uncle in Onward, but Egan had no money, and the church had stopped its insurance for the old man. There was nothing. Egan had sold his own Harley Softail, an act that broke his heart. The IRS had taken his Triumph Tiger. He had an old Nissan and no more credit at the hardware store to fix the lodge or his three churches. No more credit at the Robert E. Lee Motel, where they had cut him a nice break by the month. His wife had left him for another Christian biker who still had his Harley, brand-new at $22,000, $5,000 more in leather bags and honcho seat and tank, very righteous. Egan was looking at nothing but a last supper. He had only a hundred bucks. Without the good gas mileage of the ancient Nissan, he could not have made it to Yazoo City.

He loved to go there to visit the grave of an old pal of his, the writer Willie Morris, who had kidded him once with the question "If you were fourth and fifteen on your own one-yard line in the last thirty seconds of the game, would Jesus know what to do?" Egan had laughed wildly. "Of course! Bomb to Peter. No other choice."

"Peter dropped the ball for Christ at the crucifixion, my friend," said Morris.

"That's why he ain't ever going to drop one again, Willie."

The past weeks, the weather come over his own grave now, Egan thought deeply of killing the both of them, nephew and uncle, with the gun. But he couldn't. He was not good enough to see God yet, and the old man was worse. An alternative had presented itself, but Egan was not ready to admit it.

Feeney's dogs were all over the trunk, and the boys had to kick them back. But the Lord smiled on them then. They heard the old man go back to his lodge, called loudly by his nephew, who had a new car in the drive. A big shiny luxury SUV.

Harold always had the tools. He was from an old stripe, those who fixed everything broken in history. You do not understand how they carry the right tools in those thin white overalls, but they were there around the P-51s and C-47s in the Big One. Nobody cared about them but the fliers who knew. Such a mechanic was Harold.

He popped the trunk and pulled up the lid, and the two boys and Sponce ran backwards like hares through tall grass and bushes. So fast they were out of sight, and Harold was left caught in a cloud of rot, so bad he thought these things in the trunk were huge dead catfish for a minute. They weren't, and he got back quickly too. Missouri tag. Who would leave the tag? Only a drugged idiot, the man who was now walking swiftly through the four acres of trees and fronds, having heard noise. He held his uncle's rifle.

The mother and child were collapsed in soured meat. So vile they arose with smell and commenced being skeletons almost instantly. To Harold they seemed to sigh while doing it. The boys had come back to within fifty feet.

"This bitchin' car's older'n me," said Harold. "Sorry for cursing, boys."

"Ransom," said Sponce.

"How you know their name?" the smaller boy asked.

"Ransom is a *thing*, dickweed. Somebody kidnapped these two and held them out for ransom but cheated and killed them or nobody paid."

"These folks is ours," said the older child.

"What could you pissants do with them old folks?"

The children began to behave as interns of science, walking and thinking, not too close to the trunk yet, but seeing the car might be saved.

"That is a mother and child. You could boil them bones so they not putrid and set them up with wires and it would be a family, him Jesus the baby and her Mary at Halloween, and you could have Christmas both."

"They start Christmas the day after Halloween at Big Mart, anyway," said Harold. "But what you mean, have? Where would you have them?"

"Like on a float in a parade, or you could make that car into a convertible if the top's not no good and ride them in the backseat."

"Why? Who the hell would be looking?"

"To scare 'em."

"You mean the man that did this, if it is a man?"

"Well him too, but he'd be dead too, wouldn't he? If he was older than this car, or you, Harold."

"You boys ever hear of Sherlock Holmes?"

"No."

"Well you ain't him. You got your detective work running around the barn to hump itself." This speech by Sponce made Harold very uncomfortable. Despite the T-shirts, he was on a new program to stop using the little bad language he did. He wanted to be an influence on these children, in hopes of giving Dee another one someday.

Egan looked on from the last strand of scrub pine and winter wheat. *My God. If I run them off and get that tag.*

If I can even make myself do that. You go through life asking when do I use the rifle. These boys aren't even trespassing. The thing is, I could kill myself after I crawl in the trunk with that pair, if they would leave and give me enough time. What they want is that car. All the rest is my hell, not theirs.

It is this far I am now from my Christ.

Take me back.

Or forward.

There ain't no standing here, Lord.

I just as much as slaughtered Mary and child seven years ago.

When Man Mortimer got out of the hospital, he wasn't through hurting for a good long while and was almost unmanned. But then he watched his only video and felt the stirring of loin sympathy and was mildly satisfied. He drove to Monroe, Louisiana, in Egan's old Nissan, ordered a meal at a drive-in, which he never did because he might be seen patronizing one of these things, and when the car waiter came out with the chili dog and diet Pepsi, Mortimer reached out the window as if to offer the boy a long column of change, but it was a box cutter instead. He cut down the whole length of the kid's forearm, which caused him to shriek and almost faint, scattering the food. Mortimer drove off hastily and left behind smudges of the Nissan's old tires.

Last night at one of his homes, the big fifties-ranch-style one, he had watched on his large flat-screen Phillips television the film clips and recitation of a minister. A curious breed of faith, perhaps not even Christian.

"Why do people look for science, science fiction and signs of the End? Why do they seek the Revelation of the Apocalypse here and there and chant the old chants of the coming of the Antichrist, the Four Horsemen? Science fiction has already been *had,* fools. It was the Battle of Kursk, German tanks against Russian tanks, fifty-seven years ago. It was Leningrad, Stalingrad, Moscow, Berlin, idiots! What does it take, a sock in the jaw for you to get it that the Forces of Darkness fought *then?* The Antichrist on both sides. Piss on *Star Wars.* Nothing touches WW Two for science fiction and wasteland.

"What else do you need? Can't you see that things are *better* now? That the prophets are winning *more* battles? Where they are losing is At Home. Plenty and boredom and people are killing because they got, get this, no other imagination! And you have Mormons, for God's sake! What the hell is that? And who, by the way, *is* president of this Space Walk? You got any idea? You got a TV, don't you? I thought so. You don't have a clue in hell who our President or His Wifeness *are.* Now that's some science fiction. Our President will never kill himself, but if he did, as he ought, he would wonder who was performing the act. And our First Lady would name a different murderer three days running. Is this what the school of Yale does for people? My aching ass. Give me Harry Truman from our worst community college. He'd be on the roll, *The Roll,* there at last! Shut up!"

Mortimer thought he himself was the point of this address, that he was still suffering from a dizziness rushing from the nads. Behind the man, pictures of Nazis and Russians blowing each other apart in the cauldron kept running, and one of the Russian soldiers in the bowl-shaped helmets looked a great deal like him. This man was directing fire and using binoculars near artillery pumping up and down in a plain of mud. The man looked like the singer Fabian but stealthy and gung-ho, as if he had stumbled into an important movie.

The afternoon after his work at the Monroe drive-in, Mortimer was still in Egan's car, a blue thing going for a record in mileage and fading. He was not sure why he had traded cars, but now he was glad for the incognito and ease of parking. He had a feeling he would get more hooks into Egan yet. He parked under a century oak curved over the drive at Onward. He waited until the hour satisfied him and went around back. When he looked inside the door, he was clear. There was nothing to hurt in the first room, just chairs and a blood pressure cuff. In the next, however, was a nice cabinet with all of Melanie Wooten's glass animals in a miniature African-plains scene, done with extraordinary patience and care. Giraffes, wildebeests, tigers, lions, monkeys, panthers, elephants. He picked up the whole scene in the swathe of green burlap and crushed it under his Johnson & Murphy wing-tip loafers. He had dust and glass specks on them now. He heaved up the sack and set it as a bag of trash, matchstick trees, shoe-dye water holes, on the cabinet where it had waited for the patients to enjoy. Then he slipped out the back, just about on the spot when nap time at Almost There was done.

Much dither broke out on the discovery of the animals soon afterward. Melanie came in for her readings while it was going. She didn't want this, but one of the elderly patients had already called the sheriff's office by the time Melanie arrived. Dee Allison awoke without actually sleeping, as she often did. "Number one, Mrs. Wooten," she told Melanie, "I have no idea who did this. But the sheriff is not going to come out about a case of smashed glass animals."

"Oh I know. I'm embarrassed. He can't be that bored. Who would even take the time to *do* this?"

"I don't know anybody who would even come here on purpose," said Dee.

But the sheriff did come out. He had a good build and short hair and, when he neglected to modulate his voice, did not sound even remotely southern. Delaware, maybe. He admitted he liked espresso very much and was pleased there was a machine here, along with very modern books on all subjects, weight loss, sexual improvement, racy novels. Bleden's huge child-psychology tome *If They Were My Child*. The sheriff's name was Facetto. He performed in plays with the Vicksburg Theater League and had never played a lawman, even when he was in college in Mexico. Dee Allison had not seen his television meditations on the law and the world on the evening news each Saturday night, but he did have a presence. They said he was New Breed, this young high sheriff of Issaquena County. He knew, or talked anyway, psychology and the demographics of crime.

"This is the work of a teenager who may be having early bursts of schizophrenia. Most likely. I'll get prints, but it won't lead anywhere, I'll bet. The girl won't even remember doing it, I'd guess. Tragic. We had a boy in a youth group when I was young, we all went to the circus, but he attacked the bedroom of our den mother and tore it to shreds. He didn't know why, we surely didn't, he'd been urged to go to the circus with us. He was quiet, tall, barely whispered. The attack was his language. I'll never forget him. Dillon Brad."

"A girl? Why?" asked a man in a wheelchair. He had a deep crush on Melanie Wooten and was the angriest of all.

"The temperament. This was meant to inflict the most hurt on something delicate and painstaking and artful. A more feminine principle. If she had any intentions at all outside of fury. I think so. It took preparation."

Dee Allison was very attracted to the sheriff, who was thirty-six. When he slipped back and forth from southern to East Coast accent, she felt at home. She was good at her work that way. She spoke illiteracy and literacy, depending on the patient. They had all kinds at Onward now. Even

Vietnamese, Cuban, Korean, Pakistani. The ones who first owned the tourist courts had gotten old right along with the rest. There were the few vicious hicks too, of course, who had never had a right day and intended to live until they found one. Facetto looked directly at Dee's bosom and blinked in approval without being coarse. But he returned his look to the victim here, Melanie, and held up an uncrushed zebra figure, crystalline and delicate.

"This is art. It is precious, priceless. So we are talking sacrilege of a sort. There may be even religious overtones."

What an ass. Dee thought of another nasty T-shirt she had ripped off her son and scolded Harold for, which made him beg and beg forgiveness. He had not read it, bright white against black black. Medium-size. But it belonged on a bumper sticker. *If I Had Wanted to Hear an Asshole I Would Have Farted.* It seemed appropriate now.

The ex-doctor Raymond was having tenderer moments with his wife, Mimi Suarez, and she was learning to love the big cottage. Now she knew that animals listened when she sang on the back stoop, because she saw them hearkening. Once two little boys were hidden, doing the same thing. The boys were in love. It was a difficult love somewhere between the need for an actual mother and the affection a pagan yard ape might have for the Madonna, with the delicacy of all women's laps and breasts. The voice was what brought it all together, though, the night when they first saw her and she didn't see them, out under a wild magnolia with its pod mulch underfoot, and she was bare-breasted. In no boastful way, no criminal way, no way wicked. Because who would she be seducing?

Max Raymond no longer liked to think of himself as a former doctor at all. He had met and chatted with a real doctor, Harvard, many times, and he understood that much of his life consisted simply of a failure to fail. Now he was a saxophonist and bad poet. He thought more and more of his mother, was working on writing about her. Most thoughts that were any good, he recalled, were merely getting frank with an ancient truth.

His mother was a powerful Baptist who thought constantly of the Lottie Moon Mission and its Chinese orphans. His father was a former gunner on a battle cruiser in the Pacific, but his anguish over this remained in the form of absence. Not drink or drugs, certainly not psychological trauma, but a refusal to be anywhere much if he was not firing a gun at a Zero, the height of his life and the depth of it too. He had been aired out by a halo of lead, and his steps on this earth were light. He was not big and muscular. He remained spidery like a distance runner or a tall jockey.

Ma was navy too. That burnt-leather voice. She sucked on Old Golds, Fatimas. Smoke ran out of her like a bombed ship. She had mated twice, bringing forth Raymond and his brother. By her will, Max arrived ten months after conception. Of average height although a little thin, he was born discouraged. Too big for grade school, then suddenly too small for life, he felt.

Raymond's mother would grab him by the throat when he was a lad. "Love the Lord, you little nit."

"Ma, these swimming trunks are too big."

"Excuse me, but I am feeding the heathen orphans of the world. What is your difficulty now?"

I was sent to my room to beg the Lord to have me, Raymond wrote, hitting whiskey straight from the bottle but only twice an hour. *When Ma got the sad fairy organist at the church fired, she said, "What he is stays between him and his Lord. But his music blent poorly."*

It was the movies *A Mighty Fortress, The Life of Luther, Ben-Hur, The Robe* and others she approved. Then, for myself, I slunk to the old Royal Theater in Jackson to see the vampire films and their women breathy and innocent in their nightgowns. Like a pink supper in the rainy Carpathians. I had a mental woman, imaginary I mean, who wrote me letters from Dracula's castle, surrounded by her friends, the beauties from the Bible movies, also almost naked and looking down at their Jew sandals. My replies to them would do whole peoples in. "I've had it with them. My dears, the French must die."

I didn't have much left for the local girls except Ruthie, a majorette, who slapped me for my thoughts and told Ma, now small and whispering like a husk in the wind. She forgave me because Ruthie wore her legs bare, spangled and strutting like a field slut. It was staggering what a humanist Ma became when Pa stepped out the last step. Her mercy took on the softness of a hound's ears. I don't know if this was love or only understanding.

Now that you're dead, I have your life to play with, Ma, Mary Perkins Raymond, and forgive me for it. Guide my mercy. Endlessly rocking, and she died. She did so much good she was never bored until the time of her final sweetness.

Ruthie did love Ma and her memory. It was not this writer but Ruthie who put flowers on Mother's grave once a month. I brought along a cup of steaming coffee from the truck stop for her tomb, unable to think of much else she enjoyed but cigarettes and orphans and Baptists. And Pa with his own tomb right beside her. I believed he had missed so many

Japanese with his gun back in the forties that, dis-
heartened, he could not smell the roses. Could not
find the silver lining. I did not know a firm thing
about him. A near acquaintance of his informed me
that Pa was stone deaf from cannon every minute
he knew me. I always thought he was a mystic. He
couldn't hear, he didn't want to see us, he ranged
solitarily I still don't know where. The money he
returned with, it smelled like dogs sometimes.

I did not throw myself on Ma's tiny form in the
coffin, but I wanted to. They keep you so far away
with that last taxidermy. So much I had not done
for her, never mind her orphans overseas. I was now
forty-five, married twice. But I was still a boy in some
kind of trouble in the room, needing to pray for
myself in a smaller room, needing to regret this worm
of me. I lost my bones, it felt like. They had spilled
clicking around my shoes. But I was not given to
histrionics, as Ruthie was, her whom I never married, regardless of all her postures.

Ruthie sinned, again and again, and cheated at
cards, even stole cattle. Deceived her boys and her
husbands. Then she would pick her Sunday and
appear in a small church where theater had never
been. She was now sorry in public for everything,
everything. In a new meek dress accenting nothing.
From her midheeled sensible shoes.

"I have sinned in automobiles, airplanes, under
trestles, in warm ponds with cattle watching. This
was partly liquor, that liar, or the chemical cocaine,
that serpent. I was Jezebel who fell out of her window onto the street and the dogs licked up her blood.
I have betrayed my marriage, over and over. I played

all evil rock bands that there are on the stereo, at deafening volume. Lynyrd Skynyrd. Can you call this life?" Everything she should have whispered, she yelled. The churchgoers were cowed. Small children laughed or applauded.

Christ loved sinners so, better than the pious, she went on. He loved the hot blood that flowed under his cool fingers. She'd brought her own sermon and redemption with her.

I barely realized I was mad for her. There was a time, very tender, when that was possible. Just as John Roman is mad for Chet Baker, who was made for love and for horn, Chet at the end with toothless bony soul. Fell out of a window and died, I think, after being everything God gives a man. He never played the horn loud, never. Never showed off. What an car. No running around jagged, like me, he was mad for love. To be more like Chet Baker in my heart. My good Christ, give me talent please, no more art. I loved Ruthie.

I was a success, but wrongly, deeply. Each year there was a new record of giving to the Lottie Moon Mission fund led by my mother. And I needed an appointment with Dr. God, as the Oak Ridge Boys sang. The better part of my malformation was my own. Beyond the saxophone I had no dreams. Well, a few cigarettes and looking out the window. I wondered what my essence was all through med school. As if I had one. Then the Peace Corps and back like a lost hound to the delinquent Ruthna, the hospital bed, the narcotic line. She now called herself Ruthna of the suburb Rathnar. What in my glassy delirium to do except begin dating her? But is there

anything wronger than your young daydreams coming true?

Her man Harb got into a wreck. Harb, his woman
and car stolen and defaced. And Harb striking me,
the last blow an uppercut right through. He began
hitting me in the face right then in the hospital, where
I worked but was currently a patient on fluids. Now
was I sorry I had run with Ruthna? Harb was a small
man even at bedside. "Harbison! Harbison!" I appealed to his better nature. Such names as they give
down here they make you desist when you call them
out. "Have patience, man," I pleaded with him. "I'm
already in pain every minute. She hurt me too, remember? Would you like a high heel in your ass? In
your dead mother's bed?" While she spoke, standing over me, in some unknown tongue of lechery.
There's no use looking like me, she said, *if you ain't going
to act it out.*

Her old lover Crews was showing off his mangled
leg in the parlor and collecting pills from visitors far
counties away. This was Ruthna's infamy. Nobody
wanted to miss her next spree. It might be her last.

There is no doubt I carried my same love for her
straight to Mimi Suarez. My Coyote. But Mimi is
innocent. The band was playing at Nubie's in Memphis, and I had to have her. I was mainly good, I
thought. I was no longer a racist. I knew I could
exceed their saxophonist simply in pure fury. Yet I
disliked most people. If diseases could come attached
to something like an ambulant dummy, I might still
be a doctor. But her hair meant more to me than . . .
Well, there was Malcolm in the way, and I took more
than his spot in the band.

Few liked me at first, with my hunching toward the Coyote as she drove her hips. You can play a lot of jazz in a mambo, actually begin lessons and finish right on the spot, which is jazz. But I opened my eyes to find myself on her, horn grinding away on her thighs. She moved away, threw out her brown arms, to howls of execration from the front row and farther back. I was middle-aged, that was the main horror! But women often like a mean man. Those women who write to killers in prison. It must be for those punks like writing a letter to God. Mean is the diploma of the artist. I was an alleyway myth, but I strutted. She may have married me out of fatigue.

When my thrusting on the stand, a dreadful thing to behold, became lawful, my fans thought me lessened. But I was good. I swallowed the horn during my feud with music. Mimi screaming like a cat in a bath but with actual talent. I had friends, and they had solid names like Jim, Whit and Alexander, and only one of them asked to borrow money. Well, two. One had designs on the Coyote, the way he grabbed her and lurched at her rear. Lucky I was middle-aged and beyond jealousy.

I have left out almost all of life that's beautiful. Its small acts of kindness. The pier crowd over there, who invite me in a little more every time I go to fish. Mimi Suarez almost eternally at ease. The small fame you can get by practicing some dumbish thing over and over. The sleepy awe of these grounds and lake and house. The evil I feel close at hand to know I am alive. The evil thereby. I must see the devil at hand. Then Christ.

Sponce Allison and Sidney Farté came across each other in the elder Farté's bait store. Food, engines, devices. Two bass boats, wrecks in progress on trailers on the west side, two gas pumps out front. The last of the black-and-white televisions over an open drink and meat locker. A fine greasy television, studded high on the wall, under which the sullen could eat a dawn-prepared heat-lamped meat in a roll swamped in mustard, mayonnaise, ketchup. Except for the bait, an excellent beer from a microbrewery in Louisiana was the only item of real quality.

The coffee was bad, the standard for parsimony and contempt at fuel stops. Even fresh, in the prelight of dawn.

Two tables. Pepper Farté charged fifty cents to sit and eat there if you did not buy grub at the store but ate your own and needed only a drink. The television was free. This bothered Pepper a little. He would rather have put blindfolds on the mere loiterers he suffered around his linoleum.

Sidney was only fifteen years younger than Pepper, his father. But he was in far worse shape. They were scions of a pusillanimous French line too lazy and ignorant to anglicize their name in a pleasant manner, and they had been laughed at plenty by squires and rootless trash both, and even blacks. In the matter of blacks, Pepper's hatred of everything was so full it left nothing over for racial distractions. He looked at all the same, his eyelids raised only a bit as if asking silently, *Why in hell were you born to trouble me?* His being eighty-eight now should have made him resent the hip-hop throbbing from the cars of the bloods out at the gas pump while they came in for a beer. But for Pepper it was only another small pestilence, like his son, seventy-three with shingles and in chemotherapy and radiation, always threatening pneumonia, sent to plague Pepper by the same Overlord who had vexed him always.

Pepper looked awful, but he was in good health except for wear and the scholar's spinal curve he had gotten behind the counter, despising the chore of making change. Many of the prices in his store were rounded to the higher figure for this reason. Change was precious and his arms were feeble, holding it, and he had to fight going higher by a dime on all his goods.

Sponce Allison, matched with Harold Laird, was in the alley of the tinned meat, saltines, fireplugs and prophylactics and salt and coffee. When they collided, Sidney coiled and puked a bright yellow line that never even made an arc before it smacked Sponce in the cheek.

"Ho doggit!" The boy was amazed. Gravy ran down his eyes and dripped in a beard off his face.

Sidney still drooled in a lip-wide stalactite down his own chin. He was undergoing stress, a rapid melancholy that overcame him once he had vomited on another person. This thing wanting out of him so quickly, like a hot weasel in a tube.

Old Pepper, behind the counter near the screen door, raised his hooded scowl. Last night he had seen a mother and baby skeleton in one of the ruined bass boats, he thought, and heard a scurrying off through the edge of his porch light into a stony field. He did not credit it fully, but neither did he tell anybody, because his son wanted this store and Pepper knew it and he would give no psychiatric evidence against himself else the sheriff or Onward might be called. He enjoyed a beaked scowl now before the odor hit him, over that of weltering meat under the lamps nearby. He almost smiled.

His boy was staggering out from the mouth of his premium aisle, now toward all the bright spinner baits and bush hogs and jigs, the solid Rapallas like Picasso, the Sluggos, the salty worms, the wobbling deep-running torpedoes, the high-tech sonic ones that rattled and rolled. The single fishing video entitled *You Are in the Wrong Place*. A wet boy behind Sidney.

Sidney had not apologized, and the boy was stunned by this discourtesy. But Sidney feared a second eruption and so did his father. Others wanted him out of the store too. But the Allison boy now held him across his neck. He demanded some acknowledgment.

All his working life Pepper had sold instruments of violence against fish and game and some people. He had war-surplus bayonets from Korea. But he had never struck his son, wife or enemies. He was too remote in his hatreds for this. He would have shot his son just then if he had owned the energy. He did hiss as Sponce rode the seed of his lap out into the porch.

"Here now, here now," called Harold Laird. He was a born remonstrator.

"This old man vom on me!"

"I'm sick, sick, you sons of bitches! Don't you see?" swore Sidney, then threw out his arms to free himself. His long-sleeved shirt was spotless, the drool gone. He seemed hardly involved. He walked over to the end of his car and, breathless, looked upward dead-on at the sun. Now he was a blind old puke and swore again.

"By gawd you're stunk out," said Harold to Sponce. "You ain't aiming to get in my ride thataway?" Laird had a nice old Camry. He had left Hermansville last year and never looked back, except to retrieve his four-wheel ATV and tools.

"Tell you what. I'm standing here waiting on a goddamn explanation. Or manners at least."

"Old man, don't you want to tell him something?"

Sidney turned away from them toward the horizon. Shingles, colon cancer, psoriasis, mouth ulcers, dysentery. In his mind these old friends called out to his young tormentors.

"All right then. Here." Sponce walked up to Sidney in the gravel lot and hit him in the right jaw with a quick round-house left, then knelt in pain himself for the damage to his hand. He might never work on that side of his body again.

Pepper was in the door watching. He was satisfied. Sidney was out cold or stunned, one. But he still stood, arms at hips.

It was an awful thing to watch a sick old man slugged. The boys were uncomfortable. One was in severe pain. So they entered the car, which was suddenly irreal, out of all space and time, hurtling fast to nowhere with its points of chrome light on the hot blue wall of sky.

Nobody came near Sidney, no customers, not Egan the preacher, with his own problems and oblivious. It was Egan's habit to purchase one pack of Camel straights, light and smoke one, then throw the rest of the pack in the road as a sign of his conversion and for good luck. Cigarettes were $3.20 a pack. He was deciding, needing a smoke badly.

Sidney spoke. "Well then. I can make other things die." He staggered back up the steps of the bait store. "Pepper. Give me a pack of twenty-two long-rifle hollow points. The Winchester. Not the cheap stuff."

Pepper handed on the little box without comment. There were many snakes around, but he didn't care about that either.

The boys did not feel right. Bereft, divested, exasperated into sickness from the old man. It hit almost immediately. They drove in circles, then they walked that way.

"It ain't been right since them skeletons. Them kids loose with them." Sponce was irritated at Harold for wiring the skeletons together for his brothers. "You promising that car to them."

"We made a deal, a square deal."

"Remind me, genius."

"They would pay on the installment when they could. Or get parts for me as they found them."

"I stink."

"Don't I know it. I'm sick myself, son."

"I'm sick as a dog, Hare. But what do you get if you keep taking us all out to eat at night. Steak and Ale, Red Lobster. I'm too sick to talk food. Aw."

The deal that had been struck without Sponce's knowledge was that the little boys would persuade their mother to put out to Harold, and then Harold would become their father, in the proper way, after a divorce from their gone father.

"I can still afford it. Mechanics is big money if you get serious, which I have been since eleven and started smoking then too. I quit the smoking, you notice. The swearing too."

"But you ought to get a new hairdo. That one's too college."

"You don't know but what I might go on up to Ole Miss or Southern, even State if I'm good enough. Your own mother went to a Jackson nursing college. High education's in your blood, son."

"I remember that zoo over there. A good un."

"I didn't notice a hell, heck of a lot right before we found the skeletons, and the car came with it."

"You got a rust bucket. And the bullets in they's head. Them skeletons belong to the law, Hare."

"The law didn't care to find them, did it? Seven or eight years. And that car ain't rusted that deep. You just can't see the form like I can."

"How long till you get it running?"

"Seventeen years. They said teenage car," Hare joked. They would have laughed but they were too sick. Then they got back in the car and drove some more. Sometimes, in fact usually, a man had to just burn gas. Let the big dog eat. They wanted to drive across the Vicksburg bridge for no reason except to change states, but they were too sick and had to come back home.

"Hare, you ain't given Dee the prize yet that'd make her . . . that'd move her toward that surrender. I mean marriage. Them two old guys gave her this, that and the other and she laughs and says it don't get them anywheres. Even if you're in love with her."

"I got patience. And I'm changing quick."

"Yeah. You're all wore out from being nice."

"I ain't had but one day since I met her that I wasn't in love with her, and that wasn't her fault. That's when the flesh boiled off them skeletons."

The sheriff was doing a five-minute commentary on the Weekend Review on television Saturday night. Both Dee and Melanie watched.

"The world is full of middle-aged men who seek revenge. The anger passes for most when they see there is no way. The rate of incarceration is very low for first-time offenders of sixty. For some, there is a bigger engine of hate even then, running at the red line and very vigilant toward what they might consider insults or even bossiness. They aren't just having it, the engine, like the others. They *are* it. They have not been aware of this, and their acts confound them. Those are ones you see on television or in the newspapers discussing sodomy, rape, kidnapping and murder in the passive voice, something happened, somebody was killed and so on, sometimes even giggling. 'Mistakes were made, yes, when she was killed. I can't remember, really.' Such as that."

Such a pompous ass, thought Dee. Though she admitted the guy was hot. She had seen him and Melanie, twice his age, having a moment as he went out the door at Onward. Mrs. Melanie Wooten of the linen slacks, black slippers, a Martha Stewart hang of bangs. Dee could not believe the sheriff was gone for an old woman. But he was beginning to be.

Besides acting in local theater, the sheriff rode a Norton motorcycle. The people of the county were not clear on what man they had. He was handsome and very verbal. These things were measured against him. Many women, however, wanted to see his warm gun and dreamed, since there was little else to do.

FIVE

THE SMALL BOYS LIVED ON RAISINS OUT OF A BOX TWO nights in Blackjack, a ghost trailer-home village. There had never been much of the natural graces here. It was just a hill with a curved narrow pavement across it like a bad part in tan hair. Winter wheat, chaff stalks, stunted pines. Right up to the right of way. Old electric poles, downed wires. Kudzu stopped at the slabs of the old precincts. Repeated fires from years gone by, cigarettes tossed out, the seepage of chemical toilets. But still a town of hulks, with alleys.

Both boys kept combs in their pockets and groomed their strange but pretty hair often, sensing their beauty in this desolation. They were on a fast without knowing it. They were not particularly hungry and their energy was high, their heads clear and visionary, with the Benson & Hedges 100s they puffed now and then. They were in minor ecstasy.

The black T-shirts with the obscenities on the chest were baggy and stretched out. Sometimes hung out to dry after washing in a creek. The boys were thin and muscular. Their line had furnished the crafty retreaters and battlefield scavengers since Shiloh. Such men whose craven disappearance had only begun the troubles of their enemies.

Mortimer had seen them on the highway shoulder with the bones on a cart. He was driving a Lincoln Continental at the time and was incredulous until he drove two more miles, then credulous but confused, then in Rolling Fork he turned around white with concern. He parked his car in a square two miles from their home and worked his way in on foot, so he would not be seen. You could not heave a big cart without at least a path, he thought. He could not go to the Allison house yet. He would see Dee soon enough. The physical absence from her was hurting him, so he knew he was at least a third healthy, although not right, or he couldn't have borne it at all.

He seemed every minute to cross the borderline of a small foreign land. He had not spent any time walking in the country. Otherwise he could have hidden the people better himself than the idiot Egan, who would pay soon. Egan the man of God who had borrowed Mortimer's money. What a fraud in all ways. *Does everybody just act and lie?* Mortimer thought. He felt in quicksand, in alligators.

Now he was in Blackjack, near where he had seen the boys and their cargo. A great bomb might have hit here, deeps on either side of the road and the ghost of the trailer park hove into view on the right. He immediately saw a child running between the burned-out hulks and got out of his car, the engine still on. In his right hand he held an absurd knife such as you saw only in pawnshops. Of not even commando utility, it was so huge. It had a saw blade on one edge and most likely would have been more shiny than it was sharp had Mortimer not made it a project. You could hack off the stump of a yucca plant with it.

He trotted down an alley and looked in the blasted and rusted door frames. Past a ghost fence that was barely an idea of wire and rot. Then he had one cornered in a trailer with his nasty black T-shirt on. He could smell the boy and raced into where it was nearly black and caught him by the arm. "I'll cut your head off if you. . . ." The boy resisted, then stopped.

It was noon and no shadows and Mortimer was sweating hard in his sports jacket. A little pistol fell out of his pocket, but neither of them noticed this. The other boy came running toward them, bounding, enraged and driven by fear at the same time, like no animal.

"Believe me, boy. Your brother best stop right there too. Ease on up." Now Mortimer had the boy by his hair and grabbed for the other with his knife hand. This was not a good idea. He nicked the boy fairly well on the shoulder, and the boy shook loose as his brother plunged his fist into Mortimer's gonads. Mortimer held on, however, and now the hitter saw the blood on his brother's shoulder and desisted altogether. A lamb shaking with fear.

Mortimer grabbed the boy's hair again more tightly by the trailing rattail in back. "You come over here for a haircut or you run and it's . . . a head cut," he said slowly and way short of breath.

"We ain't hurt you."

"But you stink and I don't like you." Mortimer sawed the boy's hair loose and it fell in a black lank. He indicated the other to come over. The first was holding the back of his scalp but looking at the enormous knife, almost a cutlass. Mortimer sawed the other's beaver hang, really just touched it, and it came off in his hand too. "Now you look more, more nicer. Like boy people. You shouldn't wear your hair like rock and roll when you your age. Like you mated up with some old Mexican beaver." He bent down to chat on their level. "Now where's your cart with your friends on it?"

The boys simply ran. Why could he not have thought about that?

He looked for them awhile. Too tired for the same rage, he took on another one, a cold haunting in the cells of his blood that would not leave him until an awful thing was done. He hollered out into the thicker woods, though still scraggly, all around him. "I see you with it, I'll put you in the orphanage or the penitentiary!" He walked short distances yelling this.

When he left, the boys came out. It was within the hour. You could hear a car a long ways here, could almost hear the browning pines bake. So few cars came by at all. You would be cursed to have trouble here, amid the trailer hulks taking on shadows and figures down alleys, mouths. The boys ate from the box of raisins and vowed to go on home. The cart was way back on the other side of the lake, not too far behind the bad restaurant and Max Raymond's cottage. Then Isaac looked down and saw the little pistol. He picked it up very carefully.

"That sumbitch's ass is *mine*," he said.

"You got to beat me to it."

They were ravenous and they decided to go to Pepper's shop and get what they could. They walked three and a half miles with the pistol, which, small as it was, became weighty as a hand steam iron. Weak as they were, trading it back and forth by the mile. They went in the store and did what they said.

They were clumsy shoplifters. Pepper stood right there and he knew. But the younger boy's shoulder was bloodied, and hadn't he seen a gun in the other's back pocket? You just had no idea nowadays. Never did.

In the early morning hours, Mortimer watched again for the prophet, on a television big as a closet in his British Tudor house in Clinton, hoping for more science fiction and apocalypse. But the prophet did not come on at the regular hour. Instead was an ordinary bloated carnival figure and his wife, evangelists. His wig of slate waves, her towering nest of curls and paint thick on her massive eyebags. An ex-hooker, shouting and laughing in raptures as she explained she was actually at the moment walking with Christ and his apostles on the shores of Galilee, hearing their laughter. *Their laughter*, thought Mortimer. Here was a new one. Repentant whore laughing with God's men. He thought about some of his own women. He offered no retirement plan, no health insurance. This was no worse than he treated himself. What you did was just make money and watch out. He fondled a new purchase. A rainbow-painted clasp knife with a fillet blade.

Outside in his driveway his ride was a long black Mercedes. He could not find the pistol in any of his cars. He had to cut down on the coffee. He wrote this down. Then he cried a little for having no friends.

Sponce and Harold were very sick. They hallucinated odors of burning oil and monoxides to awful intensity. They smelled their own life tenfold. They could not rid themselves of the odor of sunbaked vomit. Both stood under headaches that drove them to the darkened back of the house. On separate cots they rolled in nausea and the jitters. Head of black air shot full of spangling pins. Sponce thought he would upchuck his heart itself. They could not keep down even Tums, only cold Gatorade, which Dee brought them in such quantity that she began to make it from powder. She took two days off from Almost There and was nervous in her home, but she didn't mind.

She saw they were clammy, too pale. She wore her white uniform and sat in a chair long into the night with a thermometer in one hand. Then fell asleep like that. She never turned on the television and did not think much of Man Mortimer, more of her real husband, which she seldom did. She had turned thirty-seven the day before. The boys were finally asleep at dawn. She amazed herself by her energy and tender domestic feelings. She had taken Emma to the Mennonite couple down the road two days ago. The couple had tragic pity for her. They took the child in with hardly a word.

The small boys had been away three days, but that was not unusual. The little scutters. They were devoted to their skits. She had little say in their lives anyway. They seemed like vagrant lies she had told once, in the form of children. She wondered if she loved them or should.

In the back, Sponce moaned at noon. "Feels like that old man puked straight through to my brain."

Harold whispered, "Lord God, don't leave me hanging. Decide." So sick he was not in love for hours.

Out of torpor, Dee watched a religious channel finally. It was the Assembly of God folks. Appease the Lord, the absentminded Big Skull. You always had to get his attention or he wouldn't recall you from an hour ago when he directed you up shit creek, and it raining. She decided these folks needed to be laughed at because their lives were otherwise flat and cold.

On Saturday the next round of fishermen in their old cars and muddy boats and ragged families would buy their ice and nothing else at Pepper's store to furnish a day at the spillway, where they fished for crappie and catfish or stripers from the bluffs not in sport but for meat. The men were not greedy, but they could carry a lot. The aerators chugged in the background like distant sucking hells. Miles and miles of fields and valleys had been flooded to make an entire county adjacent to Warren and Issaquena counties the biggest catfish plantation on earth. Cynical neighbors to the state had suggested the whole region be flooded so as to have a closer Gulf of Mexico to Tennessee, Missouri and Arkansas. But Alabama did not want Mississippi's brown seawater interfering with the emerald coastline of the condoed and biker-barred Redneck Riviera. This delicacy, catfish, was now Mississippi's leading export.

Universally, nothing is better for bluegill than live crickets. Pepper had them fat and brown. The inside of Pepper's store smelled like old minnow water and the stale bread he fed the crickets. Once Isaac and Jacob had caught crickets for Pepper to make pocket money. Now they left with their spoils, passing by the poor families on their rag-tag fishing trips, and on to the bad restaurant, staying off the road.

They knew the woman with curly hair might sing at sunrise, so they slept not far from their cart in the wet bottom under a holly bush and on soft pine needles from a stand of ten huge pines, unlumbered by some miracle of cross deeds. This was a hundred yards from Raymond's back stoop, where the dark woman would come for her aubade to the animals after a hard night of thick cigarette smoke and rum and Cokes. They were becoming tristate stars, the band Linga Caliente with their Coyote, found out by a crowd new to this area like the coyotes who had swum the river or trotted across the bridge from the west two decades ago.

Sometime during the night the boys awoke and took the skeletons one at a time off the Big Mart lawn wagon they had stolen from the orphans' camp. They brought them to the edge of the woods but not visible to the house and sat them side by side in high cane under a hickory, seated like church members who had waited too long in the pews for Rapture. The pistol went wherever the boys went. It gave them confidence, and the feeling let them sleep.

They fell asleep holding each other on the beach towels they had stolen from Pepper's bait store. They simply wore them like ponchos and ran when he looked away. In their dreams the woman would wake them by coming to the little porch and singing in a foreign tongue, beyond Spanish.

When she began to sing, they sat up. Whole blooms had leaped to whiteness overnight. The bones sat there, passengers of beautiful white in the moonlight.

Her voice naked and not there. They forgot they wanted to see her without clothes and became only hearkening ears, like juvenile rats. This was sublime until the saxophone came in all sick from another part of the house. An even more foreign country trying to converse with her.

They imagined for a while the woman's voice came from the mouth of the mother skeleton and was theirs alone. No saxophone could avail against it.

"You know," Isaac said when the voice and the horn stopped, "these shirts is nasty. The one who gave them to us is just another one wanting our mama."

He took off the black T-shirt rank with days of child's sweat and blood drying from his cut. Jacob did the same, balling his up. They dug into the earth, an easy loam, with their hands. Buried the shirts.

"We can get new shirts when her and the doctor leave."

"It's Sunday and they might not. He might be having at her. Or watching football."

"The wife would have some good shirts that her titties woulda been in."

"We could meet them."

"No we can't. We ain't good-looking enough."

"That Lincoln-driving old fuck cut my hair off." Isaac touched the back of his head.

"You know it."

"That one's ass is mine."

"And what you ain't finished with, I'm gonna be on it."

Melanie slept alone and wondered if she could sleep alone another night. Too much seemed a mistake, a lack, a sucking away, she thought. Her pleasant yard, the rippling shore water, the night singing of the wetlands, did not feel kind to her anymore, in this furnace of midafternoon. Her bones felt dry. Then came evening. She wondered if this was all because of the smashed glass animals at Onward. The doves outside repeated their three-note griefs softly, never weary of them. Surely it wasn't grief. She was awake at three in the morning. *But I make animals from my loneliness,* she thought.

The next night she had a guest.

She had "Greensleeves" from Ralph Vaughn Williams on the stereo box. He had brought *Fantasia.* She was happy he was an actor with the theater troupe. Otherwise how could he have imagined this?

He drank two very fast cups of espresso and then his moves were sudden. She had planned to talk an age, but what did she know. She asked him to hang his pistol belt on the bedpost. He chuckled and then he was all over her. It was a long hour with several engagements. She could not believe it when he took her from the rear. She felt spasms and loved him backwards as if trained to this work because she was not only older, *she was old,* and she couldn't have it that she seemed naive. That would be obscene.

Then she imagined that he would want her aristocratic so there would be something to conquer, not a pliant, grateful old woman to make jokes about later. On the CD the violins were trembling, deep and long, into retreats and sighs. Moving things around was one of the great pleasures in life. Finding new figures in ordinary stuff. *Like an artist,* she thought. She believed they both were artists and not silly at all, not absurd unless air was.

She held her own against his withdrawals and frantic reentries. What a gift to hear him cry out vanquished as his long spurts made ropes in her. She felt very rich in secrets for hours. Blushing with them.

"I guess this is trouble," she said to him after a while.

"I don't know what you mean, trouble."

He was marine-cut and muscular and did not smoke. She did. She lit a Pall Mall left from a pack John Roman forgot when they went fishing together with his wife.

"Child, our ages. Us."

"Nobody is married. Nobody said no."

"That's true. So, modern times. This doesn't feel like sin or what . . . ugliness to you?"

He watched her with her cigarette. She smoked rarely but truly needed this one. She watched the pistol butt in its holster, the golden bullets, the belt hugged to the bedpost. She needed sin.

"Well," he said, "it felt good, that good, like sin. If it hadn't, I guess it would have just been ugly."

"Will you want me again? I'm asking at the wrong time."

He grinned. She wondered if he was handsome or just a fine package.

"Maybe. But even now, a sapped ape, I'd say yes indeed."

"You were sapped?"

"Sure."

"Thank you. One more thing. I'm sorry. Believe me, I believe in quiet too. But will you stay interested in me?"

"Yeah. You're what brought me to the dance. I wonder what it's like to be as good-looking as you this long. You've got style too."

He dressed and drank another espresso rapidly. Then he was gone.

She walked around the house, and then she cried for a few minutes. Extremely happy. He had asked her to go with him to a high school football game. The end of August. In this heat. At Edwards, a town back east twenty minutes or so. She had forgotten this was possible, even though she had gone with Wootie all the time those years ago. "The season is hot and school is too early and this is the subtropics," she said aloud. Then she was sad a moment. There was no seduction. She was stunned and needy and already too attuned to him. Thirty-six years old. Did he have to be exactly the age of her only child?

He had told her nothing about his business, although she had asked were there murders lately or what were the crimes he went to besides glass animals. Somebody had seen some skeletons on a lawn cart somewhere, and two fourteen-year-olds were missing from the orphans' camp. But he spoke as if these matters might be local delusions. He had not left her out, but he had not been garrulous, as on his television five minutes.

He stood at the door just briefly, saying these things, and she was almost deaf looking at him, tall but without cowboy boots. Here was your seduction.

They knew no old things about the other. No months of dances, no convertible under the moon. But in the old days you always knew the end. People could look through you and see the children, the house, the lawn, the dog, just up the road. Not like this.

Let me keep this sweet life in me for a long while, she demanded of nobody.

Were they even friends? Or simply something else, like nothing in the old books, the old songs.

"What was your name meant to be?" asked the deputy, eyeing Mortimer's license.

"It was meant to be what it is, goddamn free to be itself like this goddamn country."

"*Man.* You don't hear that much. Never, in my experience."

"Did you go to a name college?"

"Sir?"

"You stopped me for having an uncommon name?"

"No sir. I stopped you for running a stop sign on County Road 512 and Hill Bagget's Road."

"A country stop sign. And for having this Lexus. You thought I was a dope runner."

"I couldn't see much at all through those windows all smoked. These windows make us nervous. We don't like them, you know."

Mortimer relaxed. "You see I'm not a black man now. You must be pretty fresh on the force." The car might look ill-gotten around here unless you were a plastic surgeon or an antique queer, but Mortimer was part of the fabric here. They were lucky he didn't move off from them, not even after that tornado came close to one of his houses and tore the third one to pieces. *You got forty thousand employed by the casinos in this state, sure, but you got at least forty thousand wrecked lives to go along with them. More. You got Cash for Your Title civilization, you got pawnshop villages. Me, how many lives have been wrecked? Twelve. Maybe thirteen or fifteen, tops. I even brought Edie back from Valiums. You got me who got stabbed in the wang from loving a woman.*

Big Lloyd and Edie were on a mattress in the rear and had stopped eating each other briefly while the patrolman talked. Mortimer had been driving them and watching in the overlarge rearview mirror above the dash. For his personal entertainment. *Personal* was your operative word here. *My country 'tis of me.*

"Mr. Mortimer. Do you have farming land in Sharkey or Issaquena County?"

"Farmland? Would that be a high crime?"

"No. I just thought you might know some of my folks."

Mortimer could not believe this fool.

"No, I don't know farm people. I'm driving on your soil, your folks' soil?"

"None of my folks talks like you."

"Are you saying I got stopped for talking?"

"Sir. You know, you look like Conway Twitty. A good man, I hear."

"Except he's dead, Officer, sir."

"Yes. But they say things about the King too."

"My aching." The license came back to him through the little slit of window.

"The Kang. What if I called your boss?"

"The sheriff? The High Sheriff?"

"Yes, Deputy. The sheriff."

"Well, I'd just say I had probable cause. But I'm not ticketing you this time."

Mortimer said nothing until the deputy had driven away. "I have a life. Shoot me."

The deputy told the sheriff privately in the office who he had stopped and why, and how sassy the man was. The sheriff seemed unimpressed. Mortimer had no record. Then the deputy described their nasty conversation.

"He didn't really miss the stop sign, did he?"

"Sort of."

"No. You stopped him because it was a black Lexus SUV and you'd never seen the inside of one, or you thought you had a dope-hauling African-American sort of dude, or a casino entertainer. No?"

The sheriff threw himself on his knees in front of the deputy. The deputy had seen a minor version of this theater offered to others but never had he come in the way of it himself.

"God, please save me from Boy Scouts." Facetto put his hands together in worship.

The deputy was astonished, sick with embarrassment. He worshiped this sheriff. "Sir?"

"Yes, Lord Deputy?"

"Do you know any Conway Twitty songs?"

"Your life began about the last season of the eight-track tape, Bernardo. 'You're standing on a bridge that just won't burn'?"

"I'm what?"

"One of his tunes, Bernardo."

"Yes sir."

"Get rhythm, son. I beg you."

"Aw."

"Or just read a book."

"Yes sir. Could you please get off your knees?"

"But I love thee, Lord Bernardo."

"Personnel are gathered at the window."

"Get the book, Bernard. Look up the difference between *deputy* and *rubbernecking fool*."

The sheriff got dreamy. "I seen this movie the other night, deputy old son."

"You don't talk like that, Sheriff."

"No. But a priest in it knew karate against zombies. He said, 'I'm kicking ass for the Lord.' Is that what you're doing, or is that what I'm doing?"

"You're embarrassing me, sir."

"Now get out there and troll amongst those sullen crackers along the roads. They're used to talking to their own dicks and staring offwards, looking for cars. I implore you, Bernard. Don't just be hitting on strange cars."

Those gathered at the window felt much more for the young deputy than they did for the sheriff. The murmurs had been going. The histrionics, the Norton, the fact he might be gay, the lack of hate, the little zeal he showed for his gun.

Hare and Sponce were not doing well. Sat on either end of the porch in ragged lounge chairs and reclined, with the radio tuned out and in on the tape box and orange Gatorade in a cold thermos next to each, brought and refilled by Dee when she was home. After three days she had had to go back to work, but she had no dates and this was sweet to them both. They did not eat. They were drawn, pale, whimpering, like things called by Legba. They expected the virus to pass each day listening to a radio song about rum and the sea. The health in the song was miserable to them.

They were some better, then not. They marveled at the disease. It had its own dreams. Big violent birds and prehistoric sauria. A man with an enormous head who searched for a hat and killed many. Hats or people. Johnny Cash in Vietnam. Neither was alive at the date of Cash's appearance for the soldiers. They fell asleep at any time and went into somebody else's story, somebody who also seemed lost and sick. They awoke to another singing about dope, seawater and dizzy sophomores. A one-note faked happiness, rhyming names to *malaria*. Inside, the television flamed with others talking, dying. Nobody watched. They were too weak to turn a button off and weary of listening to the bubbles of their own selves. They hung as in caves for lost days, aged hermits at twenty, twenty-one. To the bathroom if anywhere. Wet feet on tile.

Isaac and Jacob came out of a culvert they could almost stand in and walked into the yard. The grass was thick and good in large parts of the yard. Zoysia. Sponce saw them and imagined the culvert ran back miles into the woods. The boys wore clean tank tops, coral and blue. Sponce thought they had been in the culvert for hours, maybe days. He wondered vaguely why Isaac's shoulder was bandaged. If it was the monster from his dream they had been fighting.

One of them went up to the radio and tuned out the fuzz.

"Where you been?"

"What's wrong with you?"

"We been sick, Isaac. You don't wanna know."

"Where's Mama?"

"At work. She about to quit. Some old lady is asking her sexual advice. They think Mama smashed up some animal glasses or like. They think our mother did that."

"How can she quit?" Isaac said.

"She's got Daddy and them men supportin' her."

"She needs taking care of anyway," Hare put in. "Her health is important."

"Her job's the part of her isn't nobody else's," said Jacob. "She can't quit."

"You want more money for her staying on?" asked Hare.

"I never thought the least about money."

"She heard what you been up to. Hare lied and told her all y'all had was dummy zombies. Where are they?" Sponce demanded.

"Sitting in their own peace."

"You a wart."

"None of that's the point," Hare said. "The point is you were somewheres like two stray dogs. Off. Else I dreamt it."

"You get well and fix up that car, Hare. Or we might go to the sheriff and stand back and wait for the reward. That was a car like songs are written about, and we goin' to have it in red and a gold hood. Or else I'm gonna tell Mama alls you want is your weenie in her."

"Mama doesn't need that anymore," Sponce snapped. "You shut off your pie hole, wart."

"Here's a story," said Jacob the skinnier, taller. "These people is our ticket unless that car gets done. It might be some old rich man in Missouri missin' his wife and child all this time. He'd be laying on his deathbed cryin', and all this money and it never been no happiness since they were stolen. He misses the car too. Then you see us on television and him light up. And we would be friends, we wouldn't need no daddy or dating men ever again. He wouldn't let none of us six need nothing again, aside from the reward. We'd have a new house on a brand-new lake. If not a ocean."

Hare turned even sicker. If that were possible, heaving a new tomb in a dry rock face from his bowels.

But he spoke in a whisper afterward.

"I'm going through some purification here. I got to have it. Them old stories hit at me. I'm all reamed out of

everything nasty. I'm not listening to any more nasty stories. That ain't right. We all better get us a better story. When
I'm well, it's going to be a good story."

The next morning Hare awoke on the recliner on the
porch in his pajamas. July was well on. The house was too
big for its window air-conditioning units. Some corners
sweltered, eighty-eight at night. He snapped his mouth to
cut off a snore and slept. He had on no shirt. His lean muscles
were packed closely.

Dee saw him when she went off to Onward in her
whites. Her knees went a little weak. *When will I get any better about men,* she asked herself. She walked in a trance most
of the day. Cautious, polite, gone milky and holy in the head,
abstracted into kindness.

SIX

MORTIMER PICKED UP THE MAGAZINE. HE COULD NOT quite believe it existed, the gift of an old girlfriend who had found it on the Internet. *New Deal*, the organ for reformed country people who now hated nature. People who had lost farms. Settlers between town and country who wanted even less. The homes pictured were like mausoleums beside highways, no grass and not a stick of a tree in sight. Paved lawns. Good-looking women and whole families in chairs on brick and concrete lawns. Homes in bare sand neither in the desert nor near the ocean. Not a sunset in the magazine. No visible seasons. The only length of prose was an article about Hitler's bunker in the last days of Berlin, not for the history but for the architecture.

Some dwellings were high-fashioned storm cellars. To hold off grass, leaves and the elements. Nearing airlessness even in the photograph.

Mortimer was loaded with himself. He had dreamed his history, and in this heavy automobile, in heavy calm, he was a creature of great velocity. He had forgotten to tell her what to wear, and this annoyed him. He went in the casino with her full of self-worth and clarity. It had been awhile and he was mysterious. She was intrigued. Then they walked across the lot and entered the hotel, a huge monster waiting for them.

He wondered why he was not three countries away, but not long. Edie and Large Lloyd were waiting in the penthouse suite. They drank drinks. The wallpaper was flocked with red kudzu and catfish forms swimming in it, gold traces. Somehow not trashy.

She told him in the elevator what a suck-up the sheriff was, coming around Almost There. He liked hearing that.

"Are you attracted to him?"

"I believe it's the other way around."

She thought she could hear the din of gamblers, glasses rattling, shouts expressed from a gilded maw somewhere. Impossible at this distance. The very air perhaps.

Large Lloyd and Edie waited in the room, wore sunglasses.

"Let me make an introduction."

A show about sharks and rays was on a large television. Dee had not watched television since nature began to play such a part. The sharks weren't bad, although Mortimer seemed frightened of them and presumed she would be. He looked without wanting to and could not even manage to get pensive before looking away.

On the big vanity dresser, his collection of knives stood in their case. Huge machetes to slivery stilettos, even razor knives. Velvet backing two inches thick, scarlet. Gold and silver instruments of despair against people in the golden excess of the room. They all simply stared at the collection.

"Here it is. I've shown you the houses over in Belhaven and Jackson, those English cottages and lawns. You didn't want that. I'm going to play you some more nothing for two hours, and you can't turn it off or I will come back and you won't like it. It is a rehearsal of a man named Raymond on a saxophone, from a band called Caliente something. His wife, the Coyote, sings, and she's good. But you see what you think about him. Then you decide between me and Frank Booth, who won't be looking very good soon."

Lloyd the Huge spoke. "My actual name is Lloyd. You will remember this night and my name. Large Lloyd."

"And my name is Edie," said the woman in the elegant dress, the ballroom heels. "I go deep."

When Dee had listened to the dreadful saxophone, the endlessness of its despair and whining, then gaseous punctuations, she turned off the tape deck but kept watching the television for the sharks and rays. She was certain then that Man Mortimer was a disease and had assumed she knew this too for a while. He did make things happen, but the flow of these things had been redundant until now. He was only a man, even with this interesting disease. The others came in immediately.

Dee was not that averse. She had finished many men and loved to reduce them. The woman, when she began with her endearments, was not nightmarish or painful. Dee, who had never had a woman before, was thrilled by naughtiness more wanton and liquid than any since the first naked night of adolescence. An actual departure, as distinct as first leaving the Garden of Eden and perhaps the heavy air of earth altogether.

Lloyd, a mathematician and animal lover, was not accomplished, and they brought him to sighing infanthood quickly. But Man Mortimer was watching, fully clothed, and near the end of something. He rushed in and cut Dee's thigh.

Edie shouted out, "Oh God, no!"

Lloyd remonstrated but held Dee. Until then she had been winning and asserting her pleasure on others. She felt the long cut on her thigh. It stung and then throbbed. Mortimer left the room. Perhaps never to return to her in friendly form again.

The three remaining were embarrassed and sad. The woman had expected just to slap her a little and Lloyd to insist on familiar desecrations passing for ecstasy in pornographic circles. They brought her a wet towel and then played poker with her while swallowing pills. She swallowed them too. She knew she had been sliced long and deep by a razor of some kind. Her own blood, in this prison, was a relief to see, curiously. Because that had to end it, she could still win.

She believed she had wrecked them all and they were burning now. She had reduced Mortimer to spite and outright crime. She could look him in the face, but she doubted he could look back at her. She guessed she knew him fairly well. But she drank too much and took narcotics with Edie and Lloyd, the towel bunched around her thigh. They tried to play cards but were numbed in giggles. Dee did not understand what trouble she was in until she called Edie a name and Edie hit her very hard in the mouth. Then Lloyd twisted Dee's arm out of its socket. They were gone and she was in the elevator riding up and down when she woke up. A fifty-dollar bill was pinned to the front of her dress.

She stumbled into her kitchen in early morning, brought all this distance by a sympathetic Vietnamese cab-driver whose family fished out of Biloxi. There were a few hundred thousand of his citizens on the Gulf. They even had gangs now, he explained.

She did not know what she wore or what her hair was like. She was after ice water, then many aspirin in a large bottle. She missed her mouth with the glass. She spilled the aspirin bottle and it clattered on the tile. Her lap was full of melting aspirin when Hare walked in to see her under the hanging light at the table where nobody ate. The little boys sometimes cleaned fish on it or ate cold cereal and used the toaster on it. Enriched white bread, molasses, jam. Some of this food was on her forearms.

"You sick? Hurt?"

"I couldn't tell you."

"You can't hardly talk."

"You can't know."

"You're woozy. And faraway. I'll take care of you."

Her lips were swollen, saliva in the corner, her nose chapped. A dried rivulet of blood out of one nostril.

"You're not in love with him, are you?"

She looked at him as if he had just sung in Latin.

"I'll fix things, Dee. Not to brag. I've used this home to grow up in. Now I'll take care of you."

It floated, it worked, it launched against a bottle of cheap champagne swatted on the bow planks by Melanie. It was August, and they all wore boat shoes. Ulrich dressed, as usual, as if he had shoplifted in a hurry from a clothes barn in the seventies. Military jacket, purple jean bell-bottoms. Harvard had a cravat, a gold chain from Melanie. For being captain and largely the builder and finisher. Engineer's cap like Admiral Halsey's. Because it was somewhere between a railroad saloon and a boat. Twin Mercuries carried them briskly. The pontoons made an oversize wake. You could fish and swim from it. There were lockers with this gear. Sidney, after mocking them like Noah's neighbors during the laying in of planks, the rail and pews from a razed country church, the stained glass on either side of the cabin, the teak wheel, was aboard as if it had been his idea and he'd never doubted it. He loved hawking into the water the phlegm that rose easily like a permanent natural resource. They were eating burgers cooked on a grill right on the afterdeck and close to the happy engines. John Roman was aboard but not his handsome silver-haired wife, who was sick with something bad, they feared. Life jackets were everywhere. You sat on them, you used them as pillows on the pews. The big cabin was much like a chapel simply portaged over out of the church.

Sidney wore eyeblinding Rod Laver shoes, the old original leather ones his father had got ahold of by lot last month. Pepper worked with people who looted stores that neither had sales nor declared bankruptcy but whose owner simply up and walked away from their stock after a failed fire.

The huge lake today was a suspension of silver. At creek mouths and around treetops you saw fishermen like ants on sticks, this side of a moody horizon. Another barge came out from the orphans' camp dock, loaded with an extra adult, Man Mortimer. He wore a blazer, double-breasted, with khaki linen breeches and high-gloss rubber-soled moccasins. The two teenage girls, Minny and Sandra, were near him and all aboard were happy, especially the insane couple.

They could not tell their mood from Harvard's boat, but it seemed roisterous even from a half mile away. Sidney wondered if they would collide. A short-barreled .410 shotgun and a flare pistol were on board and he knew where they were. Inevitably the two pontoons plowed toward each other, as two cars on a desert highway must mate.

A storm could be making. The old ones hoped so. The roof had not been tested, but it looked as sweet and snug as all of Harvard's work. The pleasure barge had taken a year and a month to build. None of them knew how to build anything but Harvard, and Ulrich, putatively. But all but Sidney had labored with care.

They were roofed, windowed, unsinkable. They stormed forward, a chapel on the top of adventure. They were going uncharted places up the river and into the new catfish reservoir flooding down from Yazoo City.

At Yazoo Point something raced out from the creek. It was Sponce Allison on Ulrich's old Jet Ski. The rooster tails high. Driven in anger at troubling speed toward them, they thought. Closer, you saw a pale boy clutched aghast to its arms, as if the vehicle had stolen him. The boy didn't seem to know how to slow down the ski. Sidney went for the flare pistol, interested in its stopping power. Sponce barely missed the barge, then came back in a circle beaten seriously by their wake and flying high, wobbling. The smackdown knocked the boy away, and the Jet Ski slowed to the boat's spirited crawl as the boy looked over at the passengers in both fear and spite.

He saw Sidney gawking at him and straightaway collided with the pontoon.

Sidney had been seasick since the first movement away from the pier, but in an angry active way of his own. Now possessed by three nauseas, he was tamping down a cylinder of puke by main will until it backed into the last of his gorge. A major muscle group undeveloped in other men sprang forth so hard his head recoiled. Nigh ten feet out, some specks may have found Sponce's foot. The boy went wild with incredulity. He had set against this man void of any purpose and without a final destination. He shrieked over and over.

Ulrich noted that this was his old Jet Ski bobbing, wasn't it?

Sponce floated on the dead thing and it would not start again.

The old man peered at him. Wren, with skin you could nearly see through. Lewis and Moore, the sexual gymnasts in chemotherapy, were dressed for fun, and she should not, as the girls would say, be wearing a bikini with green stilt cabana heels. The boat stopped.

"No. You ain't towing me, and I ain't getting on neither," said Sponce.

So they left him, and ahead the oncoming orphans' barge puttered down to bump into them. They were no longer feral, these children, but disciplined by a uniform glee like that of their counselors, the insane couple. The Ten Hoors, Penny still a svelte looker, Gene in better shape and seeming savvy with his freckles and mustache, were distinctly in charge and adult. But they were in beatitude still. The whole group shone, and were much cleaner, and knew what they were doing on the boat. They were having love and the outdoors was what. These things were good. The four engines of the two crafts stopped entirely and they shuddered up against each other. Melanie, Lewis and the Ten Hoors tied up the boats with the wharf lines.

"May we come aboard slowly and singly? You've done a splendid job," their captain, Gene, cried.

"What are all y'all so goddamned happy about?" demanded Sidney.

"Mister Mortimer brought back our silly runaway girls. Minny and Sandra tried to break in his Clinton house and he brought them back to us. He could have turned them in to the law. He's what this world is made for!" said the woman at high volume, thrilled, radiated by the deed of another.

"Ain't that forty-five miles or so?" Sidney wondered. "Well, unlawful hitchhike, true."

Sheriff Facetto took Melanie Wooten to the high school football game in the last week of August. It was in a different county, east twenty miles in the town of Edwards, out of the loess hills. Facetto had once played the sport and done well. Big and quick but not a fast runner. A dodger. He was first team. He now reflected under the lights, sitting down with Melanie, that every other cop he knew was a second-stringer. Usually the ones who knew the game better than the starters, as they explained full-bore. The players tonight were a third again bigger than his team. He wondered if he would find his younger self here, running toward a line as if it mattered hugely.

God help me love these country lizards, he asked during the before-game prayer. *Lord, may there be significant but not tragic hits made to the other side.*

I run back and forth between them. So they sleep safe in their beds, thought Facetto.

He had gotten a call that afternoon, a wild, high voice on the other end saying, "My uncle put out cigarettes on my forehead for twenty years." "Why didn't you do something, or move?" the sheriff asked. "What could I do? He was blood," the reply. His uncle had just died, the man said. He wanted his uncle's corpse arrested.

Some fans recognized Facetto as they found their seats, and they thought he was there with the newly divorced governor's wife. They could not fathom this bright scandal, but who knew? Mastodons, tapirs and buffalo had roamed here once. Coyotes had made a vast migration east to Connecticut. You just couldn't tell even who was where anymore.

They adored the scandal until somebody said no, that isn't her. Then they turned their wrath on this person, for otherwise that night was charged with wild meaning, and their lives attached to it, like the football. "She's an actress," the person said. "I seen her playing the modern queen of France."

"There isn't a queen of France, liar."

"Fuck you." A squabble broke out several rows behind Melanie. Facetto made a pacifying gesture and it settled.

Melanie looked ahead, understanding a bit of the game from her years with Wootie but more delighted now. Blown by the first cool breezes of the season. Once or twice he touched her knee. She went wet as an oyster, blind with tears.

A blond cheerleader twisted and hollered for the love of the night and her own fame. Usually the cheerleaders were watched by their parents and pals only. Except when a flash of thigh. Mortimer was watching.

The sheriff told Melanie, "Men don't want eternal life so much as the years sixteen to twenty-three back, with what they know now and their bodies no longer middle-aged."

"You're not even middle-aged. Don't try to impress me."

The cheerleader struggled on. *You don't know me yet,* wing and thigh launched in air. *Know me. Eat me up.*

Mortimer went to the men's rest room and waited, leaning on a wall, then standing again. Between urinal troughs, doing nothing else. The teenagers, children and few fathers who saw him didn't know his function. They couldn't read his troubles. Nobody lingered in this bunker. There was no leisure space here. Somebody said he was half-time entertainment, but shit, why would he loosen up here? Maybe to escape pesky fans. Sure, but who was he? Not dick if he was playing here. Some were disturbed as by the ghost of Twitty, but they couldn't identify his age, if he was supposed to be dead or if it was his son. The tall thick waves of hair, the thyroidal eyes that swept them, then looked out at the concessions. A celebrity down on his luck. One said he was Russian. In black polished loafers with that special glare when you're either from the casino or in sales.

Then a small boy came in alone.

"You having a good time? Having a good game?" asked Mortimer.

"We're not having the game, we're watching it, mister."

"Could I play?"

"I said we're not playing it."

"Come on. Tackle me. Show me some touchdown."

"I'll go get my daddy."

"Sure thing. He could play run up my ass. But sonny, you see that man at the hot dog counter. That's my friend Mr. Booth. Please go tell him to come in here. I've found his wallet. Call him *Mr. Booth*."

The boy went out and Mortimer watched him call Frank Booth in the line. Booth felt his pocket, lifted out his wallet and looked puzzled. But he came.

Booth walked in, and by the time he had opened his mouth to say thanks but he had his wallet on him, Mortimer had seized him by the face and cut him so quickly over and over on his cheeks, brows, even neck with a carpet knife that he was not yelling until it was over and his face was streaming blood. Then as he knelt squealing, Mortimer straddled him, knowing he could strike across the throat. But he did not. He said something about higher law and Booth's not wanting to find Mortimer because he might want to keep his eyes, then ran from the blockhouse with a clap of loafer heels. The concessionaire who watched him said, "That sonofagun went out of here like a running back."

Mortimer entered a strange car. It was his but strange. The car was new and had a grumbling muffler and nobody on a bet would guess he'd be caught dead in it. It was a Trans-Am with a firebird painted across its hood such as the car punks of every trans-Appalachian district would use to demonstrate muscle and arouse fright and disgust. He had never had the thrill he had watched richer boys have, North and South. Burning gas loudly and for no point whatsoever except to warn the universe. He saw them chase girls, the cars of troubled librarians, teachers at the end of their rope. The muffler spoke to his blood. Leave rubber, leave pavement, leave governance. You got your foot in something, but it feels like you're kicking it. Cock-deep in internal combustion, metal, fire and gas.

It was five minutes before anybody could remember a sheriff was at the game. Two local officers had gone out into the parking lot, hunting between cars slowly on foot. But with grim authority, warning all others to stand back. This was not really an issue, as nobody was standing anywhere except for the small group around Frank Booth outside the Masonite bunker. Milling, they watched this stricken man, and you could not have paid them to follow that monster into the night.

The sheriff told them he had no power here. He was out of his jurisdiction and not armed. He did not offer to help, did not even arise and walk to see the man's ravaged face, and this was held against him. He had swollen up beyond the workingman, him on TV. Him and his sugar woman. They would go off and drink their wine and forget where they were from, which was where?

Melanie was not aware of their ebbing popularity. Her smile was radiant under the lights, she was a moist girl, serene. To the east the ambulance crept in with dogs barking around it. The crew took off a beswathed thing who cursed God through a hole in the gauze.

Facetto said they had better leave.

The cheerleader, ignored all around, stared at the powdered dirt on her shoes as if her face had fallen there.

The sheriff was not affectionate in the county car and let Melanie out in a mood he apologized for. He said for her to lock her doors well, and she looked at him curiously. For all his build, he seemed a frightened boy. The night, or the people in the night, concerned him, reached out and held him. She had never seen him nervous before.

At the office late, he was hoping he saw somebody who admired him, but there were either those who didn't or other subhumans. *Help me,* he thought. *I've acted my way into this job. I am now an officer and a coward.* There was a note on his desk from an anonymous hand: PLEASE REMEMBER TO ARREST THE CORPSE OF MY UNCLE.

The next morning a call came in at four A.M. and dispatch awoke him at his nice apartment near the old Catholic school and convent. They had found the old owner of a bait store early this morning with a missing head and a football stuffed in its place.

It was six before Facetto arrived at Pepper Farté's bait store. Facetto didn't even live in the county, and this was not known yet. He seemed to push them and dare them, didn't he?

The smell of minnow water, cricket refuse, crawfish aerated in a tank where hundreds of these bait crustaceans clicked together in the sound of sprayed mist on aluminum, each on its way to digestion by one monster or another. Pepper despised everyone, a deputy told Facetto, but he was up to date on bait, he missed nothing in colors, wiggle or odor that was the rage nationally on black bass, white and black crappie, blue and yellow catfish. The black bass was so sought after for its hard hit and pull, sometimes a full minute before boatable, and the expenditure so enormous per decent fish, that you came close to an industrial religion of bassers. Pepper would have sold colored New Testaments with hooks in them if that's what the bass wanted this season. Because the fish tire of the same colors, trim and wobble after a season, like high-fashion ladies. Crawfish were big this year for largemouth bass. The next year they might be ignored altogether. There was an era when fish hit bath soap as it dissolved underwater. Pepper knew all this. He knew that bassers expend a ration of money to bass almost exactly that of modern warfare. In Vietnam, for instance, the budget was one million dollars per dead Viet Cong. Bassing was a war, in fact, and the exorbitant fiberglass boats doing sixty over water spread in miles of honey holes was about like an airport where no machine did anything but taxi. This was music to Pepper's ears, if he heard music at all. He was an institution and not a poor man.

A part of his store was devoted to army surplus. This was a brisk trade too. Fishermen are fetishists about equipment. They are high-lonesome folks and need to surround themselves with goods like knives with good edges, whetstones for sharpening hooks, superior lanterns, army rain ponchos, machetes and cut-down twenty-gauges for snakes. Pepper had been done in, after general laceration by some other sharp edge, by one of his own bolo knives. These short and thick machetes will take down an old kudzu trunk, which is like a sapling. They cut so quickly the parted end stays in the air a millisecond before falling. The Bolos were frightening commandos and guerrillas in the Philippines. Heads rolled.

The football concerned Facetto. They had left it in, the deputies, one of them Bernard. The corpse had no family to horrify, for his son stood right there, conversing too cheerfully around it with the police and photographer. It might have been an exotic cargo just in that Sidney had ordered for a conversation piece. The store was his now. He told stories about the old man, none of them pleasant, since Pepper's fatherhood of Sidney at the age of fifteen. No mother came into any of these stories. Three of the cops knew Pepper for a rude bastard, but still. There was blood everywhere and one of the cops was a woman. She noted the mother was dead and now the father was dead. In this family, dead meant dead. Sidney's wife had been dead for four years, and he recalled little about her.

Facetto told the deputies about the mutilation the same night over at Edwards. It was not his investigation, but somebody had called him about midnight just to chat about committing his uncle to a mental ward or Onward. A pastor Egan. The old man was loose on the fields as they spoke, and nobody had seen him for days. So he was a missing person too, and a candidate for the bin when and if he was run down.

The football game, the football game, Facetto kept saying to Bernard and the woman corporal.

"Conway Twitty and football," said Facetto. Sheriff Millins of Hinds County, who liked Facetto, had called him earlier too, right before he left the office. A man resembling the singer Twitty standing around the urinal talking football with a child. The little schoolboy knew more about the game than the tall man. Very odd. Another eyewitness said the man dressed like a pedophile. This witness was the boy's father and the description meant little besides shiny black loafers, as far as Millins could tell. He could run fast, this perp. Somebody heard an open muffler or glass pack. A driving nun had been threatened on the road by a car with wings on it, loud muffler, she said. Wings on it.

"Did your father play football?" Facetto asked Sidney. "In high school, that you know of?"

"He didn't get to but seventh grade. He never played nothing, except he was in the merchant marine in a liberty ship that was blowed up right outside its own harbor in Port Aransas, Texas. He started swimming. He couldn't swim, but he damn well *did* swim. A German Nazi torpedo boat was chasing them sailors too. It couldn't just shoot the boat off the water. Them Nazis was mean."

This was the only near-positive story Sidney had ever told about his father, who leaned off the stool stiff with rigor mortis and with a football for a head. The actual head lay just to the east of the stool on the filthy oiled floor where he had stood for fifty-five years. Sidney appeared to have a lump in his throat all of a sudden.

"He cared about his own life, I guess, back then. Well, folks change."

"You don't think he cared for his life?"

"I don't give much of a shit for mine," said Sidney. "Do you?"

"My life, or your life?"

"Well sure you care for your life. You tappin' Mrs. Wooten. You tappin' that old pretty grandmother, son. You gone break ol' Bennie Harvard's heart when he finds out."

Everybody there, twelve, turned to look at Facetto and Sidney. Facetto simply went out and got in his car. Bernard was the only one who noticed his hurt and confusion. That was a mean little fuck himself, Sidney. They had a tradition here that broke with southern civility. French. Just straight mean and rude and unnecessary, this line.

Facetto had two idols as investigators. One was the well-known sheriff of Coweta County, Georgia, the man who had no unsolved crimes in his county during his tenure in the forties. A man of humble genius and savvy. But look. What about the population. Small. Homogenous. Everybody a cousin. Little to kill for. Finding a murderer might be like finding Frankenstein in an elementary school. What would he do with crack, folks killing for cell phones, sneakers. Fiends off the highway rearranging someone's body for some aspirin, for methedrine, sometimes just for the hell of it.

The other was a brilliant investigator in Mexico City. Plenty of unsolved untold everything. But the quick deduction. The five-minute profile. No, not a murder, a suicide. See here. Exactly the right thing. Piece of bird shot in the ceiling. Feather on a finger from a pet pigeon. The blood on it there. No other bird would stay close to a gunshot. So his first model would be Lieutenant Maury Fuentes.

The sheriff seemed nonchalant, but he was afraid. These cuttings and the phone calls drew him into a family of hurt he did not want to know. He was paralyzed.

He could not think about this case and had no interest. He wanted only to pull the panties off of Melanie Wooten and enter her and listen to her make her joyful noises again. Straightening and pumping her nice legs and girl's bottom. He was consumed by love for her. And afraid anywhere she wasn't.

It was only eight in the morning, but he drove straight for her house.

SEVEN

CARL BOB FEENEY WAS STILL MISSING, AND EGAN WAS living in the lodge by himself. He thought, *I will be going to Onward with Uncle Carl Bob soon. It could be by the time we get there I'll be fit to be his roommate. God, I can't stand this guilt. Nor the 30 percent interest. Mortimer called it the vig. Some sort of cut rate for taking him to the hospital.* At least the old man had not taken his gun, and he had left plenty of food for the dogs in the pen and the cats in the house, five days' supply at least. Egan prayed he would be back and that he wasn't naked and dead already, or releasing animals from a shelter, which he had attempted before, driven to it by a man named Ulrich in a woody station wagon. Sunday morning, and Egan stood before his flock thinking these things.

Max Raymond was in the pews. He had bought a gun, an old Mossberg automatic. Spring-loaded, with a magazine that worked off the plunger in the stock. He convinced himself he had tried sincerely not to buy it, hadn't owned an arm since rat shooting and the navy. Mimi hated even the idea of a weapon. It was that old boyfriend problem, that sin he couldn't forget. He would one day buy the bullets, long-rifle hollowpoints. Would one day probably not use them.

Next to him, Mimi and three of the other bandsmen. The chubby trombonist, a professor from Memphis with a goatee everybody adored. The emaciated drummer, color of the street, ghetto bus smoke, with exquisite hand-eye talent. A flutist who was the only regular churchgoer, a Methodist in rebellion against Episcopal dryness, people

145

like T. S. Eliot. Four dogs lay quietly. Sent as representatives of their world, it might seem.

Egan spoke. The pew crowd didn't know if what he said was a poem or an odd psalm or what. "If you see my old uncle, tell him I love him," Egan began. "He was right and Mr. Ulrich too. We should commence living for the animals after killing them for all these centuries. Go back, go back to their simple fur, their fun. Their ecstasy over the day, their oneness with the infinite. Their lack of memory. They are our heaven, our friends. Why did we imagine they looked so beautiful, only for our tables, only for the backs of selfish kings and lazy sluts? The Garden of Eden, can't you remember, children? The animals were *already there*. We were made for their kinship, and they could speak and we lived in the peaceable kingdom. Until the woman broke the contract so that we should have knowledge, and now what do we know, even when the animals look at us through zoo bars and slaughterhouse gates. They are Christ every day, giving their meat, their coats to us, and we without gratitude to these creations, these that we call savage beasts.

"We take, we take without even a thank-you, when if we open the door for some woman we'd like a thank-you, would we not? The other day I opened the door at Big Mart for a woman, a woman shall I say better dressed than I. She had just used food stamps, in her lizard high heels, and going toward her Cadillac where children shouting vulgar things waited, and this woman never even thanked me for my little courtesy.

"How do you think you would feel if you were God? Would you feel unthanked for the universe that is yours? Almost any animal is more beautiful than anybody here today. What were they before the contract of the Garden

was broken? For their eyes speak better than our best sena-
tors today. They use a language we can't understand, so we
kill them, tear them apart, even sell their parts for aphrodisiacs. The poor rhino's horn. The liver of the poor black bear,
poached by bowmen too cowardly and lazy to work alongside the rest of us in the fields of the Lord. I want my uncle
and Mr. Ulrich back, wherever they are. They are apostles
from the Kingdom. They have been Paul on the road to
Damascus, they have seen the light and quit killing."

Egan then began the—poetry, was it?

"Dee, thy charms shall not always be sweet.
Minister, thy rituals of the cross turn to babble.
Woods walker, thine feet shall be taken from you,
      and proud ladies' man, you are a boil on a
      cadaver.
Be so happy he has not made you suffer yet, like
      the animals, eaten
For our sins.
The snake may be kind, we cannot know. Even
      our gentlest kill them with
Expedition, the automatic twelve-gauge shotgun.
The snake spoke and was made to be despised,
Even though they may be babies, mothers, they
      stay alive
And as friendly as they can manage. But they
      spoke. Now we cannot reach out
To them, many of us.
Born into a bad cause, lost at birth,
We late Confederates so proud and stuffed.
There was a time when we smiled and charged the
      hills of artillery.
There was a time we did not doubt.

Now you lounge, rain in the trees outside, but you
　　see nothing.
You charge only at the sports store, the toy store,
　　the Radio Shack.
You have no cause, no belief, you don't even have
　　faith in faith,
Or a prayer for a prayer. There is no paved golden
　　heaven ahead.
It is the Garden of Eden behind. We have already
　　seen heaven. Else
What else has this life on earth, this pavement
　　among throngs
And squalling choirs of sycophants, been prepar-
　　ing us for?
Prepare to get naked and talk to the animals, right
　　now!
Given to us by the Lamb, the fisher of men.
But now the question. What are the animals going
　　to do about the overpopulation
Of so many billions of ugly people?
For we have fed on the blood of our own.
We are not even kind to our own retarded that so
　　fill the Southland.
We go off to other states and make fun and litera-
　　ture
And Hollywood movies about them.
The Best Southern Art On-screen is Stupid and
　　Heartwarming.
But you do not know what is beyond the window
　　of your own home.
The crumbs in your navel are your history.
We have pretended that Sherman caused anything
　　in the South too long.

We have spoken of the fall of Vicksburg as if it
    mattered.
Wretched spectators, heads just out of your
    mama's womb.
Buy me sumpin, Ma. Plug me in.
All this blindness without no ON knob!
Parasites flourish in the lesions of bitten mother
    sharks.
Shut up! Shut up! And talk to the animals. They
    have soul, they have art.
Shut up and live with your gorgeous neighbors!"

Frank Booth lay in the hospital for three weeks. He had
already had four operations. It was mid-September, but the
heat had not broken as he waited for the last, a three-hour
procedure by an expert plastic surgeon from Florida, in
St. Dominic's hospital in Jackson. He was fifty miles from
Vicksburg, almost seventy from the lake, but only eight from
Clinton, where Mortimer watched his big-screen TV for the
return of the perverse evangelical bard he had seen only once.
Perhaps it had been public-access television. He couldn't
remember, so he kept a vigil. He had acquired a taste just
lately for a motorcycle, a Norton like Facetto had, a Commando. He had leather suits already, and he looked good
with a knife and a monster key chain.

    Frank Booth opened a letter block-printed and ad-
dressed to his room at St. Dominic's. His hands trembled.
Only three others knew where he was and he didn't want
two of them knowing. But he owed them jewelry, and he
was an honest man. He barely recognized himself in the
mirror even still, and he liked that. He felt hidden, passing
for a thin-faced hermitic and pale sort. The letter was on
good stationery but in printing like a child's.

OLD FRIEND, HAVE YOU NOTICED MY OWN
PATIENT FRIEND ON YOUR SAME FLOOR? HE CARRIES
A FROG GIG AND HE'S BAD TO DO FOLKS' EYES WITH
IT AT NIGHT OR JUST ANY OLD TIME IT IS
SHUTTY-EYE TIME. MAYBE YOU COULD GO THE MAX
AND HAVE ZERO EYES.

Large Lloyd had printed the note for Mortimer. Lloyd was very literate and helped Man a little with writing it but did not ask what it could be about.

Jacob and Isaac fished in the cove and swam. They were childish, changed. They pretended it was a familiar activity under the gaze of their mother, who was not watching at all. She wondered too why the boys came close to her all softly of late to mimic a time with her they had never had.

She was drinking on Melanie's porch. They had one day become friends. Dee quickly realized she'd always liked Melanie, just had a wearying time believing she was sleeping with Facetto. But Dee knew a woman in actual love when she saw one. It might turn out pathetic, but it was true. Melanie did not act as if much between them had ever been less than pleasant, and for people like her, it might be they didn't register bad looks. These things were too foreign to their style.

So they drank and talked, joined by Mimi Suarez, who had recently performed at Almost There with her husband the saxophonist. The tone of his horn was sweeter now, blending with Mimi, with the lustrous hair and hot legs and little dresses. She seemed a good Cuban woman from Fort Lauderdale, and Dee could live with envy, for she had been envied and still was. Being envied was a burden, but these three could afford it, especially with the tequila and gin and vodka. Limes, salt, olives, whatever you wanted on the tray. And as for Mortimer,

Dee was still certain she had won that night, although she had required stitches from Dr. Harvard with his old kit, whiskey and her big lie about a run-in with an electric knife.

She sat up and paid attention now and then to her boys, as she had seen Mrs. Cleaver and others do on ancient television shows. They were above the cove a hundred and thirty yards, and the grass was gray-green in the minor heaven of light when the subtropics finally cools. It is all man could want of this planet's seasons. Many fall in love with anybody and vow marriage simply because they are in this lush afternoon light. Mimi bent to Dee's beautiful daughter, Emma. She gave her a few glass animals that made a family.

"I know now," said the Coyote, "that I want to have a child too. Seeing her almost makes you pregnant." The animals were exquisite in her small palms. Pins of light from hooves, snouts.

Dee had lately come to like the gin, the tonic, the lime, the tingle. When she looked at Mimi again, she grew almost weepy with coziness. Then she felt daughterly to the old lady. It was a family, if you had steady gin. She was fluid in folks. She swam in Mimi Suarez, legs kicking down that canal of hers. Crying out hello, hello. These thoughts did not surprise her. But the next one did, so she said it.

"I got no reason to live."

"No," both rushed in. "Yes."

"I'm just a nowhere cunt. I don't even have a hobby."

Nobody said anything. Mimi envisioned a helpless vagina hanging over the chair back. Melanie felt something on her spine, wet. Then this succubus went into the slope of the yard. They studied the swimming boys raptly as if they had never seen children or water.

"Well, dear," Melanie said at last. "They also serve who stand and wait."

"Crossword puzzles helped me through a bad patch a few years ago," added Mimi.

"Oh God." Dee laughed.

Melanie giggled. "Church is good for some."

The boys turned from their violent wading to hear hoots and shrieks of laughter from the porch. The women seemed to tremble and reach for air around the wicker chairs. The boys' infant sister stood between the women with a glass uplifted in her hands, into the gin.

The pleasure barge closed in on the pier from the western horizon. The engines puttered grandly, washing out the black water. But the men wore the look of mild disappointment common to travelers everywhere, having failed to find a miracle or endure a metamorphosis. Only a further gravity on the face. They could have returned from an expedition around the rim of a vast navel. Harvard, Max Raymond. Ulrich and the ex-priest, found near the animal shelter trying to speak words of love to the inmates through a door. Wren, Lewis and Sidney Farté, more confident since the hacking of his dad, a celebrity and a capitalist. Nobody spoke. Still, they were alert to something new at the pier.

It was Mortimer, down from the hill off a brand-new Norton, in a leather sports coat and fine boots in the style of the Mounties. They knew he was strange before they saw his face closely. Sidney hollered out, "You the man!"

The others looked over at Sidney doubtfully. Mortimer was still a little bent from the stab through the gonads, but he had the posture of a range warrior familiar to cow dung and burning oil. He held a child-size football in his hands, flirting with its shape, unused to it. He did watch the barge arrive and walked into the edge of the water. The boys ran almost on top of him, thrashing. Then they saw. They

froze to the bottom of the lake. He had crept up on everybody in the shadowless remnant of the afternoon.

"Say, boys. I don't know how hard you can take an
old pass. What say let's run for a few goals." He fired the little
ball at dangerous speed past the head of Isaac, and the ball
skipped toward the willows behind. Mortimer went in up to
his knees with his pants billowing. He waded for the ball.

"We got to make some memories here, boys. You
got some bones for me? You best get me in a good mood."

"I'll blow your ass off for you," said Jacob.

"Is he asking them for help or after them?" asked
Melanie, at last seeing the man new to the evening.

Dee had never imagined Mortimer in this form. She
could not comprehend this person had ever touched her, but
she felt a sour loyalty that confused her. She was fascinated
and drunk. A pipe organ went off through her head. Jan-
gling lines of nerves like she was coming or vomiting.

Three fat moccasins hung in the willow forks behind
Mortimer, and he was unaware. The boys saw. Isaac made a
motion of a receiver through the water away from the willows.
"I'll play. Throw here. I'll get her." Mortimer fired the ball
too high, but Isacc leaped and almost grabbed it. Then he
waded out and retrieved it. "Go long, Mr. Mortimer!"

The man was half out of the water pantomiming a
varsity end, for as he recalled from Missouri, you ran long
and then barely missed, every time. A sort of coolness toward completion. He was too suave to really try. He jumped
a bit in inches of water, but the ball sailed over him into the
snake roost. Mortimer plunged on by momentum right
among the fat sleepers, one of them seven feet.

The boredom of the men on the barge was inter-
rupted by a man screaming and flinging in the water. Wails
pitched like a woman's. You did not hear this much in men.

Mortimer shook his hands and you thought he might die of *your* shame for him. Then he began scrambling out of the water and up, up the grass. His leather coat was flecked by shore mud. The bargemen looked downward.

Sidney was in despair. The others could not know why he had invested trust in this man. Mortimer straightened and walked slowly to the pier and to the bow where Harvard and Raymond tied up. Raymond was drunk.

"Hello, sir," said Harvard.

"I was admiring your ship the other day, and I came over to see if I could join the club. You boys seemed to've got things all smooth as a baby's ass."

"Is that your red motorcycle up that hill?" asked Raymond.

"It is. It's part of me now. I live it."

"You can't come aboard, not now we've heard you over there like that. What was that?"

"It was snakes. I was in snakes. You're the saxophone man. You making the rules about the boat club?"

"No, there weren't any rules until you went over the line. You think anybody'd want that sort of noise aboard? You've created the one rule."

It was Harvard's barge, but he was not interrupting this drunk. He was nodding his head.

"This ain't right. He don't have to prove—" began Sidney.

"You're barely with us yourself, Sidney. You didn't believe in it. Why don't you be quiet?" scolded tall Lewis, surprisingly solid for one so translucent and veined.

Sidney was furious but quiet for a while. He was very confused because he had watched this very man hack off his father's head through the glass of the stockroom door. It seemed to him old Pepper finally looked at the wrong man with contempt for supporting him.

Man Mortimer had known instantly the nature of Pepper's heart and destroyed him straightaway, Sidney imagined, while others had known and borne cowards like himself. Sidney had never tried to hide his glee. He told his peers that old Pepper's death was the sweetest gift the man had ever given him.

"And the store, of course," Harvard added.

Now the same man who had killed Pepper almost in an accident of random frenzy told Raymond, "I don't need your club. You're drunk and I'm letting this go. Lots have nerve that's full of liquor."

"I'm as drunk as I ever get, and then I'm never wrong. I smell evil and it walks like you," said Raymond.

"Weren't you a doctor?"

"I was. At your service."

"You don't get many to just quit. You musta mouthed yourself right out."

Mortimer turned and walked up the hill slowly. He did not look Dee's way or toward the porch at all, except to mutter near it, and the women heard. "Old Sidney he said he saw through her window the other night. Little granny giving a blow job to the law."

None spoke.

Dee had passed a line where the gin no longer obtained, but she pretended to sip. She saw herself trembling beneath a ghoul in a red chamber of sin. A creature whose veins were swollen blue. They swayed in a penthouse lit with gilt over the raving casino. Grim fun against laws of God and man. Beasts crawled away ashamed. *I queen bring wreckage to my lover.* For seconds she could not remember her relation to the present evening and its people. Everything was yonder except a central burning ruin, the howl of her counterpart. Then she recalled the man in the mud-smeared leather coat.

"That man, I've seen him in some other version," said Melanie.

"He was pitiful, nasty," said Mimi.

"He seems to be wanting to join things," Melanie said. "I know who it was. The man on the orphans' barge. He brought those teenage girls back to the camp. They'd run away. And Dee, he sat at our table uninvited at the casino music hall."

"He is after me," said Dee, blank, sad.

"You know him?" Mimi asked.

"I am his woman."

"You are not."

"He was trying to play with my children."

"Child, you're too young for him. His face is a deep map."

"Oh no, Melanie. I'm very old. I'm all the ones that watched themselves move everywhere and go nowhere. Your face in the crowd that ain't quite there in every picture."

"My husband is a fool, but good mostly," said Mimi.

"My husband turned gay in his seventies," Melanie reported.

"Is that possible?" Mimi cried. "Then God will forgive you everything. Oh, God, I meant nothing by that. I meant you have license to be free, even dumb." This caused a long pause, sighs, forlorn detachment.

"You gals made your deals with college presidents and doctors," Dee said. "When your charms give out, you still got your own roof, your own music. You can piss and moan or strum a harp. You still get the roof."

"Don't you own your home?"

"I don't know. Something on the verge. My kids always felt rented. Best I could do was leave them alone. Except for Emma there sleeping, the cherub. Me and her father were just clouds she passed through. I don't think I had much to do with her."

"Can I ask you an ignorant Cuban question?" asked Mimi. "Are you white trash, or do you just want us to think you are?"

"Well, it feels like home. It's relaxing, really. I had every chance to choose and still do. I turned down another whole life in Minneapolis, Minnesota, one night."

"Why was that?"

"I think I like it on the verge. I'm from people such as that a hundred years, they told me."

"Would you be English, Welsh, French, what?"

"I would say soldier in a bus station, quick couple of spurts in a rest room at midnight with about a pint of liquor. What I am is when they repealed prohibition in Mississippi."

"You're very clever, Dee," said Melanie gently.

"But I like a clean yard now."

"Yes, yards. Light and shadow on yards down here at twilight. So much."

"You're very much in love, Melanie. You know that."

"I know that, of course."

"Well, then it is good," said Mimi. "God allows." Dee felt a groggy box of air around her, dusk shrunk down. Outside of which panic slept like big dogs.

The animals are in ecstasy even when they are eaten, Ulrich was telling Carl Bob Feeney. They stayed in Ulrich's cottage or on the barge now, setting out short distances and tying up. All were sympathetic with the two except Sidney and Wren. Sidney felt the ex-priest had turned into a dog and belonged in Onward or jail. Wren's position was that this fugitive situation would bring more law in, and you had one point in life, to get more law out. Egan, the nephew, was looking for his uncle still and keeping up his animals, himself verging toward feral because pursued by the vig.

So Ulrich and Carl Bob slept sometimes on the pews of the pontoon boat, sometimes in the unlighted basement of Ulrich's house, sometimes in a single room in the rear of the doctor's cabin. Harvard had threatened Sidney's life if he revealed their whereabouts to anybody. Carl Bob Feeney might not have been the choicest seer at the lake, and Ulrich, now his secretary general, was just bogus guff mostly, but they were the only prophets they had now. Sidney threatened the doctor's life back, but he was too busy running his old man's store now and not doing that badly. He had a car, one of the new Chrysler PT Cruisers, a silver heartwarming car for anybody in love with the sixties Volvo coupe and forties grillwork.

One night when Egan was serving a prayer meeting at Rolling Fork, Ulrich helped Feeney break in his own house and steal his gun back, along with clothes including his old vestments, which he intended to put to new use. Feeney would not go to Onward if he could help it.

Ulrich would frequently stop talking and go quiet like a thief who had forgotten his mission. Carl Bob Feeney was a good listener because he was hearing himself now, in different words. They did not humanize animals, Ulrich and Carl Bob. They wanted to learn their language, and how indeed they had kept going despite depression, despair, even suicide. For instance, it is well known if a fire dog finds too

many human corpses in the rubble, it will become inconsolable and stop looking. What of the amazing quality of
forgiveness in animals? It broke your heart. Carl Bob often
wept, but it did not weaken him. He had different kinds of
weeping, some of it murderous, some of it clearly insane, a
long purr-howl that frightened Ulrich.

"We are damned, but that is the way of the way. If
you choose, you are damned somewhere else. We are defi-
cient because we are tired of *people*. Bosnia, Ethiopia, Kosovo,
the AIDS horror. We were not supposed to know so much
despair at once. It has killed feeling for others. We are ready
for the New Testament to be about dogs, monkeys, chee-
tahs. Ulrich, you must know we hate ourselves and accept
it as right. The first thing you have to give up in belief is being
admired and a friend to man. 'Hail fellow well met' is not a
description down south, it is the *vocation* of most of the
South. It has ruined it. We have lost something precious,
Ulrich, and you must, must acknowledge this. We just don't
give a shit. Machines started it, but we finished the job. How
is it possible a man could sit and read an average newspaper
without attacking at least twenty people directly? Know that
we are dangerous zealots now. Not just animal lovers."

Ulrich had fallen asleep, but before he did, he was
agreeing with what Feeney was saying. Then he awoke and
they had a cup of fine dark coffee made on the hot plate of
the steerage cabin. The coffee was too good here in the night.
Ulrich brought some cigarettes out from a locker and they
both lit up these Camels. He shouldn't, but the night, the
coffee, the ripple of the water and slap of bass.

"Most animals live a short while," said Ulrich, "but
I had a revelation. That we cannot know the *intensity* of their
lives, which is hundreds of times more attuned than ours.
They don't talk because they don't need speech. A dog, when

it puts its head out a car window, smells almost everything in a county, a world we never even suspect and have no description for. That is why I am daft. I have flown and smelled the smells, Carl Bob. I have known life by my nose. That's why the dog looks so ecstatic sniffing in the wind. They smell a thousand times more than we do. We could only know it as hallucinatory sense. Dogs are in space and time. We can only know one or the other, plodding, toddling. Not to mention hearing. And taste. Water is fifty times more delicious to them. We must not pity them, a cheap passive hobby. They live huge lives before they die. Watch how happy sleep is to them, and right next to waking. They live both at once. We are predators of not only meat but of essence, my friend. We want to be them because they have spoken to us without speaking and we can hardly bear their superiority." Now Carl Bob had fallen asleep, the lit Camel in one hand, the coffee in the other. It was by the glow of their cigarettes that Egan found them and waded out the short way to the barge.

They were both startled by the voice from a man standing above them on the planks of the stern, just ahead of the engines. "I'm so tired, Uncle Carl Bob, chasing you. How could you doubt I loved you? How can you wear me out this way? Who is your friend?"

"I'm Ulrich. Son, he can't go with you. We heard about your sermon. You said you had to find him and help him. But you've found him and you mean to follow him, don't you?"

"I'm worn out with the dogs and cats. Come on home, please. I can't do it by myself. Nobody can. I love them too much. I can't get nothin' else done. I can't stand for one to get hurt or left out, great or small, I'm goin' round huggin' 'em and pettin' 'em and cooin' over 'em. I'm a silly ass. I'm in trouble with God. I'm in trouble for some old bodies. I'm preachin' bad. And let me tell you, somebody broke in the house."

"That was us, son," said Ulrich. "We needed some things. And we needed protection. I agreed with your uncle."

"No, I don't mean that. I knew who that was. This person left something square in the middle of the front room. They didn't take anything."

"Left something?"

"A football."

"Why?"

"It was sitting on top of the Edwards newspaper about some game a few weeks back where somebody in the men's room got his face nigh cut off."

"I saw the old bodies, the old bones myself," said Carl Bob.

"You've got to stop that. Somebody'll hear and haul you off. You couldn't have seen the bodies. They were in a car underwater till a sinkhole took the water out."

"I don't mean underwater. I mean behind the doctor's house. I looked out the window at night and there were two skeletons and some little boys sitting beside them like in church."

"That's right. He told me," added Ulrich. "Three nights ago when the girl was singing on the back porch. Some animals come up too. Two deers, a bear, a ghost of a orangutan."

"No orangutans," said Carl Bob.

It suddenly occurred to Egan that his uncle looked like Basil Rathbone and Ulrich looked like an elderly Mortimer Snerd. Then the name Mortimer passed through him.

Roman was riding his motorbike with Melanie Wooten clasped behind him. These were grave times, but they were not sure how grave. Roman's wife waited for more tests. Basal cell lymphoma. Non-Hodgkin's lymphoma, which wasn't too bad. But she had begun bleeding, masses had shown. She was up and about but weak, and they had her in the chemo now. Roman did not know what to do with disease. Except for his wounds, his wife and he had been healthy and they were not old and they had done nothing much dissipating or poisonous. He smoked a little. She could eat a great deal without gaining, and she liked two stiff drinks of Maker's Mark now and again. Melanie had helped as she could, but Bernice Roman did not take to help, although she was pleasant enough. The woman acted distinctly outraged by her luck, as if still misdiagnosed.

This was not as much fun as Melanie expected, but it was trouble of a sort that she still wanted. She had never had a black friend, and she thought it ridiculous that she could die without having this man as one. He liked her and reminded Melanie of early playmates in Texas. But she wondered if there were any left around the lake who might shoot them. She was so tired of race. She was warier since the destruction of the glass animals. The world with that person out in it, wild and needy and ugly.

A man stood in the road, just a man alone. He was staring at her and Roman, but a flat field suddenly interested him and she couldn't see a car. They came to a little bridge over a creek after passing the man, and the motorbike wobbled on twelve-by-twelves. You didn't want to catch a tire between them. But then they shook as a car came up behind them. She turned and watched as a Lexus SUV neared them. The windows were smoked. Roman drove to the right to let it pass, but the Lexus stopped when they were abreast the front passenger door. Roman drove around it across the road to his left to force a decision, but it passed them. Roman stopped. Holding the motorbike between his spread sandaled feet. Melanie tapped him on the shoulder to show the Lexus had stopped with them.

Nobody opened the door. The sun glare off it was hot. You could see the car as the house of whatever your mind held. The people inside were not visible, so you guessed many and not one. The elevation and headroom were preposterous even for a large rich fool. Still it sat blind, dumb, glaring. The whole world was the gravel and this vehicle. Roman got off the bike and kickstanded it. The two of them walked up to the window, a bright maw next to opening but not. There was some activity behind the smoke. It was a human tongue circling the glass, licking and sucking it. They could see nothing except the mouth working dimly. But the glass went down inches, and Man Mortimer looked over the top of the window at them. Devoid of expression, yanked-in tongue, flat, overall. The rearview reflected the ones in the back who did not know they were revealed. It was old Sidney without his shirt, very mottled and speckled, silvered concave chest. Marcine and Bertha, the car-lot girl, were working on him.

Then the glass rose and stopped the view. The Lexus went off at urgent speed.

"That's a lot of car," said John Roman, "to be fucking with you. I'm sorry I said that, but—"

They knew well who the backseat lovebird was, but it took minutes to get their three or four images of Mortimer together. These still did not make one man, because they had little but a forehead and a mouth. Old Sidney perched right in the love nest, at ease in the rearview mirror. He could enjoy his money and new friendship, a major change from his old man. The shamelessness of it shook Melanie, the ugliness. But she who with Facetto . . . it was not good to pursue this concept. The SUV all black and swollen, it hurried as if recently parted from a gathering of its fellows in a wealthier country.

It was getting hard to have innocent fun. All seemed driven toward a calculated nightmare. The football game, Pepper, poor Bernice with her cancer, the tongue in a fretting black ghoul of a car.

They never rode the motorbike together again. She missed the touch of Roman's fat shoulders. She had never felt the war wounds beneath his shirt, as she suspected she might.

The pleasant day erased by that thing on the window of the Lexus.

It occurred to her how many motions people made to simply present themselves to a window, a mirror, a sea of nobodies. These groomings, pulling straight the pants, licking a finger for the hair out of place. She had heard these all were movements of those before execution. Why else so circumspect? Your first impression on the gallows.

John Roman thought. He fished with a spinning rod. He had delayed the pleasure of artificial bait–casting deliberately until he retired. Times were wretched in many ways. Bernice and cancer, tongue on window, old men on the run from relatives for loving animals too much and learning to talk with the beasts, a grown white man shrieking with a sound that should not be heard when he stumbled close to snakes in the willows. But you could get as good a spinning reel and rod as the pros for cheap at Big Mart, against which there was no competition. The local fishing-supply stores didn't even attempt it but went rather for a fishing class that imagined itself temporarily detained by Mississippi until it could get to the glossy lakes and streams in magazine photographs at the doctor's office.

Roman fished long and guiltily because Bernice did not want him home fretting about her condition. She'd lost some weight and looked even more Indian now. Perhaps the last trace of the Natchez tribe. He was another sort of Indian partly, Chickasaw, lost in the South.

Melanie was on his mind, how she was doing. He hadn't fished close to her house for a while. She was a friend in a panic to live, and he didn't want to be her instructor. Life itself was not much of an instructor but more like the fits of a runaway child. It would shock you with depravity and staggering kindness within the same hour. If you could get used to that, you might learn, but life itself didn't especially want to follow up on anything.

It was his own time alone with his memories. The wash through the head, a wash of half-stories, peace and war. No screaming or banging or outer noise, just this steady action, floats of rooms and lamps, rolling of women like happy seabirds riding the first of the storm waves. No radio, no beer, but you sat there on a bucket and collected them all.

Nobody had the right to touch the stories, the pictures, the silence. That was your due. Nobody could enter. No government was here. No phone calls, no mail, no knocks on the door. You saw old men on benches and you pitied them for all bereft, but you were wrong. They had the time of their life. The deaf ones even more so. Inside and away. They were inside a pure dream.

Roman resembled his grandfather on his mother's side, a man struck blind by a train in his sixties. The old man sat in the chair grinning. Roman couldn't recall a whine or complaint from him. As if he had crashed up safe somewhere, the water of an ocean bathing his feet. You would go to him for a memory and he spoke it.

Melanie was a fine lady but didn't have enough stories in her, ones of her own. She borrowed from him. This was not so much too late as just impossible. If you couldn't sit without stirring into somebody else's life at age seventy-two, you had either bad stories or too few of them. When you had too few stories, you went mad. When you had only one, they took you away to the asylum until you got more.

The army had been a long mistake, but he could let that go. Somebody must be there as the platoon's old animal and it was him. Sergeant major, watching West Point, Virginia Military and Citadel killed over and over. He regretted he was not a singing jazz-trumpet man like Chet Baker, but somebody had to be there regretting too. The army would rise up and grab you because it was vacant. You went to it young when even an army barracks was something fresh. The place filled you, or the unplace of it. Then you got wise enough to live. Others came close to you wanting to live also.

Roman hooked into something large and squirming. All his evenings contracted into this sweet emergency. Muscles underwater struggling against your arms, the line alive down to your belly and the butt of the new rod, Shakespeare the brand, answering. It had to be a cat, very big. As clear a gift as anything in the world. If he were a preacher, he would say that fish was God's mercy. You never got closer to it than above the water for a long, long time. Here, bringing it home like a lost friend.

When he was young he cursed fish as he pulled them in. He no longer did. That was evil, stupid, greedy. Should lose your thumbs for it. For your mean and larcenous spirit. Now he loved this fishing peace above all things. He had not once been let down, even when nothing came home for him. The stories inside had been better over green water.

At the mouth of another cove near the bad restaurant, the one that he called Gristle and Sons with Cold Beer, he saw a pale-faced but arm- and shoulder-burned cracker bounced up and wallowing on a Jet Ski, a horrible and noisome bully of a water motorcycle built in spite for the northern snowmobile, on which other punks roared and beheaded themselves on fence wire. The boy was doing about fifty over Roman's quiet water. The wash from the machine was immense into the shallows, whipping water weeds and terrifying minnows and young bass toward Roman. The big catfish rolled in behind this local storm. Roman cursed the ski and saluted this bully. Old whiskered heavyweight at last snatched from its appetites. *At last we meet.* It was too big to be succulent, and he was glad to let it go after petting it.

When he turned to the lake again and threw his nightcrawlers and light sinker toward a stranded bough on a black strip of deep, he hoped he would not see another living soul, and he didn't. Heard only the distant nagging whine of the ski.

The cracker Sponce was on the far side of the lake, seeking other audiences. A mad Protestant in a cathedral too green and black and silent for him, bent on fouling these spaces with the great *I am.*

EIGHT

THE COYOTE WAS IN HER COTTAGE BACKYARD SINGING to the edges of the swamp. She was naked in her solitude with nature. She sometimes saw deer and raccoon coming up to hear. And a thickage of squirrels, red and fox and gray. She saw mistletoe high on a dead post-oak limb and wanted it for her hair. She hated guns, but Raymond shot the mistletoe down for her with his newly confessed Mossberg. Now she had it in the hair above her ear.

The Coyote was much like John Roman. The young should have been seeking her instruction, but it was Raymond after her, and sometimes hard, wanting evermore an answer to her easy talents, her simple life. Still doing homework for his soul in his forties. His nervous dissertation.

He was a late-blooming prodigy on the saxophone. She could not read music much but she knew. Grant him that, even though he bought the band and managed it toward himself almost unintentionally. He had somehow gotten good through pure want. Triumph of his burnt doctor's will. It was a puzzle why he played certain needy and vicious ways, or would even want to, like a tomcat dragging away from a long fight down an alley. Imprecations, hisses, mewlings, threats. Why develop this style when there were so many others?

They put something called a jellyball in horses' stables to give them something to do. Or they put chickens, goats or radios in their stalls to be their friends, or a Jack Russell terrier. Otherwise they would get bored and kick themselves lame. Hurt others, bite. Maybe she was Raymond's jellyball. And he needed another too, his talking saxophone. But who

171

would not? Standing alone drives most mad in a single week. Look at Castro's and Stalin's prisoners. Mimi was on the right, happily and with great health. Her talent was committed on the day the Iron Curtain fell. She felt new lightness in her voice, the old gray seriousness with its laws left her. Her dispossessed grandparents were mocked in Havana for once having money and an ink factory. She could spit twenty feet across the room into the eye of a communist.

She was needing Raymond less and this would go on, but she loved him. They could walk together like a pair of face cards. It did not frighten her that their love was sometimes dead. It would come back and surprise you. She was fierce for loyalty.

Now she parted the limbs of the wild magnolia and froze at the sight of two skeletons sitting in the soil watching her. She did not hear the six males whispering not far behind them. Ulrich, Jacob, Isaac, Sponce, Carl Bob Feeney, his nephew Egan. Choir of voyeurs? Hunters? Lake idiots? They could be tourists spying on this cottage haunted by its terrors and chaos. Rude bastards. Where was the woman nailed to the wall? Where did the graveyard witch sleep?

She gave a yelp for Raymond and shut her eyes. When she opened them, she saw every male coming forward through holly hedges and giant ferns to assure her with their kindest apologies. Hurt on their faces. Max Raymond now right behind her with the stupid mistletoe rifle. Everything absurd was borne by this ministry, like a strange rural basketball team that had lost its ball. The skeletons smelled too.

"I love you," said small Jacob.

Mimi screamed again, but with less power.

"Lady, we ain't—" Jacob was paralyzed by her scream and jumped backwards into some vines, struggling, feet tangled.

"We're sorry we seen you naked."

Not us, the adults thought together.

"We tried not to look."

"I don't care whether the children. . . . Who are you?"

She lowered herself before the two boys now standing together. She would not look at the skeletons. When Raymond saw them, he chambered a round. The skulls with their stunned hilarity. Arms resting on the soil. Now the wiring job obvious, coat hangers. Done with pliers. This was the empty swamp she had been singing to without knowing. All this lively rot. Mimi went back to the cottage and grabbed her robe off the porch rail.

"We don't know," said Egan. "These bones have nothing to do with any of us. The boys put them together with wire. I'm a minister of the Lord Jesus Christ." She'd already heard from Raymond about the tattoo of the cross on the man's cheek.

"Were you hunched down here listening to me or waiting for me to have a heart attack when I saw these dead bodies?"

"Please, lady. We meant good."

"They did. They told me," said Sponce. He was seeking the level of maturity, at least to that of Egan of the cross and gray ponytail. At least a trustable ass.

"We sharing these folks, but they ain't ours. The sheriff can call up north and get us a reward," said small Jacob.

"That's not a good idea, little boy," said Egan. He had been sweating mightily even before this conversation.

The boys now hunkered. She could barely perceive they were waddling toward her. Raymond shared lust for vision with the eldest, Ulrich. She saw they were fascinated by her black curls. Her Cuban Florida face. They wore her shirts, but she didn't notice. Blanched coffee beans with faces on them, these boys. No Indian or black. Small earnest Ulstermen looking for a mother and her music.

She began singing, incredibly, facing away from them all but facing Max Raymond and his weapon, lowered. The song was about a baby, the mountain and the sea. She sang it quietly, but there were high notes that made the boys quiver. At the end Jacob reached over to touch her wrist. She held his hand. The three of them walked toward her kitchen. Isaac and Sponce knew they weren't meant to follow.

She had become used to the smells out here. It was no longer only decay but richer life, she understood. Soldiers, slaves, Indians, lost women, all under her in the earth. Same as Cuba, with a crown of living creatures and fat vegetation on it.

She had once sung a song taken from the seventeenth-century Japanese poet Matsuo Bashō.

Summer grasses,
Where soldiers dreamed.

Now she sang that one to her new swamp acolytes, rapt twice over for being nearly in her face. She sat on the back steps after feeding them ham and Gouda on French bread with mayonnaise and a tall bottle of orange soda pop. Spanish words, Japanese thoughts, for these elves of Confederate trash. Sister singing away the last days of her youth.

Raymond had gone back inside and was sleeping. The preacher Egan had hung around for a reason unclear to her. He went back and forth to and through the border of tree arches, unseen at the foot of the swamp.

Raymond suddenly knew it was time to return to the bad restaurant and then his ache for visions would be satisfied.

The bad restaurant would stay when only zombies prevailed. It served food for the dead, tired fishermen and humble vacationers worsened the instant they sat down and had the bad water. Thousands like it at state lines, watering holes in the great western deserts, far-flung Idaho and Maine. Their owners say, "We just couldn't help it, we were food people. We never said good food people."

Raymond was in the pawnshop looking at a delightful saxophone and about to buy it when the feeling hit him. What he would see and be transformed by was right next door to his own cottage, not out in the fars, the wides, the bars or churches. He put the saxophone down and within seconds saw a shadow pass the shop. It was a man hobbling and slurring the few words he could manage, and Raymond was positive it was Mimi's old ex, what was left of him after the suicide attempt in Vicksburg, rolling and pitching up Market and the pawns to find Raymond. He went out to the walk and saw nothing but a red car leaving, and he followed it in his own. Mimi was in Miami singing with another band for a couple of weeks. He was alone. He knew this was right. He had not eaten for two days, for no good reason. The moment was pressing.

A zombie had just waited on him in the pawnshop, a man who stood there remarking on the history of this saxophone. In apparently good health, in decent clothes and well groomed, polite, but quite obviously dead and led by someone beyond. You look at them and know they are spaces ahead into *otherness*. Not adolescent either, that natural Teutonic drifting or the sullenness without content. They might still be people, but unlikely.

Everything about the zombie is ravaged except his obsession, thought Raymond, following the red car. *Dead to every other touch. They simply imitate when there is movement or sound.*

They imitate the conversations around them to seem human to one another. He had seen them in scores from the airports to the bandstands imitating one another, mimicking the next mimicker in no time, no space, no place, no history.

The bad restaurant even had bad-food loungers and loiterers, hard to shake when they got a good imitation of you going. The restaurant with its RESTAURANT sign. Its mimicking of the dining life, yet no edible food, bad water and a weak tea to go with that. *Refill that beige for you, sir?* Every dish served in contempt for what used to be human. Rations for an unannounced war.

Because as Mimi Suarez's grandfather said, *When you eat well, you are eating memory*. But here for a few cents less, you could eat no life at all. You could eat as much history as just ended in the kitchen, cooked in spite at great speed by an inmate of dead dreams. A sort of hospital food with more dread in it.

Oh yes, mambo, salsa, shake that tree, bitch, let them coconuts of yours fall down. Max Raymond heard the man in the crowd watching Mimi in Miami right then. Each heavy command resounded in his head. He'd never experienced anything like this before.

The red car was indeed heading for the lake, through Redwood, the low fields and waters. Grim bluster of new black clouds in the west. This was storm country. Vicksburg, 1959, a tornado came through, tore out half the town, created new lakes, killed scores. He watched breaths circle a lawn, lifting the leaves of a collapsed muscadine arbor. The smell somewhere as if lightning had opened a melon, electrified sperm. He thought of the hot grease pitched on the honeysuckle by a zombie of the restaurant's kitchen. In a meadow he caught a wave of dead-fish smell. Oh, the Onward cemetery. Called *There Now*. Har.

He was closer to rot and birth with every mile. This place was lodges, bulks of mobile homes, old trailer villages where fugitive creatures abided. Modern doctors did not vacation here anymore, nor modern anybody much, although the fishing was good. The town would ghost out in a bad fishing season, a hot spell, and the loneliness left behind could hurt you physically in the eyes. Long tubal aches to the grand home of migraine and hot rain at noon. The doctors took their families skiing in the West or to the Islands, where they mimicked life as best they could with the new big money. The wives haggard from hanging on to beauty.

Max Raymond realized all of a sudden he had very little doctor money left. It was nearly all saxophone money now. Or Coyote money. Not too bad. He would buy the house and make the landlord happy that its haunted memories would stay in good hands. His life, this place where something was. The red car? A boomerang on the curves now, all red.

Fifteen miles behind him, Vicksburg, city of the bluffs. Gilbraltar of the West at one time. Now into these casinos dime-store Legbas bid the weak and bored come in. See the man with the wonderful saxophone! Illuminations of the bridge over Louisiana at night. Capitulant city! Shops crying deeds and titles for cash. Children out at the orphans' camp because their parents were for sale without buyers. Drugs, car wrecks.

Lightning loved the swamp. The willows thrashed now where all the souls of dead bad poets roamed day and night. In their big sprawling cottage, what good storms Mimi and he watched together. Popping those souls that cannot die but must return to open-microphone poetry slams against an adjacent junior college. Catering by the bad restaurant. *Pop,* a soul in bliss for just seconds thinks it has actually died and is moving away somewhere beyond this green echo chamber. No such luck, only the cynical lightning.

Raymond had one model for a poet-warrior such as himself and his Mossberg. Or just forget the rifle. *Be a man, use your new long-barrel .38, stuffed in the trousers. You go by even the orphans' camp, there's the mass popping of firearm training now. Nobody can touch them. It's a legitimate sport. Then the thud of the bigger stuff. The lunatic couple ride horses now. The .38, you've got to be good. No real stopping power, no scatter-shooting.* His model was a man he visited in the veterans' hospital, a nationally honored poet, mad and with his shoes on contrariwise. The poet's son in middle age said he had suffered all this while for being a man. He now wanted a woman operation. And as a woman he desired other *women.* His father the old poet could not understand.

Why was madness ever thought to be a transcendent state? What idiot waited how long around the raving to decide this? It was the nastiest and saddest condition Raymond had seen. The man had suffered Guadalcanal, Okinawa, Saipan. He wrote long electric poems, or tried, like an ecstatic writing in sand with a pickax, or something like that, a reviewer said. But then real madness drove him to real madness. Worse, perhaps the son wanted to change into the mother so he could at last have her. And on and on. How can life take this turn? Raymond himself still felt depressed by his short visit. His pity, his terror, his absolute disgust. *But the poems. Were they worth the cost?*

He caught up to the red car pulling out of the gravel lot of the little church, continuing around the lake toward the restaurant. Raymond drove up to the window with its stained glass raised to prevent explosion during the storm. Egan was leaning out, watching the sky. Then he looked at Raymond in his car window. Egan had a bloody face and he pointed. Raymond got out the .38 and drove back to the road, but not before he heard a quartet of trombones behind Egan in the church, playing sweetly and importantly some sacred number, oblivious to both the storm and Egan. He seemed to have gotten his cuts leaning out the window.

Raymond was chilled, but he drove on. Some kill for Christ, he reflected, and cannot be Christian but are Christ's allies. They can never have close communion, only quiet thanks. They do not have visions. They have war.

He touched the pistol, then thought further about Christian soldiers. They live in a dream amid the valley bottoms of tall white pines, live and river oaks, palm trees, palmettos, wild magnolia. They live in a dream between paradise and purgatory. They sleep on hard thin mattresses. They sit down to dinner in the bad restaurant, today with its blue plate special of frozen prefloured meat, gummy white bread and gravy made from cut-rate mushroom soup in giant industrial drums. There should be pictures of ambiguous fiends through history on the wall, all dead by the efforts of the Christian soldiers. Every meal as they wait for the battle, somebody looks at dinner and says, "I've had worse."

Raymond thought. Separation from Christ through murder for him.

But in his mind he saw again the church in the dell and heard the sweet trombone chorus chording through the window. "Nearer My God to Thee" was the tune.

On the barge that afternoon, Melanie and Dee and several men, including Sidney, began a tradition of meditation on the lake. The pontoon boat was both museum and church afloat, by far the most elegant hand-built craft on these waters, which opened as they went through the lock into a new reservoir.

The first meditation was to be led by Melanie, with comment from others as the rest of church. Essentially, they were floating Unitarians. Facetto was aboard for the first time, his and Melanie's love in plain sight. Dr. Harvard was having a very hard time. Melanie was unconscious of this. They anchored in a cove. She stood at the wheel on the captain's box.

Harvard introduced her. "Today's meditation will be read by Melanie Wooten, a changed woman who now shares an altered worldview." Harvard did not know about the tongue in the car window, so he did not understand Melanie. But she had a new sadness that Harvard liked, because her careering with this confident young lawman was not right.

Dee Allison and her little girl stood wearing church dresses, but they tended to recede from the group in uneasy shyness. The little girl was fine, but Dee had never been among dressed boat crowds and felt diminished by the blazers and Melanie's smart suit.

"'There was the snow, and her watch ticking. So many snowflakes, so many seconds. As time passed they seemed to mingle in their minds, heaping up into a vast shape that might be a burial mound, or the cliff of an iceberg whose summit is out of sight. Into its shadow dreams crowded, full of conception and stirrings of cold, as if ice floes were moving down a lightless channel of water. They were going further into darkness, allowing no suggestion that their order should be broken, or that one day however many years distant, the darkness would give place to light.

"'Yet their passage was not saddening. Unsatisfied dreams rose and fell about them. Crying out against their implacability, but in the end glad that such order, such destiny, existed. Against this knowledge, the heart, the will, and all that made for protest, could at last sleep.'

"That was a selection from *A Girl in Winter* by Philip Larkin," said Melanie softly.

"Nice," said Carl Bob Feeney, less insane than last week.

"I disagree," said Sidney. He rose from a director's chair near a side pew. "And I need a drink." Sidney had taken to mixing Stolichnaya vodka with orange juice for his health. He had affected this weeks ago.

"Disagree?"

"Number one, it ain't about me, or nothin'. It's about snow and some time shit." He looked down at Emma, the child.

"Any other thoughts?" asked Harvard.

"Well I'd like to know who she thinks she is," said Wren.

"You mean the girl in that passage?" asked Melanie.

"No. You. 'Unsatisfied dreams crying out against their implacability' or such. Who the hell you think we are, schoolkids you're trying to impress? You're implying you go around the house saying *implacability* often? Ever? Or hoping many of us dumbos wouldn't get it? Why, I understand the word quite well. And I find you and the author posing asses. Christ, I thought we'd get some Robert Frost or something. This is worse than Faulkner."

Melanie was stunned.

Another man, Ulrich, wanted to speak. "You need to change again from wherever you've changed. You would have us think anybody gives a damn what white people think anymore. They are the killers of seals, baby seals, by clubbing. They shoot polar bears just because they're there. What do *these* creatures think about our thoughtful moaning?"

"That's not fair," said Facetto. "It was a meditation to invite thought. It wasn't her own writing."

"She didn't read it because she hated it," said Wren.

"Maybe she read it because she ain't getting enough dick," said Sidney. You would not know he was drunk until he went suddenly about it at the drop of a dime.

Many turned. But nobody called down Sidney. He seemed satisfied. Statement, vodka, orange juice, his tweed vested suit, everything.

Melanie tried, but she could not help weeping the rest of the day. The sheriff left her early.

Sidney led a disordered party far into the night. Whores were still coming aboard at nine P.M. Large orphans mingled with them, and Minny and Sandra, now fifteen, had on backless cocktail dresses. John Roman and his wife, Bernice, who had not been out in weeks, were aboard celebrating the end of chemotherapy and the beginning of remission. The launch rocked. Chet Baker was heard in the middle of it all, though he was not a noisy man. The pier lit up with fireworks or gunplay. You couldn't be sure. Harvard's hair became disarrayed. He waded in the cove and cursed and howled, holding a bottle of Jack Daniels aloft, baying at the moon. All this practically in Melanie's backyard that Sunday night.

"The best thing about dogs and kids," Ulrich cried out near the end, feverishly intoxicated, "is they ain't going anywhere. They're already *there!*"

He dandled Emma the cherub on his knee, breathing tortuously, from the emphysema, in long tugs and seekings of his lungs. This angel was not frightened of Ulrich. She thought he was a train. Then one of the fifteen-year-olds took the baby girl in her own arms, saying, "Oh, this one's coming home with me!" At one time Melanie pressed her nose against her own windowpane, watching down the hill in miserable incredulity.

*   *   *

And, thought Raymond, pulling into the parking lot of the bad restaurant, *back almost to my front door*. He didn't shake as much as he expected he would, and he put the pistol in his belt against his stomach, put the coat on as he stood from his car. The red car, a Mercury Sable, was here all right. The tag wasn't Memphis. It was local. He knew now. But he wasn't certain why it should go on. One would make a quick move. The other would pay. A hum of grief came to his ears.

The air was solid with earth- and tree-frog song. They went *kecka kecka kecka* in the early night, the storm blown past.

The man was at a table next to the wall, tall even in his chair. His eyes were in shadow. Nobody else was about. His hair seemed too great for his neck, which had gotten thinner. Raised and swept to width, set like soft wire. He could be a singer, an evangelist, a small-town sinner living out a sneer established at seventeen. An almost effeminate elegance too, a man deep in self-study, a creature of mirrors.

Raymond looked into the backs of the man's hands on the table. A meal hardly touched in front of him.

"I know you. What is it, Man?" asked Raymond.

"I came out here to get a second opinion. You the doctor?"

The doctor of yester-Memphis stood in the aisle. "Sit down," Mortimer said. "Unless you planning your way out already."

As Raymond sat, the trance that had brought him here was broken. The man at this level looked frail, whining, "You called me names and wouldn't let me in your club. There might be a new vote, though. It's a democracy everywhere you look. Sidney wants me to come aboard."

Raymond had not expected wit, if this was wit. Could evil be witty? If this thing was evil. The hair almost its own life. The Everly Brothers. God recalls them. Two boys packed into one hairdo.

Somebody was in the back. They were the only ones still in the dining area. The hour was desolate, dim, redolent of fried meals. Scorched crust of meat in the nostrils.

"Raymond, let me tell you something that might get your attention. I had to see you. Where is that big knife or whatever? Show it to me." Raymond reached inside to show Mortimer the butt under his coat. This did not feel unnatural. If he missed him here, he had the longer gun back at the house with the hollowpoints, and he was very good with that one at age eleven.

"You want some of me?" Mortimer raised his hands. He had thinned a good deal, almost to gauntness. He seemed ill.

"I came to destroy you. I don't know much, but I know you're bad straight through."

"No, not at all. You going to help me find some friends . . . acquaintances that went wrong, let's say."

"How would you get help from me? Can't you see I've got a pistol?"

"I must have been blind." Mortimer had a face under his face, grinning like a blanched skull. "You ain't got the goods, sonny. After the oath you took. 'First do no harm.' I've had many a doctor acquaintance. Put them to work too."

"Shut up."

"Like the orphans'-camp job. There's an opening."

Raymond hated the word *stare*, but it was a verb that occupied half of art and life and that was what he was doing, as in a French movie. As if his eyes were, beyond God and law, the single powerful arbiter in the room. "I'm going home," said Raymond. He was shaking.

Mortimer laughed. "Not *that*."

Raymond turned, relieved totally and sopping wet under his arms. He was beginning the walk. A noise broke out behind him, but he wouldn't look at it. Then a huge pain entered the flesh near his spine. He could not account for it, then did not believe it. He tripped and stumbled, flailing at chairs, never falling. Only at the last, before he knocked his head on a chair back, did he crane his head.

Mortimer sat at the table with a silver penknife in his hand. It was a thin short blade but not short enough. Blood was on its hasp. Raymond held his wound and staggered out the door, then into the gravel, where he thought, *There is a gun in my car.* But he was wearing the gun, or rather now it had slipped, the long martial thing, into the crotch of his underwear with the barrel down his right leg, sinking lower even then and trying for his ankle. He was stiff-legged. The monster of pusillanimity. His house was a hundred years away. The Mossberg was in there. His interest in the avocation of gunning was on the wane, however. He felt Mortimer right behind him. He had fled nothing. The man was swift and quiet to boot.

"Let's go right to the bone people in your backyard. I got the lantern, good buddy. You want to take a leak or anything?"

Raymond struggled with the descending .38, which was making for his knee that moment.

"Oh, go ahead and take your time. Go on in the house there and take a long leak. I don't want you uncomfortable, Max. Sure, let's both go on in. I'm wantin' to look at that foxy lady again. Been missing her." Mortimer walked ahead of Raymond, up the steps crowded by thick Carolina jasmine vine and honeysuckle, dead bees underfoot that got drunk and fell. He opened the door for Raymond. Raymond felt this was as lowly as his existence could get, but he had to sit on the couch.

"Can I look around? Boy, now that was selfish. It was *me* who had to take the good long leak. You can't beat a good piss for clearing the mind and putting a plan to things. Boy, I might not leave. Uh-oh! Your bedroom, Max, somebody left their gun right on his *pillow*. Great Lordy son, this is one horny ol' lonesome dude. I got girls too, Dr. Raymond. Your missus, as I recall, would be in Miami getting leched on by all the old folks from Cuba? The Cubans, now, they're hung I hear, and greased, with a golden earring, bandanny. But she got you. That's a good one. She ought to be wearing you for a Tampax. Little music boy don't wanna be no doctor no more."

Raymond was pondering the depth of his puncture and wondering how long it had been since anybody called him Max, as Mortimer did. High risibility. *The wound's nothing. He's going to hurt me.* He had hands on both kidneys and arose as a token of manhood.

"Come on now, Maxy. Follow the old lantern and let's just see some bone, my man. I had an interview with Pastor Egan, the ponytailed cross-cheeked boy, and he told me just about where. Said you wouldn't mind my dropping by and smashing up a few with me."

"I don't mind. They're almost kids' toys now, anyway. Wired-up."

"You want to bring your gun for snakes?"

"I really don't."

"I'm afraid of those things. Well, snakes and guns. You remember how it was with me and snakes?"

"Yes."

"That old—Christ, they're all old, it's hard to re-member which one—said, 'We don't hear sounds like that from a man around here.'"

Raymond slapped at the fronds and walked him di-rectly to the site of the people. When the lantern beam found them, Mortimer jumped past him like a dash man bobbling the light. He hurried straight to the woman and kicked her head off but it tangled in her rib cage and swung on the coat-hanger wire. But he followed with a field-goal boot to the plexus that sent the remainder of her affairs clattering.

Then he jumped on the skull over and over, grind-ing it with his Mountie boots, waving the light and demand-ing Max Raymond join in, take the child.

NINE

ISAAC AND JACOB WERE ODDLY WELL BEHAVED, DOMESTIC. They straightened the house and talked around the old Ford that Hare had pulled from the swamp. It was behind their garage, a sagging building with stacks of *National Geographic*s in it from a previous tenant. The boys would ask if the house was really theirs, and Dee told them she was pretty sure it was. Her gone husband was bad at details, but he was a good provider, sometimes a flush one. She and the boys could satisfy myriad needs in Big Mart. They straightened the house again.

They hunkered in prospect of manhood, waiting on Hare to build the beam and trestle faster. The sun-grayed back of the garage was Hare's drama curtain, they said. He had to tell stories in front of it while he worked and they sat. They pressed him for tales of other machines and major explosions.

Harold Laird stared off as if in conspiracy with other mechanics near the horizon. It was a labored stare of either profound stupidity or alienation. He had looked constantly in himself for a likeness to his progenitors but failed. His large teeth, big legs and no chest or much rear. Too late, but he had entered the black church up the road and stolen a book from its meek open library called *How to Be a Teenager*. He gave it to the little ones later, but they discarded it because it was about how to be a nice teenager, which Harold Laird had been. But he had gotten it for himself to see what he had been, and he was going back for *How to Be a Man* and wouldn't share it. Laird had hung in the background of his

191

own history. He could not read well and hoped that in the next book there would be pictures of Christian women naked, since he was going to be a husband.

Actually he had once, with others, participated in an event with a woman from Edwards in the bed of a truck, but he was still unsure whether he was manned or not. He was betrothed before to the silhouette of a woman on a bottle of some good-smelling Oil of Olay he found, but could break it off. She had owned him for years now. He could not leave himself alone sometimes, a sin.

The boys' voices were quiet. They were hesitant to laugh or dream or curse. The heat kept up its unsurprising late misery. The mind was brown at the edges, the tongue dry and slow. Dee slept in the weak air-conditioning of October. Little Emma beside her was so good that her mother expected her to die any day, as angels were snatched away early to paradise. Once, when Dee had a migraine, the child she now held in sleep massaged her temples the entire night. When Dee opened her eyes at dawn, the child had fallen asleep with her doll's hand on Dee's forehead. Dee wondered if they were born twice as sensitive as normal women.

Emma was gone when Dee woke, knowing it was too late to get out of a story she had dreamed. She had few powers. But she was trying. The better part of her was that she liked to heal old people once she knew their pain. She was not a cynical nurse, not at all. She just did not like letting on to her sincerity in front of fools. She could change languages to soothe folks of wild diversity and wants, though her most natural posture was that of the slut paring her nails. In her dream she was chained in a basement with many sex parts that howled on their own.

Then she had dreamed she was running up a hill with women, hundreds of them, arms out to what beckoned at the crest. A row of cannons blew down on them, blasted them apart, but they were happy and they sang, like Japanese infantry, exploding into mists of ecstatic nerves. Then they arose and became everything, even the cannons. The hill, the tree, the barn, everything. She woke feeling she could commit suicide this minute with huge happiness because she would leave the world a finished job.

She was not sure the meaning of her dream. Without the help of gin, she felt no common sisterhood to women. She also knew she could not leave Emma until the girl was strong and ready. Like the younger boys but not Sponce, who shouldn't even still be home. Thing was, Sponce was in love with her, her own son. He feared the uglier world.

Hare was at her door. He was not a bad-looking boy, and he seemed to have acquired more and more manners, even unnecessary ones. "Where is everybody?" she wondered.

"They took the baby for a treat," he said.

"They never do that."

"We're alone. They cleared the way for me. Us."

"Of which there isn't any."

"I have changed since I first saw you. You are beautiful. So beautiful. My thoughts were animal-like. But now I'm like family. We're all in it together."

"In what?"

"A home."

"Who are Mommy and Daddy?"

"They could be us."

"Do I look pitiful?"

"Not at all."

"Just checking. I'm kind of married."

"I'm proposing me as husband. One, I am steady. Two, I am good with my hands. Three, Mortimer is out of the picture."

His hands were nice and he could fix things. She studied him across a moat of indifference and time. His throbbing youth softened her. He looked filled now, thicker. Like some boys she knew who had come back from the army.

"It just seems like you need a home, Harold. I'm already here. My roof."

"I never saw a girl I needed before I met you."

"Is it the nurse's outfit?"

"It's everything that gets to me."

"One day soon I'll look in the mirror and see everything you like about me is over. I'll know the day. You'd be stuck with an old bag of flakes. I'll turn into an outhouse overnight. With heavy lipstick."

"No."

"Then you'll know how bad I am. It'll be on my face, every damn story writ in wrinkles."

"How can you say those things?"

"Go up to the casino and see. It's where us old party girls go to die and have a club. Some turned, some just about. Sulky old things with the girl cut out of them. It's not the same with men."

"I'll stick."

"Such hope."

"You're my reason to live."

"Do you get it? I'm what men remember. I'm not what they need. It's been said to me. What I am is foreign pussy."

"You didn't mean to be."

"How do you know?"

He dropped his head. The long gentle fingers of his right hand covering his face.

"Stop playing house," she said. "Build what you want on your own."

"But you're clean. You don't smoke or drink, much."

"They aren't my drugs. Please go on now. I don't care to break your heart."

Laird went out onto the front porch, shivering in the warmth, lost between homes. Engorged by despair and desire. He had heard her words as the wail of a kidnapped queen. Unransomed these two decades of his spindly life. He thought of the marines, or the long honest life of an expert mechanic.

Both of them seemed chores in hell now.

Life was just this, you got a lot of money and you bought things. No other game. You bought her, a house, a family. You didn't pull fifty-three-year-old things out of a swamp and fix them. He was angry and small. A gnat. He turned and went inside.

She was staring at the blank television.

He had no story to put on its screen for her. But he would have her and then tell it. It would begin with an old Ford coupe, red with a gold hood like the boys wanted. He would dump this bucket of rust and just steal the one he'd seen at a junkyard on the south edge of Vicksburg, not well protected. The lot belonged to Man Mortimer and a junkman who lived on the premises. To steal Mortimer's trash and make a classic from it would be a story, not just life. Moreover, he knew the junkman, who was a Christian and had cheated or betrayed or connived at no man.

The junkman, Peden, was a Baptist lay preacher, but cars were to him like whiskey to an Indian, his addiction, and they kept him poor. He had preached before to Harold about the naked Bathsheba when King David saw her at her bath and betrayed her husband, Uriah, sending him to the front lines of battle to die, so that he could possess her and know her forever. David who had all, Uriah who had nothing but Bathsheba. The story implied to Peden that Bathsheba had no choice. Who would not lie with the king? Peden would turn through the Psalms and say he had found the one David wrote to Bathsheba but that it was too dirty to read to the young.

But Sponce could get him to read it while Hare stole the coupe right out from under him. If he was successful, God would forgive him, probably.

The boys had real power over Dee, Harold Laird knew. She was guilty and served them. Now he was helping them mature. They were becoming, not overnight, but steadily more and more, Boy Scouts.

The day would come when the couple would stand in the yard, each actor glistening in happiness, the little boys especially. They would have a long talk with her and she would discover the truth that Harold Laird, genius mechanic, body man, paint man, was her future. He could see her in a bridal peignoir with her hidden softnesses all meant for him, but he couldn't think long of this because he hurt himself, again and again.

John Roman saw Mortimer, looking pale and bent, in the aisle of the bait store. Roman was picking up a beer and pig knuckles and saltines for his lunch. The slab crappie were biting near the spillway. He drove a car this time, wanting to fill a freezer box with this succulence, which Bernice in normal times would broil or fry lightly. Eating didn't get any better. It was so good that many thought the fish was French, *crappé*. *Sac du lait* is its name in Louisiana. Speckled, a frisky white steak swimming. They bite softly, like a suckling child.

You take them with minnows and jigs. That was why Roman was in the store. But he was there also in curiosity about Sidney's run of the store since Pepper lost his head.

Mortimer made a quick movement past some cans, knocking them over, and didn't bother to set them back, didn't even look back. Roman was fairly sure he was the man with the tongue in the Lexus, but that afternoon was vague. He and Melanie had not spoken since the event.

But Sidney in the Lexus was a thing of utter clarity. Even thrown into that rear seat in the black chariot between two sluts and caught unashamed like some mollusk in the light all of a sudden. Gray hairs on the chest of an oyster.

Roman had noticed how sensitive Sidney was to the pain of others. He was not sympathetic, but he was deeply concerned when he heard or saw the hurt, then took its measure against the longest disease of all, his life. He was just alert and, well, hungry for news of his fellows' ills. He began to sort of eat the air and whimper over someone's asthma, scabies, cancer, chest wound. You might make the mistake of thinking he cared, but it was simply an emotive topic and began the peristaltic writhings of his gorge, always about to blow from various bloatage. On the other hand, Roman was sickened by sickness.

He watched Sidney behind the cash register standing and watching him back as if he might be a common shoplifter. To his left in the mouth of another aisle, Mortimer walked out from his own shopping with a sea gaff in his hands.

"You know John Roman, Mr. Mortimer?" Sidney began, strangely formal. "He's a veteran. Wounded. One of our brave ones from the lost battles."

"Oh, I've heard. And he dates white women, I've heard. I have knelt on my knees at the graves of such white women. Is your name Ramp?"

"No. John Roman."

"All right. Guess my name."

"I know it. You've stood five feet from me."

"Death by sea or death by mother. *Morte de Mer* or *Morte de Mère*. Merman, seaman, see. Did anybody tell you I now own a big piece of this store, John? Your feet are walking on my—"

Sidney began to protest. "N—"

"Oh for pity's sake, sit down, Sidney. I was just going on."

Sidney seemed relieved and did sit down on his proprietor's high stool, a swivel chair new to his regime, fairly swank. He immediately jumped up and out in the air, screaming, holding his bottom. He pulled his hands from behind. Tiny points of blood on them. He held three or four map tacks.

Mortimer squalled, "He fell for it! Fell for it!"

Sidney grinned.

Who were they? What was this?

Roman thought they were like two little brothers. Who was leading who? His stomach turned. He drew off one of the ancient dusty cellophaned white handkerchiefs from a snap display and handed it over the counter to Sidney, who began eating off the wrapper and getting the cloth out with his teeth and fingers. A kid, a not unhappy kid in an old boyhood-prank cutabout. Buckwheat, Spot, Spanky. The other freckled goony-haired one. Alfalfa with center-parted hair, cross-eyed a lot. These two men were brats, that's what they were. They were neighborhood bullies. *I took three shots to the collar and jaw for them and their recesses.*

The tall one with rock-and-roll hair was still holding on to that fish gaff, that shark gaff. *What is the verb. The word? They are in* collusion. *Noun, I guess.* Roman walked down the front steps with his new jigs and good minnows. Various geezers, Ulrich among them, were bunched at the base of the steps having at it.

"What was we looking at?" one said.

"The mother lode of weird," said another customer.

Ulrich was in a bomber jacket with fleece and it eighty-five. He was real.

"Bad news with big preacher hair on it."

"I don't know what that cocksucker was. But this old fist would be his watch-out if he chanced to come close to me."

"That man was crossbred with Lazarus."

"That cut-up preacher?"

"I seen him before."

"Said he ain't said word one. Like he talked to a devil."

"You don't see nothing like that twice. But we did. That old boy in the Edwards football-game lavatory."

"He seen maybe an unclean spirit, like."

"Or trying to exorcise one, like."

"You here one day and Stagger Lee cut off your face the next."

"Or your head like Pepper. We ain't never finishing talking on that one. Your hotshot sheriff wandering around like a mascot."

Ulrich in the moth-eaten bomber jacket, the corduroy trousers much too big now in this skinnier madness, spoke again. "Spiders hold the altitude record for earth-bound creatures. Mount Everest." He seemed on the verge of tears, then was over it. "Up there above the murder of men, these fine little creatures. Their thin legs. Having their families. Those delicate eggs. The winds must howl and howl outside."

Roman was sorry he had not gone straight to fishing, but these were fine minnows. He might seine his own, keep a little pool of them behind the house. He headed off to his car.

When the fishing was over, he would be glad and sorry both to return home to Bernice. She was suddenly an old sick woman like Harvard's Nita, and he felt just paces behind him, unable to drag her back from the maw of huge nonsense ahead.

The spider of Ulrich, he considered abruptly. Wind howling on the jagged mountaintop. Their little legs. *Shuh.* Down between them rocks. Icy winds the only weather, only world. *Get aholt of something heavy, don't never quit. New babies coming, feel the wind outside their shells already. Get born a half foot from ruin between a rock and another rock.*

When you knew death was not far off, you always got a strange arrangement of the usual facts. You almost saw the spirit itself. An essence of the familiar, shifted. Sound, smell, dirt, sky. Thirty-three years ago, three times he had left where a sniper's bullet struck seconds later. Then on a hot afternoon he had known the strangeness but was weary and, he knew now, curious. He had made no move and gotten shot.

Roman hummed around the remnants of a tune. "Time After Time," Chet Baker's version of airy sweeter days. He kept a pistol in his kit for snakes, but he knew he didn't need that much caliber. You lived long enough, mildly on the lake. That was the plan. Nothing greedy or hungry about it, hardly even a dream. Now some sullen force came in to take away this small existence. No harbor. *Us small craft, cracked against the wall by mean winds.* Now he realized he had bought the pistol for men and lied to himself about it. Men in this new newspaper headline shoot-out, even on the school yards. How many niggers drove down a road like this to die fifty or a hundred years ago. They'd looked wrong, they'd whistled like wolves, they'd voted.

If, say, some fool in a smoked-glass car came up beside him running parallel and wouldn't stop it, kept looking at him, he would pull the gun and fire a magazine through the glass. Death worked on Bernice at home. Here, Whoever, here's some for you too. He had changed and hated his changes.

Pastor Egan lay silent. The other patient was watching a television show about a hospital as he lay there in the hospital. Maybe he wasn't convinced enough he was truly here. Egan knew better. His inner voice had just returned and he liked himself again.

Episcopals, your rituals are babble, it muttered. *Robed baboonery. Lukewarm, I spit them from my mouth, even while loving them and their gold and whiskey and cable-knit sportswear.*

You are postwar, postmodern, posthuman. You sweep up, is all. The waste of the stores and storerooms find their place in each consumer heart to rot and reek. You are lukewarm, my people, my people. No decisiveness. Saith I the pastor. The man who owes thousands to the pimp who butchered him. Something large is in the woods. Not what you planned. You have not decided, so the thing in the woods is deciding.

TEN

IN THE PAWNSHOP WHERE THE SAXOPHONE RESTED IN its velvet-lined dark alligator case, Max Raymond had not been as misled as he supposed. His nemesis Malcolm, the afflicted past lover of Mimi Suarez, had gone by the window. He knew where Raymond was and intended to have a showdown with him but was in no way connected to the red Mercury Sable. He was looking for a weapon, probably a twelve-gauge double, when he missed the pawnshop and was led on by another rank of pawnshop signs down the way. He'd turned into an alley by mistake, tired from hitchhiking down Highway 61. Seven different rides and a grinding wait in all weathers, October going hot, cold, rainy and balmy, freezing. He could not drive, and his old gang did not approve of his pilgrimage.

Malcolm walked out of the mouth of the alley after Raymond had followed the car. Had he bought fast and, leaving Raymond dead behind him, taken the man's car, he would have arrived at the house with Mimi Suarez away visiting relatives and singing in Miami. Neither he nor Raymond had seen the other. But they never lived a day without the other on their minds. In the next pawnshop was a more comprehensive collection of guns, and in this state of enormous sympathy for gun owner and hunter, where the legislature has even designated a specified season for dwarfs to hunt deer with crossbow, he found sympathy surrounding him on all sides. The pawnshop owner wanted stroke victims armed for whatever.

In the shop were the Ten Hoors and many bigger, meaner orphans and the now fifteen-year-old girls. It was not just a summer camp anymore. It was also less announced what it was now. They were not survivalists, nor religionists, nor paramilitary exactly. They needed guns, ammo, water and canned goods, barbed wire, and already had dynamite and four live grenades from the National Guard. The percussion kind, which they needed more of. You could add shrapnel to the outside of these very easily in the shop. The couple and the others liked Malcolm instantly and they had a much better gun for him. He left with them, he who was skimping on food to buy the twelve-gauge.

Carl Bob and Ulrich imagined they had a temporary grand theft going when they started up the luxurious pontoon launch that Harvard had conceived and largely built for Melanie Wooten and sailed it directly across the lake to preach to the orphans. But it was part Ulrich's already by original charter, and the keys stayed in it all the time. The men were senile, sometimes raving and unkempt, but Ulrich had handled the launch several times before, and he did pilot well and knew the lake better than Harvard. Also he had no fear of water, although he would forget whether he could swim or not. Carl Bob Feeney simply couldn't. He wore a fair barrel of life-preserving with two jackets, one in front, the other on his back. You couldn't have held him under with a semi wheel rim and chains.

They plowed. This vessel required patience, although the Mercuries were powerful and magnificent. Patience and meditation were what it was all about. They had brought their own sermonettes to read when the orphans got aboard.

Ulrich would talk about the white teeth of animals, especially those of the lesser creatures. The traveling was perfect in late October, the sky orange-lit at midafternoon.

The trees along the shore were still green, but a few were on fire in that incandescence born of lush summers, fat sopping roots.

Forgive us, little children, he rehearsed, he prayed. *Our long years on this earth are an obscenity.* They carried pictures of McJordan, the Jackson policeman notorious for shooting two smallish dogs, with a red *X* across his face. They had had it done at a LazerPrint in Vicksburg owned by an angry animal lover.

Ulrich wished he could sing, write songs and sing, but mainly just sing. So much so long in his bosom that could have been shared and vented to his auditors through the years. They would have liked him instead of fleeing. He wished he could sing all out, in a long exquisite howl for the animals and flight, but he was just croaking here and taking a nose hit now and then from his oxygen bottle. He had heard a story of a man, Roy Orbison, who sang so beautifully that he turned permanently pale. He wore nothing but black and dark sunglasses to memorialize his grief over his wife and children dying in a fire. That was a wonderful fate, thought Ulrich. He wanted to be pale and a bird with a deep throat. The animals would elect him their tongue.

We will have a ceremony in gratitude to the animals and then I'll kill myself, he decided. Carl Bob Feeney bore straight ahead with his stare at the far shore, trying to piece together any orphans' tableau on their pier that might be ready for them. He could not see well, though, and he was looking at a crowd of heifers with buzzards over them and trying to figure. Carl Bob loved the launch as his, an almost bold late gift to his years on the land with his dogs and cats. Loved his nephew, Byron Egan, a prince of the spirit, a boon relative. Blessed his sister, Egan's mother, for providing him against this darkness. Sometimes old Feeney forgot he was not still a devoted Roman Catholic. And sometimes he felt he was a whole torn country, afire in all quadrants.

A greyhound, alert to kindness, stood next to Melanie on the pier. It was a gift from Facetto. They had come out after loving and discovered the two ancient loonies had taken the launch. They called Harvard, and he was a little concerned but said gruffly that he did not care to come down to the pier if the sheriff was there. He told Melanie, she thought bitterly, that it was consuming all his care to watch his beloved wife of all these years slowly slipping away. He had begged her not to smoke, to exercise, to eat better. So here they had the results of another individual, fully warned, taking her own road in mild spite against the odds in the newspapers. Betting on Harvard University upsetting Alabama in football. Oh, to be holding her hand again when they were twenty-three! Melanie said that sounded right and it made her cry.

She hung up the phone, bereft and held in the sheriff's arms at the same time. She had never disgusted anyone before.

In their haste to renounce Melanie, the pier crowd did not notice that their cheerleader looked better than she had since middle age. The evidence was that she was reclaiming middle age right now, however briefly, and enjoying it backwards. A smile on some old women does not become them, and they look macabre in their glee. Not so Mrs. Wooten. She was backlit, it seemed, into severe blond on a blue field. She had admirable teeth, for one thing. But the sheriff was drawn and bag-eyed, more like a throttled immigrant at the turn of the century than the video lecturer. Some did now mock him for his race. They weren't used to

Sicilians except around the Gulf Coast, and he was noted as *Mafia-eyed* by several older viewers, as well as *lying fool*, for his failures to indict or even locate the killer of Pepper Farté and the butcherer of Frank Booth and Pastor Byron Egan. These people did not fear his wrath or respect his office. Sheriff Facetto despised being unpopular too. For the main part he had acted himself into this job and had intended to grow rapidly in office.

Melanie and Facetto. Love and despair go hand in hand. Sleep in the same bed. In full light she was not confident of herself, but she could not know Facetto was gone in love for her much deeper than appearances. The love was ruining him, he slept with her soul and never got enough of it. *What lines bred Melanie? They ought to store the blood in a safe.* He was twice in love with her just for lasting.

She studied the large bent dog. Its face made her think of T. S. Eliot's famous line, "some infinitely gentle, / infinitely suffering thing." It was an emeritus of the tracks in West Memphis, where Deputy Bernard had confiscated it from a man who had abused it. For Facetto, the greyhound stood for something. What else could comfort this startling creature better than another startling creature, with eyes haunted as if alarmed by its own creation. He gave it to be there in his absence from her.

"When I come back, I want you to've named our dog. We don't know it. You'll be at the door of your house and tell me the name, and then drop your gown and I'll get on my knees."

"Sweet man."

He thought he knew his killer now and cutter too. It was long quiet work, but he would have him soon. Bernard had seen something and a church trombonist had seen something. But Facetto's memory of their last acts was driving him around the bend, riding his Melanie to the tune of "Sorcerer's Apprentice" on the stereo in the next room. She was taken by several supreme moments, a happy crisis she did not know as a possibility. She was sad after the outflow and wept deeply in gratitude. He said he needed to bring her home good news and wouldn't return until he did. Then he was gone.

Melanie was very weary of what regular people thought. Their thoughts began to hurt and make her weak. *Come let me be your grandmother harlot or whatever it is I'm called. Let me be the source of dissension. I never knew Ben Harvard loved me. But fine, fine—let me serve as not only sin but evil around here. I meant to be a scandal all along. Add me to all the hauntings and chaos and lunacy. I am so tired of these old jaws cracking about it.* She went back into the house.

For his own pain, Dr. Harvard decided to come down to the pier and see Melanie by accident in his mission of concern about Ulrich and Feeney at large on the barge. Others had gathered when word got out they might be in trouble or lost. Wren, Lewis, the dog Son, who frightened the greyhound back indoors, John Roman and the pale and butchered Egan gathered at the end of the pier. Then Sidney dragged down from his bait-store duties, making a show of anger about his lost trade. Nobody remembered who'd called him. He was off on a mad consumer's ride, a revenge against lost time and missed women, fun, dice, fine liquor. His language was tougher, glibber than his old talk. Nobody knew quite who he was now. He emulated Man Mortimer, who was changing gravely himself.

They could see tiny specks of life across the lake but no boat. They spoke of the boat as if it were at the bottom of the lake and the old men bobbing and yammering in their life jackets. And what each had planned to read next meditation way up the reservoir near Yazoo—the Indian word for death ghost, was it? Sidney reminded Harvard of all the artistic and nautical effort he had put in the project, forget the pile of money, which nobody else here had, combined.

"All for Miss Melanie too. We know that. A grand boat for a grand swank love, wasn't it? And your poor wife dying at home all the while, smoking them cigarettes and building up her sad neglected ass with chocolate."

"You are scum," said Harvard.

All agreed the sheriff was a strange do-nothing about these troubles. That he was just another fraud of vocality like Bill Clinton. The law was fast cars with whip antennae racing around from one unsolved atrocity to another, screaming radios. Shield on the door ought to read *Late, Lard-ass, Last to Know*. But expert marksmen on small dogs ruffing in a driveway, or puffed actors in dinner theater, a fit of exhibitionism. Your taxes at work.

Then they spoke of Melanie. "There'll come the day when it's right, Harvard. You'll propose marriage, she'll accept. The two of you were made for each other. Get married on the barge by Parson Egan here," Lewis said.

Egan watched the water east and west. He had not uttered a word, and he was ashamed of his carved face, the cross in stitched pieces.

"If you don't care old sheriff boy been a-tappin it," said Sidney happily.

"Please." Harvard had found his own small voice at last.

"The two of 'em come 'round, why you can smell it on 'em," Sidney insisted.

"You're a wretched man, if not evil," cried tall Lewis.

"Not no worse than the truth. Yeah, she got her glass animals and her books and music and now her lawman. She a complete woman."

Harvard turned and walked up the hill, in grief, they presumed.

John Roman was about to reveal Sidney's late career between the whores. He liked and admired Harvard tremendously. But then Wren spoke again, hopeful that the lying he had done about Wake Island was forgotten.

"You had to move your mouth and break the best heart here!"

He stepped forward and slapped Sidney across the face. His arm was long and he still had surprising power in it. It was not an idle blow. Sidney sat right down on the beach grass. It seemed Wren was not through, and John Roman moved up to restrain him. But you thought he might be wanting a piece of Sidney too. Everybody did.

Sidney, huddled down, delirious in spite, was glad to see that in their unhappiness the others now turned on each other. John Roman got Wren in a half nelson and started dragging him away from Sidney. Lewis kicked at Sidney's face, missed, came again. Sidney took a blow right into the heaving place and began rolling and firing projectile vomit. Got some on the poor stitched Frankensteinish Byron Egan, who was attempting to intervene. Son pranced around, barking and wagging his tail. Across the lake they heard at an immense distance what sounded like serial gunfire and turned. All this while, Egan, silent about his attacker, pleaded for the flock to return to itself.

Ulrich and Feeney approached the pier and slowed, observing the etiquette of the small wake. They were doing fine, nothing going over had been senile or forgetful. It was just that Ulrich was relying on Feeney for a bit of navigation and Feeney didn't see right, nor did he acknowledge this to himself, so he had taken them out of their way a bit. Now he thought he saw a sail come up on the pier, and a boat, hoisted by its small crew. What was happening was that armed children were making a barricade on the end of their pier at the behest of the camp founders, Gene and Penny Ten Hoor.

The couple was armed too. They did not expect the oncoming barge to be armed, but they guessed Mortimer might be aboard and intended to deliver a volley that would part the man fifteen ways.

They had made a flag, orange, black and white, with the letters OASS in black. They called themselves Oasis, *Orphans Against Smiling Strangers.* A slogan stitched on it:

WE HAVE ALREADY LOST, SO WE WILL WIN
WE SHALL LOSE MANY, WE SHALL KILL FEW
THE ONE WE KILL, SMILING STRANGER,
WILL BE YOU.

The changes were inspired by the awful revelations of the fifteen-year-old girls. Man Mortimer thought he had charmed them and sent them back to recruit fresher younger subjects for his new video company. But Sandra, the littler one, had been injured by Large Lloyd, who had grown angry and impatient in his work and felt ludicrous in a cape and mask. They intended to kill Mortimer, and Lloyd too. And Edie, Bertha and especially Marcine, who was hardly older than the camp girls and helped betray them. Both ruined for life by intimacies distributed widely as underground art.

Minny and Sandra had turned on Mortimer when he explained over the telephone, with compassion and sweetness, he thought, that they were too old now for his projects. One day, he promised, he would take them away and set them up in fine style. But day after day, Mortimer failed to show. Then came the day when they exposed him for what he was. They did not say how glad they had been to participate, but they mentioned drugs, blackmail and death threats that had never occurred. Gene and Penny were in violent sympathy with hurt children. A new spirit took over. They would not assassinate outside the camp fence, but anybody from outside who entered the grounds, well, the new spirit was on the end of the pier behind a canoe. They began to string razor wire from the cab of a pickup, but several were cut and the going was slow. They glued glass onto percussion grenades with Krazy Glue. Many a little one glued the grenade to his palm too. No discussion. No trust in the laws of men. Death to smiling strangers on the spot. Death by long-overdue Higher Law.

Both girls now knelt behind the canoe barricade with seven others, all taking aim not on the man in the wheelhouse but on the one standing and trying to unblur his impressions, Carl Bob Feeney. Minny, the girl with breasts, had the honor of handling a Winchester lever-action .30/.30 with hollowpoint bullets. A telescope for sighting. She had known for a long time that Mortimer was not aboard, but Feeney looked a good deal like her second stepfather in Galveston, Texas.

Ulrich performed a slow turn about fifty yards out in a hail of lead. The pleasure boat was riddled, its windshield and stained-glass cabin windows shattered. Only the ineptness of the orphans' rifle training was on their side. Outside of real estate, the Ten Hoors had no talents, though they presumed to emit rays of instruction by simply riding horses and setting a good example. Minny fired over and over at Feeney through the telescope and must have carved his outline in blue space around him. Somebody threw two grenades. Thumping, pumping geysers and minnow kill out of twelve feet of clear green water. The barge was on the way back at full throttle. Twin Mercuries churning all-out. Ulrich must have caught up to the point where most of the bullets and buckshot were going in their error, for the back of the right stern disappeared and smoke crept up.

After a year, it felt to Feeney and Ulrich, they were out of range. In another place and time they would have been commended to some award. Soon they were pretty well afire back there but making good time to Farté Cove. The Ten Hoors stood arm in arm behind the firing line, hating the vehicle that might have brought another Man Mortimer to their shores. An armed Carl Bob Feeney would have shot down the both of them.

The Oasis flag still flew on its pole at the front of the barricade. The couple considered this a victory, and they celebrated with hot dogs and a long movie that night. Outside, older orphans patrolled the fence and beefed-up sections of unrolled barbed wire. Rifles slung on a rope across their backs. They gathered around the campfire for chats. An unwise salvo, bad military instruction. But there had been army error everywhere. A tradition carried on apace.

The pier crowd watched as Ulrich brought the barge over across the lake. There was a fire in the stern near the gas tanks. Saner men would have jumped overboard five minutes ago, but not these pilgrims. They plowed, they felt the power drop back to a single Mercury, they felt orange and hot on their backs. One of the tanks seemed a wall of flames and threatened to explode the next tank. *It will blow, it will immolate, it will soon be over*, Ulrich thought. *Not a bad thing, as I am ready to go to the dead animals in that other world and spend my next life atoning. Carl Bob Feeney alongside. This is the hell never described, where you get a second chance to correct your miserable life by daily ministry to those you harmed or made dead. Perhaps these are the reincarnated ones, the saints we still have scattered among us. Hitler and Stalin working as good men in obscurity somewhere. And Mao, who never took a bath except in the organs of his young lovers, as he put it, and who murdered even the sparrows of the air to bring a pestilence of grasshoppers. Feeney and I will recognize them, workers in the vineyard.*

Feeney would have been long gone in his double life jacket except he feared water so much and thought it capable of melting off the buckles. All deeper water to Feeney was a sucking vortex activated by contact with any warm thing that thrashed. Then there were the sharks. Great fat blond lake sharks that lay on the bottom until stirred by that music above, men flapping, kicking their legs, yelling for help.

"We'll have to run her aground near the pier and call for help," said Ulrich.

"Friend, there is no help here. Try to make the shallows out of the shark beds."

"Feeney, you're an old priest from Ireland. There are no sharks. Leave it to me. I know nature!" This was a lie.

All considered, Feeney thought, *those children blazing away were very charitable. They might have killed us easily instead of this warning. We could have been the church, the state or landlords. Preachers and destroyers.*

They neared the pier, jumped down from a fully engulfed floor of the bow and cabin. The pleasure barge was a collapsed charcoal hulk by the time Melanie got the Redwood fire department there. No obvious evidence of foul play, only the vague idiocy of two old fools. Ulrich and Feeney never mentioned they were fired upon and took the abuse with equanimity.

Nevertheless, sane fishermen avoided fishing the weeds and lily pads of the orphans' camp shoreline. All that rifle range going, you might get into something stray.

Sidney was back at the bait store when he got word and almost wrecked his fine car several times racing over, wallowing on gravel and twisting on grass, fishtailing. With water on the road he would have hydroplaned. Then he limped wildly down the hill where others gathered. Ulrich had done this trying to light a cigarette aft, near the gasoline, he was told. One more chance before they hauled him and Feeney to Almost There. Sidney Farté was in ecstasy.

Sheriff Facetto had a lead. The last to see Pepper alive seemed to have been Ruthna, a somewhat notorious woman, and two men called Harb and Alexander. The sheriff had tracked them to the tame and brick-streeted town of Clinton, where the Baptist college was, and where Grant had once stabled his horses in a chapel in the midst of giant cedars. Now its suburbs defined it. Pine forests ripped down for the blocky bunkers of new businessmen and computer Christians fleeing the blacker Jackson to the east.

The sheriff met all three in Ruthna's ragged house, an ersatz hacienda with failing cactuses and yuccas about. It was the home of her fifth husband, Harb, who was her ex but still came around to visit with Alexander over a bottle or two now and then. They were friends of Max Raymond and did see Pepper a few minutes before ten that night. But they were depressed and godless, divorced and alcoholic, and their memories were random. Once they were not suspects, they began to be drunk and pathetic in a short space, fighting for narrative time with each other. The sheriff was sorting, writing, reacting. Then he just asked them to shut up.

The night in question they had gnawed bones in a booth of the northside restaurant, Near 'Nuff Food, far superior to the restaurant right at the saxophonist and singer's cottage. Raw beams, linoleum, spiderweb Formica tabletops, leatherette seats, happy waitresses. A theme. A waitress hurried out and dumped ribs on a heavy paper tablecloth, two rolls of paper napkins.

They wanted to be higher when they left to visit Raymond and the Coyote. They considered themselves urbanites, ignorant of philosophy but crammed with half-remembered songs, which served. They were unhappy, and if God existed, they blamed him for much. The whiskey still worked on them, but they needed more. Ruthna pulled the Jeep Grand Cherokee Laredo into the gravel lot of the bait store for a last beer. At least ice and cups and Tums. The ribs of Near 'Nuff Food were loggy and scalding in their tender stomachs.

Harb and Ruthna had already begun to fight regarding her past. Alexander went inside and left them to it. A hound watched them all from the porch. Soon enough the fight grew tiresome. They passed a man on a high stool, a note written on an envelope on the counter before him. He was asleep, a football was in the aisle of the store and this was a curious thing, as if somebody had just left off a game of touch. They had a sense somebody was in the back but just left this old man to his sleeping. He was a dry white old creature, leaning on the bulwark of a Lucky Strike display case in which all brands of smokes were stacked. Old Camels, Chesterfields, Pall Malls and Roitan cigars, brands that seldom moved in modern towns. The note under his fingers must be a message to customers, they figured. *Out to Lunch* or the like, even though he was there. They got the sack of ice, the plastic cups, the soda, lemons. For a geezer he was well stocked in the needs of the drinking life.

Maybe he was deaf as well as asleep. They couldn't get his attention. Alexander turned the note around, thinking maybe to wake him. The note seemed oddly personal but scrawled in excitement or carelessness.

I SEEN THE LIGHT AROUND THE CORNER OF THE TUNNEL THEM BASTARDS WAITING FOR ME.

His face was perhaps more purple than was good for a fellow. But he could damn well sleep and they decided this was quaint and in their sleepless tossings they envied him.

They grabbed a bottle from the shelf behind him and went out with the goods, pocketing the cash. They thought this was what the sheriff had come about and this they apologized for. The drink, the weirdness of the scene, their lightness of spirit. Really it was only a prank.

They continued a bit just to hear for themselves what happened the rest of the night once they got to Max Raymond's. They told Raymond about the catatonic man. Old Pepper harked back to Raymond's adolescence, his first night here in a cabin with other boys. The rare night it snowed here. A January with only a few crappie fishermen around. Somebody had insisted Pepper look out at the snow falling thickly in the porch light. He went out, peered briefly and returned.

"Nasty," he said. Nothing else. Raymond insisted this was modern poetry.

Two thought Raymond was affected. Another fight broke out.

He and the Coyote had been drinking too. She told him the way he clung to his past was morbid. He accused her of having no memories. Fort Lauderdale, Memphis. What was that? She was nowhere, just tits and hair with a voice.

The others took her side. Mimi Suarez said she was not pregnant and was glad.

After a while Alexander and Harb insisted Mimi sing. For song was what was left in the world. Ruthna felt her powers waning and began taking off her clothes. She went out to the back stoop like that and thought she heard boos from nature and her feelings were hurt. She came in and the Coyote passed her and began singing out there with her back to them. Raymond passed the naked Ruthna, dancing. Harb was swaying before her in boxer shorts and black shoes. Alexander watched Mimi's back as she faced the swamp and sang. Presently Raymond accompanied her on the sax. Then he tore her dress off.

Raymond and the weak porch light on Mimi's shoulders and buttocks. Out there kneeling and spying, Sponce, Harold and the little ones were at pains to keep their faces behind the fronds. Mimi was the first woman Harold had seen naked. He looked straight through her as through a lens to his beloved Dee. This woman was not his stopping place, pretty as her voice was, strange as his vantage. The younger boys stayed close to the skeletons.

"I've got more confidence. I'm not scared of melody anymore," they heard Raymond call to the others. Nobody cared.

The guests lumbered about the rooms in a great sweat, dancing, one nude, wishing themselves lost from their species.

ELEVEN

CARL BOB FEENEY WAS DEAD, THE SHERIFF LEARNED, arriving at the mortuary in Vicksburg. Feeney's nephew had identified the body, but he was not here now. Loved ones do not linger in these precincts. Only the women who sought Christ in the tomb to pay their respects and discovered the resurrection, announced by a frightening young man in all-white garments. Perhaps the writer of the gospel Mark himself, who had fled the law and run naked out of this garment one night long ago at Gethsemane.

But Facetto was not here about Feeney. The mortuary staff had called him with a problem. It was after nine, but lights were on in the basement. A man had been telephoning them at regular intervals, then random ones, about the embalming of an Uncle Ricky, who was not there in any form. Yet the caller insisted they save Uncle Ricky's *head to be arrested.* Who would arrest him? the mortuary director asked him, the caller. Sheriff Facetto, said the caller. He knows this case. Uncle Ricky put his cigarette out on his forehead for twenty years and now his head needed to be arrested. The calls became harassing and then stopped, but they threatened the mortuary and the sheriff both if Uncle Ricky's head did not stand trial alone. It must not go underground or into cremation.

Have mercy on these people who see the living become a thing, thought the sheriff. Look here, said the dead, I'm going now, but I'll leave you this gray meat to lug around a few hours more. No matter what rattlesnakes the dead were, the living had to salute the leavings. All must submit. He thought of his father, a small savage marine, proud of his dry heart. The old soldiers around his grave, lying through their teeth. Oh he was the salt of the earth, a man's man. His mother a tall beauty desiccated and driven nearly mute by his company. Like an old television antenna finally, obsolete decades ago.

The man at the car door surprised Facetto. He was already scared.

"I'm Sheriff Facetto. You called?"

"Oh yes, Sheriff."

"This is about the telephone calls. Uncle Ricky and all that."

"Yeah, he called again just now."

"What was the cause of death on Feeney, by the way?"

"A coronary, I think. He had very bad lungs. His nephew said he had become a chain-smoker since leaving the Catholic Church. He was once a priest. He had other diseases. But Lord, he was eighty-two. He came from Ireland and was a missionary to Mississippi. My wife informed me this was a third-world mission field to Irish Catholics."

"Ireland. All their broods and terrorists. Well."

"Anyway, we wondered if you could put a trace or stop the calls."

"This isn't my county. I don't know who's calling, either, or I'd act on it. Sorry, friend."

Facetto drove off. He felt pulled by dread to nowhere. He'd never even gotten out of his car and had spoken only through the window. He might wobble if he walked, or thrust headlong like a swimmer through this fog. Next week he was onstage again in a production of the Vicksburg Theater League. Now he couldn't remember who he was playing, or what he spoke.

He acknowledged he was a fearful man, but why had this Uncle Ricky call shaken him so much? Horrible laughter and Facetto's ruin were in the voice over the phone. That specter every man might feel at his shoulder. You would turn and here was the shape and face, the awful laughter, the thing pointing at you. It knew who you were and had caught up with you at last. It had seen you faring back and forth in that old woman. Hot Granny. Pulling a long one out of Granny. Hiding her false teeth. He needed sleep. He needed to be out of love.

He felt he reigned in a county which everyone of worth should have left decades ago, all breeds. He dealt with refuse, squatters, the ones gathered around their own nastiness, their own echoes, like night dogs.

Max Raymond returned to the church in the glen where Egan had beat his fists, demonstrated his hypodermic, tossed his ponytail. It was empty but open and he walked to the pinewood altar. All was poignant since Egan's uncle had died and Egan's face had been mutilated. Egan still refused to name the mutilator. Raymond remained silent as well, the bones, his disgrace, the stab wound, which still throbbed in his buttock when he walked or played the sax or even stood too long.

Rain hit on the tin roof. Early shots from the pickets before main engagement. The rain pleased Raymond immensely, as it always did. It whispered, cancel your duty to the outer, get fetal, think of caves. He had loved it at Tulane, where he went to school forever, it seemed. Rain out of Texas and the Gulf. Twilight now, the last of radiant heat sweeping out in the new breezes under the cracked windows with their purple and green glass. Last swirls of color before you drowned, maybe. You could imagine yourself purified by them, you wanted it. *Clear this mess, Lord. Save me while you're at it.*

Raymond waited and then picked up a hymnal. The altar was lit by a single bulb in a reading lamp. He was about to tear out a page and leave a message to Byron Egan.

Outside, a car crunched alongside the church on the pea gravel. He went to the window and saw two boys in an amazing automobile, a 1948 Ford coupe in deep red with a gold hood. The driver could barely see over the panel. The driver did not cut off the engine. The car pushed out a considerable white cloud from the rear. Perhaps blown or crippled by a break. But the thing kept throbbing. The boys seemed to have been stolen by it and made to do its will. *Well, if you can shoot and drive at ten, then it's still the South,* Raymond thought. He raised the window and leaned out as Egan had done many nights ago and lost his face.

"Are you the preacher?" asked the boy behind the wheel.

"No."

"Are you his friend?"

"I think so."

"Tell him we wanted him to do this thing right. We gone to have some fun. Might even shoot somebody if we can get him to follow us. We think he seen us and took the bait all right."

"Stop the car and come in. Don't be rash or dumb now."

"We carryin' his own pistol. Mortimer's."

"That's what I mean. No reason to make more trouble."

"You think the preacher'll be back soon?"

"I imagine. It's Wednesday night. Prayer meeting."

"You know any other preachers that smoke cigarettes, mister?"

"No I don't, not right off."

"That's why we chose him. We like him. But we gonna come back when we see his car here with yours."

They were underage, undersize, underfed even. But in the vehicle they had dignity, and you did not think of children but grim little men. Wild smoke out the back and the two meager heads, pledged to this red and golden absurdity. A casino roundup car. They drove off very solemnly with the bad shifting. The car lurched from its own colors, then went smoother in the third gear.

He waited for the preacher a while longer. Maybe there was no prayer meeting here. Or canceled while Egan was mourning for his uncle Feeney. Yet Man Mortimer might be close to the boys. Raymond could stand being a coward only just a little bit longer. He left.

When the preacher did come a half hour later, there was a pile of crushed bones on the top step of the church porch. He knew at once what they were. He had money in his pocket for an installment on his loan. Mortimer did not need to go voodoo on him. But the man was apparently enjoying the reach of his evil now. Rushing into symbols, always a sign of some disorder, decided the preacher, much reformed since those years of the Maltese crosses and crossbones of the bikers. He wanted to ride, to drink, to smoke. He had started smoking again several weeks back. Nobody liked it, and he tended to hide his butts like a schoolboy would. In trees, rest rooms, the cup of his hand.

Egan was not too mournful. Taking Uncle Carl Bob to Onward would have been sadder. Now he had a surplus of money, really, a home, dogs, cats, land. Two priests had attended the small funeral in Vicksburg. They were nice gentlemen, fond of Brother Carolus Robert still. This helped Egan's heart.

He'd come to sweep the church and check the space heaters and radiators because the cold was on. But he would preach if any showed. The rain chill lay in him still. The heaters were old donated units, probably illegal. The clay grates red with heat. They ran off a propane tank behind the little church. He liked them because you saw immediate hell in them. Hell was loose in the world and it had its colors. Beings came up from its reaches in a reverse resurrection and got among what righteous flocks remained.

He knew he had no more life span than a dog's left to him, and his face might ruin his chances for marriage, but he would bring a righteous posse into this fight, beginning tonight with even one sheep. These bones were merely death, reminders there was only one road and the road never changed. They were only the last litter of life. Perhaps his methedrine run seven years back was meant to show him this. Here they were where they belonged. He might preach about them. Or lacquer them for display in the chapel, carrying them with him to his other ministries. He did not quite understand yet his duty to them, but on the other hand he had not known what day would follow the next since he surrendered himself to the Lord Jesus Christ.

Serving his Lord had been a joy and not insanity at all. It was joy even when none listened, even when he was cursed for a Christer in the casino aisles. When the right triumphed, Egan knew they would build cancer centers and Christian motorcycle-repair shops, and bookstores and even colleges from the casino buildings. He was not waiting, he knew there were others of the same mind. They would see the tails of the godforsaken backing out the greasy way they came in, Donald Trump, Harrah's, whoever thought they were at home here. He had heard Russian Mafia too. Wherever it went, you knew the money was siphoned off to out-of-state, out-of-grace pigs somewhere, not into an education fund for small children as they boasted. *And Lord*, he whispered, *I know these counties better than any living man. I rolled in sin in every quarter, every dark province. Even Moses wandered in the desert forty years. To compensate for former lost years in narcotics, I have been blessed.*

Like many another reformed smoker, he had returned to the habit twofold. He smoked incessantly and drank nearly a gallon of thick coffee every day. Because the minister smoked openly, he could not have a denomination, only a flock. He knew smoking was wrong, he was weak. He was positive the Lord frowned on it. Some things were sin and others just math. You smoked a number of cigarettes and then you got ill. You watched television a number of times and then you were a television, empty until turned on again. The casino was math become a monster. But even with wrestling and prayer, even tears and spasms into the wee hours, he could not quit cigarettes. Maybe a sign to the weak ones they would be let in and forgiven too.

He felt sin more deeply than the rest because he had seen it from its early infant sleep. And bliss too, the bliss of relief from his sour burdens. A bliss next to flight itself. Dear old Ulrich, Egan had tried to tell him this, but the warrior soul of the man was still angry about Feeney, his pal, and sad past words. Egan and Ulrich sat long on the end of the pier watching the ring of red around a cold moon. Ulrich told him he must love the animals even more and help them. Yet Egan thought the heart could stand only so much concern. Sufficient unto the day is the evil thereof, no more.

He took the broom and began sweeping in the pale glow of the altar lamp. He did not want lights overhead yet. He wanted silence and shadows and the rain outside on the roof for a while. Then he found the torn page with the note on the altar.

I AM YOUR SERVANT CALL MAX RAYMOND.

The number beneath it.

Egan had seen Max Raymond and his band, especially the wife, performing in a casino where he had once dearly loved to gamble and walked trembling past the tables still, his pockets full of stiff little cards. John 3:16 on one side; YOU ARE IN HELL on the other. Quietly handing them out to the annoyed and angry, some frightened by his cheek tattoo. When he came into the music hall through which Cuban jazz was throbbing, he saw there were not many revelers at the tables. Few dancers. He saw the Coyote onstage, curved around the microphone like an old torchess, and straightaway coveted her, sailing into fantasies so sweet they seemed beyond heaven or hell. He whispered his thanks for her existence, then departed quietly.

But he asked questions later, came back to the casino, his ministry bent somewhat to the earthly appreciation of Mimi Suarez. Who was the husband with such luck? He saw him, heard him play the horn and could not understand.

In the church he turned on the overhead fluorescent bar. He continued sweeping into the corners, invigorated by the cool drafts. For all his philosophy, he avoided looking at the pile of bone shards on the porch. Then a voice called from outside. The man was still in his car, leaning out. Byron Egan stood on the threshold.

"Oh Pastor?"

"Is that you, Raymond?"

"No, no."

"Are you with the bones?"

"I am related to the bones." A bent man stepped from the car and stood at the bottom of the steps. He seemed unmindful of the mist on his face.

Egan recognized Mortimer. "What are you wanting?" he asked, shaking, holding the broom.

"Oh, my money, but no idea after that really. I just seem to want to go a lot of places," said Mortimer.

Egan dropped the broom and whipped out a great switchblade, nearly a bowie, from the hip of his jeans. The blade jumped out with a loud click and lock. He waved it beneath the porch light.

"Why Pastor, I been sick. I know not what I do. What could have happened to your face?"

"I could see you now a hundred yards off. I lived in sin an age and I know you well."

"You look a devil yourself. Like you in some far pirate tribe. Old Burt Lancaster swinging from the ropes on a boat. But they're doing not a half-bad job on it."

"I am the Lord's servant, branded."

"I'm taking these old scraps of bone off with me. But they might be employed again. I'm getting to be the caretaker of these slivers, looking for the owner."

"Get out of here. You're the black seed itself." Egan thrust the money at Mortimer, who gathered up the bone sticks haphazardly, dropping pieces, unmindful. Then he got in the car and went.

In this life, last things are never said, nor can they be. The preacher pocketed the knife. His knees were weak, his neck stiff. He was certain the Lord moved in his fingers and did not understand this fear, or even the words he had just uttered. He thought he heard a crackling, or a sigh, just outside the south window, and he watched out for what glistened in the mist. He listened for the living sigh of evil, if it was bigger now. Echoes from the casino were all he heard.

Then Ulrich's old woody wagon rolled up to the church, glistening. Both ancient and new, phantom of a heavy past but joy manufactured right into it. First Ulrich climbed out slowly, then on the other side Max Raymond. Egan was very happy.

"We've come to worship, to discuss, to live," said Raymond, somewhat practiced, Egan thought.

"I'm scared, I'm alone. I've come to ask you to let me move in with you and the dogs. I'll be no bother. I must be close to Feeney's dogs. I'll clean and watch the house for you," said Ulrich.

Egan did not doubt he was given two miracles. He loved the old man. The man needed him. The dogs needed Ulrich, even with his oxygen and nose tube. The man who had once flown and dreamed himself away all his life afterward.

Egan himself was suddenly wrapped twice by a high lonesome and a circle of fear. But this night was good. The wine of gentle conversation, other like spirits directly near to hand in the nights. Good, good. The old friendly strength came back to him.

"I want revenge," said Max Raymond. "I'm a dog myself, the dog of a zombie."

"Come in, come in. What we have is one old sinner out there trying to be legion. He doesn't even trust his help anymore. He is nearing his breakdown. He took my money and drove away muttering, afraid of my knife."

"You are an armed Christian?" asked Raymond.

"I believe the Lord approves if they get you in the

face. And no little slap on the cheek. I don't think the Lord is training any knife bait no more."

"He called my home and offered my wife a job as queen of whores if her performance with him was sufficient," said Raymond. "Said she needed breaking in a little and English lessons."

CUBANISMO! GOT TO HAVE IT! read the flyer.

The band blared and chopped along, aroused by itself, uncertain of ever descending. The weekend crowd was big, less derelict than usual. A few college people, a bus crowd from Wisconsin, stunned dentists and their strap-shouldered wives, some of them without a social event since high school. Lone dancers from dead Protestant crossroads where meager churches jutted like tombstones with steps. Ignited, undulant, gay, half drunk, friendly. The rage of the casino just behind them, red and gold, a lost football crowd.

The wives and husbands were startled by the Coyote, who shimmered under her black ringlets, curved in her gown like promise itself. The women wanted her for a pet, the men to be an anonymous head eating away at her. Many changed race. Some tried to have ecstasy in Spanish. The band made them doubt there had ever been another life.

One who danced alone was John Roman, who could no longer stand the pain at home. His shoulders went up and back. His gray head sweated, his eyes closed. He wanted down the river of trumpet, saxophone, trombone, the raft of rhythm underneath him. *Dance some of the gray sick off me,* he prayed.

Max Raymond searched the crowd even as he played the horn. This was half impossible for the spotlights. He did not play so evilly tonight. His playing was not firmly anything. His coveted wife was nothing to him now, his horn nothing, he was not certain he was clothed. His entrances and choruses with the trombone and trumpet were tepid, staggering, reeling without heart, like a tune wounded but still carrying on down the road in bedroom slippers. It was Costume Night, and many of the crowd were wearing masks. The Coyote was always in the contest, he thought grimly. In her natural stuff, the minimal mini memorable, her legs. *We have a winner.*

Raymond began to relax during his break, when he did not see Mortimer in the dancers or tablesiders or anywhere costumed or uncostumed. He settled into a fine jar of Wild Turkey on ice, with a soda and lime to the side, and began his lean, bumped by a few fans, those angry and sullen laggards to whom he could play no wrong. Some of them had homemade CDs of only him. Anybody could make a disc now. Our great democracy. Perhaps he and the band were due one. This Latinismo thing would fail, he feared, but it would always be around as long as there were butts and rumbas. It was a shame these baby nihilists creeped him out so, with all their love, and always too early drunk, and their females too, little skanks latched on to the wrongest punks in town. He could not know he was looking straight at his own youth. All that was missing was a war and a pet wolverine.

Beside him was a strange figure, unmasked, hooking his drink with a claw made out of only natural hand, and moaning, perhaps a jester ignored for all his private comedy. Except for some vision half suppressed since the awful night with the bones, Raymond was not aware that Malcolm was lakeside. Now, with a thrill to the pits, Max Raymond recognized him, accompanied by the leaner and sterner couple to his right. He turned away quickly. It was Mimi Suarez the three of them were watching, onstage alone now with piano, bass and drums. Malcolm was the only one who watched with love. The other two seemed saddened by her ballads and intent on suffering. As if they were reviewing their own lunacy, their own love, their own cause. They each seemed alone. Separately crucified once more. Penny and Gene Ten Hoor.

Raymond would play the rest of the night with his back to the audience, like an old idol of cool, Miles Davis. His punk following would think he had outdone himself. He hurried back to the stage now, through couples panting and sweaty. A college football man misunderstood Raymond's need and slammed him across the shoulder. He went down into the legs of a screaming mulatto woman bigger than he was. He rose through her kicks while somebody screamed, "He's with the band, bitch!" He wondered where this had commenced as her curses followed him through the crowd of masks, Reagan, Nixon, dancing together even without music. Donald Trump's rubber face on a very short man. Even Alan Greenspan. Hillary Clinton pouting but with mouth open, perhaps raving, pop eyes. Momentum rang through him like an urgent telephone somewhere ahead. He rushed past John Roman with a handkerchief to his neck and then Man Mortimer. He could not credit they had been dancing together, but he did not slow. Drugged women passed like a discord of mannequins. Or was he drugged? When his head cleared, he was high but did not know quite what floor he stood on. It was the curling bandstand.

As he held life dearly, so he also yearned to leave it. But now he would play himself somewhere on the instrument. Play it well, with heart and no more belly lint and asthma.

Now, when the music began once more, it was John Roman, dancing, who was incredulous. His partner was

Mortimer, uncostumed except in a silk bandit's mask and the slick beam-shoed costume he felt compelled to wear against all contigencies. He raised his hands and shuffled violently, an enormous grin on him. "Can you boogie? Can you do the dog? Get down, get down, John Henry! Oldies but goodies. C'mon c'mon c'mon." He was an uncommonly bad dancer, Mortimer, and here with a solitary black male with silver hair, he did not mimic one well either.

Just behind him, perhaps betrayed in partners, was Sidney Farté in a very large old-timer's party suit and vest, white shoes. He troubled the floor with some spastic revision of anything right, perhaps clogging or just stomping. But he was happy and grinning and drunk. Looking on the back of his bad influence, and not a finer man in the county, old Man Mortimer. *He the man!*

John Roman ceased the dance and decided this was the worst possible outcome, to have danced himself to Mortimer. Nausea struck him. Danced to hell and didn't even see. He wanted home to Bernice very badly. Old Sidney slid by, bumping in a kind of march, hands in the air, aimed toward a table where blond, blood-lipped whores laughed at him. This was enough.

"John Roman, the night is young! Come on now, man. You ain't showing us nothing!" called Mortimer. "We in the Club! Get in the Club! *Club of the Now!*" He clamped his hand on Roman's sleeve, and there was a too-mighty squeeze. Roman tore away. It was a nice coal-brown sports coat with a rep tie. Mortimer's fingers themselves seemed coiled and toothed like serpents.

Roman did not realize he was bleeding from the wrist until he was in the car and cranking up. He leaned his head on the steering wheel. He felt sad, weak, small, eking away. His wife would die, he would be one leg in the grave. No more dancing. No song would speak to him. His wrist was wet and he raised it curiously. All his hand was drenched, sticky in its white dress shirt. He felt the pain and now saw the gash. What vicious tiny thing had snagged him? Then a car passed him in the lot with two lit skulls on the shelf of its rear windshield. Roman groaned.

I used to be a man. People did what I said. I advanced under fire. I had dignity. I walked toward crowds with my head up. Now I hold hands with nonsense. Gnats of spite around my head. I do not know where the fight is or where to give up.

Now he supposed he would have to kill Mortimer or start back going to church. With that ponytailed fool Byron Egan. Now that was a man who might have laid a couple out in his days. Lost his old uncle now. Like Roman had almost lost that nice old child Melanie Wooten for a friend. He started the car and drove home to hold the hand of his wife, Bernice.

Chet Baker was on the tape deck as Roman drove. Nothing. A painful irrelevance worse than silence especially in the love ballads. They seemed a fraud, they didn't hurt enough, there wasn't any shame in them, only that whimpering lapdog studio tribute to some ghost broad.

Vines climbed all over his housefront and there was a dim light within. *Bernice would shoot the motherfucker, no doubt of that. And she's still got a God, last I asked. I ain't bothered her with him. She's got the chemotherapy, she's got the sleeps, she's got the nausea and the marijuana pills, the THC. Now she's a legal junky, but not even happy when she's stoned. She's got the baldness that's humiliating her. That wonderful silvery hair gone. She didn't want to look like no fortune-teller or woman wrestler.*

All she wanted was her man and a house, waited half her life to get it. Set in the depopulated reaches of west-central Mississippi, Louisiana across the river. Swamps and flood on both sides, bayous. The great fertile lake that Roman had fished so good, so long. There was no starving here unless you meant money. People got by on enough. Too much electric have-to greed out there anyway. Roman thought he had gotten rid of the disease of want. His life was simple, near good fishing water. In their house he and Bernice shared the easy devotion that comes when you wait and wait. Little rhythms, unspoken speech of love. It seemed not to matter where a mad god was. They had earned this shelter beyond his wrath. Roman knew he was alive somewhere, this god. He had seen his work. And now he had seen Mortimer's.

He held the handkerchief to his wet hand, his face cold. His shirt ruined too. Roman had seen such monsters in the service. Only question is whether Mortimer's worth doing any kind of time for.

Chet Baker, what is *it? It was always there, but we hear it only now and then.*

Bernice was asleep.

One day you say I'm not moving, here is my country, I can't help it, I've fallen into my place, no budging. I'll die here with the ghosts of my old everybody. My Indians, my Africans, my uncles and aunts. Where half was grief, home was at least a hole to have it in.

The Allison boys still drove when they had gas, but they did not come near the house with their hot rod. They had washed it for free at several homes and car washes where there was a good machine. *We may be next thing to dead children driving this old car, but we will run out our minutes in it.* The car had come out of the water and was delivered by the sinkhole and they knew a true miracle because when Hare dragged it off to put on the last touches, it wasn't but rust and slime yet and in five days he'd come back riding down the road in this. Even Dee was impressed by the car all painted and running, and she didn't impress easily. Now, Isaac and Jacob believed, she had to give herself to Hare at the church not too long from now.

They dreamed Mrs. Suarez would hold them like puppies for a while and let them listen when her song started. She would sing and they would live high on these notes on her bosom before they were dead by Man Mortimer wanting the bones they had lost and the car they came in. They still had his pistol. *Bam, bam, bam. But knowing Mrs. Suarez,* they promised, *we can't kill, we can't be mean no more.*

The dogs were pleasant strays, all grateful, shivering. Made to be a friend of man. Happy for the hands that now led them and pulled the burrs, ticks and deer lice from their coats. The hands that gave them their heartworm medicine, their vaccinations. Their eyes were bright and their coats bushy and shined. They were a smiling lot, bidding for attention from Ulrich and Egan. They snuffled over Ulrich and took him down like a short rugby team, a scrum all over the laughing man. He required them for his soul, a new shape taking up its own just lately, and felt distinctly by Ulrich as a pain in his chest.

Fixed with Ulrich as his housemate, Egan was feeling better. Another five-hour surgery at University Hospital in Jackson was over. Ulrich drove him over and back daintily in the woody wagon, wanting to stop and chase down every stray on Highway 20 past Bovina, Edwards, Bolton and Clinton. Egan allowed only two severe cases, starving and spiny. The odor, road-carboned and grease-gamey, was not that bad. At home the dogs fell on a bucket of chicken and lapped water from bowls, then slept on old blankets of

Feeney's. One a spotted hound, one a corgi and shepherd mix they named Wayne. The other after a while they called Woody, for his profession.

Egan had shaved his head, which the surgeon liked. The black cross had re-formed whole, even blacker now that it was out of the gauze. With its Gothic menace. He wore the knife back to St. Peter, who cut off the centurion's ear before Christ could stop him. Such bad faith, such minor work. He was not proud but he was scared.

Both of them missed Feeney very much. Ulrich was certain the old man was killed in the service of his animal ministry, but he did not tell this to Egan because he himself wished to die in this manner, it did not matter when. Just let him serve. Given this tenure, he was at peace. Without cigarettes, he was even something of a worker.

Egan had a good oblong head on him. Ulrich saw this as a sign of intelligence, although the biker hair never mattered to him, he who had just a pewter scrag on his own head, and large ears. Egan joined the part of the elders, and he spoke with them on the pier more as they cleared the burned hulk of the barge and began a new one. What else was there for Harvard?

One afternoon Egan told Ulrich, "It's time we reached out to the orphans. Get up some of the friendlier dogs, say four, howabout? I'll help. The kids'll love petting them."

"I don't know. They're not outgoing folks. But all right, Feeney'd been with us."

"He'd be there."

They drove themselves and the dogs, singing songs of faith, anthems of dead ravers and prophets, Luther, Longfellow.

TWELVE

Today

Maxwell Raymond
Eagle Lake, Mississippi
copyright at Vicksburg Public Library

My forebears prayed give me Sherman, Grant or a
    lesser general.
Ptoom and bummf, hit square.
This old mistress my rifle.
Nasty bite. I call her Mingo, the old bopster.
Blooooom! Above the eyes the nice wide forehead.
My headshot, our whole lives.
Fill your head, Ulysses S. Grant, William T.
    Sherman.
The visionary like the loaded gun.
If he waits long enough, something will happen.
Unless he rusts, unless his eyes collapse.
The dark diarist, his last words shouted, "I'm
    dying, watch this!"
You knowest not what I do, Rag on the cross.
I always loved You Jesus and didn't understand
    much else.
These claims, What the Lord Wants Me to Do,
Greek, Greek to me.
I would like the straight Aramaic right from His
    lips.
And why not?
This long wait with this much posture gives you

the blue soul.
I dab and idle, attendant God.
I insist my art and path be crooked, in fear there
      will be a herd
Of the simple where I want to be.
Help my eyes and ears,
Or just show up, why don't You?

Raymond was speechifying to Mimi as never before. He was nearly coherent and it frightened her. They heard a mass of gunfire across the lake from the orphans' camp one evening.

"Now I can feel the madness of grief in the kitchen where Penny talked to the limb. When they lost the boy, I believe they became just people at last and couldn't bear it."

"Became people?" asked Mimi. "What were they before?"

Raymond said aloud, looking past Mimi, "Movers, actors, I'd suppose. Sellers, takers, keepers. Some come apart when they discover themselves. As somebody said, Acts mark the land, words are only its smoke, or something.

"I despise, but am in awe of, this couple, Mimi. They simply ran out of words, don't you understand? They dealt with things you touch and hold and appraise. Bodies. Bodies and acts is what they knew.

"With drugs or without them, bodies and acts. At my deposition nobody wanted to talk drugs, but two lawyers wanted Halcyon and Xanax, I tell you. I told them, sorry, I'm a saxophonist.

"Sure, Gene and Penny were sad. And they were absent the usual compulsion to be *good* in sadness. Goodness is respected and often mistaken for a cure. Not only words, though, they seem to have lost even their taste buds toward the end. They went naked or wore clothes to no effect on each other. They collected money. They collected fish. They had destroyed wetlands and aviaries. Now they began nailing it all on the wall."

"Why is it that you adore the pain and suffering of your family and others? Tell me." Mimi stared hard at him without warmth. Now he was silent. At last. "You are in love with ruin. You get a contact high from it. You play your horn like you are sick of the notes sometimes. Why is that?"

When Mimi left, he had, he *did* have, a vision of his old poet mentor, speaking out of a fog at the vets' hospital. Speaking as he had done in the late seventies.

"Oh I found my feminine side long ago, Max. It's Edna, an old navy dyke."

The poet did not smile.

Ulrich and Egan returned home with their petting zoo intact. They met Malcolm, who carried a rifle negligently at his left leg, telling them he was the victim of Max Raymond and he loved Mimi Suarez. The proximity alone seemed to please him. All this he told Ulrich and Egan while they looked at a few bullet holes in the woody wagon. Gene and Penny were on horseback. An accident. They were sorry.

Harvard, who worked to salvage what good timber might be left of the launch, was annoyed when Ulrich and Egan's dogs came to the pier. He was querulous in his suffering over Melanie. He pouted in her presence and scowled. This might be her last year of radiance. Harvard hoped it was. She was unbearable to him.

America is dreadful for the emeritus, or so Harvard thought. Once a god, a surgeon of few mistakes, now an eccentric out to pasture. His neighbors connected him to more charming days when doctors made house calls and bespoke themselves in soft benisons. Some might hit him for a drug now and then.

He began searching the aisles of the launch, through cinder and ashes, and finding bullet slugs. He knelt and studied them. Mushroomed .22 Magnums, .30/.30 and buckshot. Harvard raked through the coals and could hear the slugs rattling.

He cleared the embers, the broken stained glass, the half-pews, the quarter-wheel. He had once lived across the street from a man with thick glasses. He owned no car. The neighbors called him the Walking Man. He walked everywhere, morning and evening, and nobody knew his mission. He did not sing, laugh, play. He had no work except perhaps at the library. In his thick glasses, he seemed to be taken up with the traffic. Going and returning was a demanding event. You would stop to offer him a ride and he would brusquely refuse. He did not answer his phone. He once drank, but he stopped. He smoked, but he quit. He may have been a failed scholar, a torn philosopher. The thick glasses controlled him. Earnest and officious, even fervent, in his walk, without humor. Never smelled a rose. It was a free country. Harvard wondered why the neighborhood boys hated him so.

Sheriff Facetto and Bernard were in the bait store one evening in khakis and T-shirts and canvas shoes, a johnboat in the gravel out front. The weather was mild and the winter crappie season was in and they had in mind filling a freezer box with fillets for a county beer-and-fish picnic the middle of February. Big slabs lurked thick as necklaces in the brushy sinks near the spillway.

Mortimer in the back did not recognize the sheriff and his deputy through the storeroom window. But these men were not leaving until they learned the color of jig and depth for the slab crappie. The locals were leaning around freezer chests close to a potbellied stove with a good fire. Two of them were having a sport on the sheriff and thought he ought to find out himself about the jig color and technique. It wasn't something you just handed over to a foreigner, it took years, many bad mornings, many frozen spines. Mortimer could see the skinny younger one, Bernard, getting angrier over this matter.

Mortimer recognized the sheriff and deputy the same moment he saw the thing on the top rack. Two full-size footballs secured in tandem by foot-long black strips of canvas webbing with Velcro at the ends. It was a life preserver, worn around the neck. Pepper's old footballs. Sidney was having a go at invention. The weekend after the costume dance, when he had gotten with three large women for special tastes right out of Mortimer's service, the experience of which, he told Mortimer and Lloyd, was like "rolling around in a warm room," he had worn Mortimer's silk bandit's mask all weekend behind his store counter. The effect on a fishing Sunday was disquieting to his hungover clients, drinking beer rapidly before they could decide whether to stay.

Now Mortimer was staring dead-on at Facetto, through the glass and quite unknown to him. He could have rammed a bolo through the two-way storeroom mirror into the man's very face without his ever knowing what nightmare had struck him.

Years ago a man had driven into the bait shop at night, hungry and with the inventory of an entire bankrupt sporting-goods store in a four-ton truck. It was hot summer, tree frogs and gnats having away at the air, aggravating the man's thirst. He was broke, bankrupt and alcoholic, and he knew not where he was. He figured perhaps Kansas. Nobody else was in the store. He appealed to Pepper's charity, spoke to him curiously, as if he might be the governor of the state, who was at that time a graceless yahoo whipping up racial purity among even lesser yahoos in confrontation with the Brothers Kennedy, who wanted one black man in the university at that time. He spoke as if Pepper were in charge of large fates and was known far and wide for his special attunement to the troubles of the little man in this often heartbreaking and deceptive land. He indicated waves of wheat and torrents of oranges out through the door. "I will do anything for a drink and a sandwich," he told Pepper. "I have a truck full of sports equipment and not a dime. For a bottle I could give you a whole lot of sports equipment. Playground, floor play. There might even be fishing stuff in there, I'm sure there is. Isn't there a good bottle, two bottles, and a hamburger?" He looked over at the greased meat and soggy bread under the heat-lamp row across the way. A man on the television was pouring down a frosty mug of beer so sweet it seemed to create new muscles of pleasure in his throat.

"First," said Pepper, unmoved but interested, "I want you to get out a football. Go get it out of the truck there. Something might be waiting on you. Take your time and get a good football, your best."

"My best football. I got one kind, the best. A Hutch. You got it." When he came in with it, a bottle of Maker's Mark sat beside a greasy burger on a napkin with a bottle of mustard next to it. Pepper seemed to have moved no place nor fretted. The man held out the big football.

"Now I want you to suck it. Suck this football. Get a lot of it in there."

"Aw, man. Why, do you love football? That your game?"

"I hate it. Suck it, now. On in there, moan around on it."

The man did, caterwauling and gagging. "Is that all right? God damn. You reckon it's really pig hide?"

"Go on, get your drink now. We can be trading for a while now. There's a place for you. Some old crazy man's tree house, he left it. But the tree house is professional. The tree'd blow down 'fore the house would. He left meat around on the floor like. You goin' to want to clean some with the critters comin' after the smell at night."

The man stayed for six weeks, fed from the store, seined minnows and caught grasshoppers and crayfish for Pepper, and stayed mainly drunk, high in the boughs singing with a transistor radio. There was a wire up to it for reading or coffee. Then he left, and the truck was all Pepper's. He had sold off most of the gear to fairly delighted people who had hobbies. That is, outside fishing, hunting, weather discussion and church. But he kept the boxes of footballs in the storeroom. When he saw the boy children come along with their fathers to learn the way of the world, he would look at them with no expression and refuse them a football for their own. It was believed he kept the balls as a memorial to the ungodly humiliation he had wrestled from that bankrupt creature those many years ago.

Mortimer felt suddenly that he had to buy a new pair of shoes. He was doing this a lot lately. He felt a bit sick and nervous. In the storeroom thinking about the footballs, looking at the sheriff, he felt dirty and low-rent. He went out the back and almost immediately drove at breakneck speed into Vicksburg to purchase a pair of shoes. He wanted bright white ones. Perhaps a boot, a soft suede pair you could hold in your hands while you went off to sleep in any house and feel perfectly at home. The next day when he went out to talk to the lay preacher who kept the junk-car lot, he would buy yet another pair. Sandals and it cold. He knew he would probably never wear them, but still the excitement held.

Out in the bait shop, a geezer was telling the sheriff, "You got your chartreuse with sorty beige spots, throw it out there with a sorty small fireplug weight on her, and you'll want a good rope size, say about like a venetian-blind pullrope on her, them slab crappie is big and mean with the teeth too like a band saw sorty." Bernard the deputy was incensed, being an actual fisherman.

The sheriff spoke as if nothing had been heard, nothing mocked. He said to Sidney, who was smirking behind the counter, "You don't think the football contraption is a bit in bad taste, considering your father's murder?" He quieted the air. Something like church in there now.

"Family tradition is a man's own lookout, like his choice of faith, sir."

The sheriff did not miss the *sir* and was astounded that Sidney spoke of faith at all. He was slow to anger, but these crackers were getting confident around him.

"The faith of your fathers is a chicken hawk and everybody knows it, Sidney. Tradition."

"I don't guess you'll be welcome in my store from now on unless you got papers, friend. But by the way. They're taking slab crappie with a light cork, a foot deep on a fuchsia and frog-green jig, sometimes tip it with a small minnow. I seem to be all out of those substances at the moment, but good luck."

Bernard and Facetto proceeded to the spillway, where there was another tribe entirely, honored to have the sheriff and his man fish elbow-to-elbow with them as they waded the little rapids over gravel and worked the pools with a light spin cast, lent them jigs and corks hand over fist in that almost belligerent hospitality the state of Mississippi is famous for. The two felt much better and had a full chest before long, and it was splendid to get out of the cold water, rip off the waders and toast in the car, alternating on hot espresso and cold Louisiana beer.

"I'm sheriff of these folks too, thank the Lord," said Facetto.

"The truth. Folks is all right. It just seems tense at the lake nowadays."

The sheriff grew solemn. Melanie. Did the deputy know? Or was it something else he meant? Trouble at the orphans' camp; the immolation of the oldsters' barge; the disappearance of yet another pair of girls from Oasis. Old Pepper's seated corpse, bleeding in ropes from the neck while a football stood for his face. The tracing of that jackleg preacher Byron Egan to a methedrine ring of long years standing; a '48 Ford coupe reported stolen from the St. Aloysius Junkyard and replaced by a filthy rusted-out car of exactly the same vintage. And that stolen car had been reported running down scarcely known county roads, driven by minors, and then parked in a cemetery near the home of Dee Allison, the sex bomb, about whom a groaning man had said, "She'd fuck a snake just to hurt it." She had four kids, great legs and other acreage, but the talk was she was getting married soon, right there in the cemetery. *Shut your mouth. Right* in *it.*

THIRTEEN

MORTIMER HAD FOUR DREAMS IN A ROW ONE WEDNESDAY night. He had performed a small amount of manual labor in his runaway years, and the work itself was nightmare enough, although it trained him never to go thereabouts again. In each dream he was fired from a different job, jobs he had done in real life. Offshore drilling in Louisiana. Lumberyard. Car salesman. Offshore drilling again off the Chandeleurs out of Gulfport. In each dream the boss man came up and said, "Get out, that's enough of you." Then came a fifth dream in which his own mirror told him he was an impostor in the body of Conway Twitty. Then his mirror fired him. But he killed it. A funeral was held with a coffin and pieces of glass. The woman and the boy showed up. They were trying to have a funeral, but her father was late and they could not start. Mortimer said, "He just can't find his clothes, that's all. You don't know the outfit for a mirror funeral." But he knew he was lying. The news was that her father was coming naked. So they waited at the graveside next to the hole. But instead came Frank Booth, with whom Dee Allison had betrayed Mortimer. They walked in naked like two crabs locked together. Booth was saying, "Please help me. I can't pull it out of her. Somebody's got to cut. Help us."

Mortimer woke in horror, the sun streaming in his window. Yet he had only a few moments of relief before he was in full need from waking life. He was going to have to cut again. This matter was no longer spontaneous. He knew exactly what he would do when he saw the junkman Peden again. Fire him? In his dreams. Peden, his lackey, who owed him money.

Peden was a Protestant. Why then, Mortimer mused, did he spend his idle time making graven images? What did *graven* mean? Of the grave, serious, heavy? A graver, he graved nearly all his free time. Over there graving, is what. Peden carved wood. He was one for animals like Mrs. Wooten and her glass. Mortimer said out loud, "You look at me, I don't seem the type to go about having such thoughts on my own, up high in my Navigator, this new green buggy, swank, but look again, looker. I have these thoughts." In fact he could not quit having these new thoughts that gave him a hand on the common man and the old life he was rushed from by such forces as he now despised.

He recalled the mobile phone he had bought Dee once and the first time he saw it in her hands, in the BMW he had also given her. Must be two years ago, they were new then too. He thought the phone, deep red, was very intimate, and her words, it didn't matter which ones, excited him. He saw now the red phone in her fingers, her fingernails very red, her toenails too, and then he imagined the razor scar down her thigh and he could not stand it. He wondered if she would ever forgive him, how crazy he was to do it. But that red phone next to her fingers, her lips.

He wondered would there be a day when he would open the car door for her to get in, and on the backseat would be her two younger boys sitting there. He could play with them, make new games. There would come a day he could change, nobody'd recognize him. He might even resemble nobody at all, or a pleasant television star. These things happen. You can get a lot with money.

He thought of his sequence of good cars, and then the whores. His work was his play. That's what they said of players. He was either moving or flat-out dead asleep, it didn't matter under what roof. Probably he was a sea shark, even if he feared the sea. Death by sea. Life by eating a great many others. But he had his kindnesses. He was not tight. He set a plate for the unlucky, like the lay preacher Peden. Until this car, under his eye, rode off. Just the core of the apple of his eye, it just rode off, and its mud-bottom rust-faced sister is your date. Old preacher boy Peden eating from the plate and whittling his idolatrous beasts and strumming his psalms. Great hell, he *lives* there! Otherwise it would be Haven House or a box in back of the Salvation Army. *This man's been passing for a sound old junk general too long, he's got himself into trouble. Well here comes Not Hardly*, Mortimer said to himself, dressing for battle. *Peden has his coming.*

The shack at St. Aloysius Junkyard was an old shotgun house weathered to a pale of gray and re-tar-papered and tarped in spots on the roof for rain. The two snows they had in the decade, the edge of a horrendous ice storm. It was warm inside, burned a good modern Franklin. It was electrified, telephoned, a small pawnshop refrigerator did its duty for beer or milk or bacon or the whole old hams Peden often bought at the discount grocery. A stove of propane. Peden liked to keep a soup going during a major bender. He would make the soup days in advance, and it worked so that he was not detected incompetent until a fire broke out or he drove some elected junker queen all around the lot honking the horn and plowing into even more terminal junkers. The law was not necessary. A neighbor black fellow phoned in. Grandson of the owners of the house and the original property years ago, still proprietary although sold out. Then Lloyd or others would come and settle Mr. Peden, clutching his Bible and tearfully spouting out hard plainasyournose truths from the Book of Revelation.

His recovery usually lasted a week, and he was a very good man afterward for a very long time. When he was sober, he expressed the sentiment that he wished the Book of Revelation had never been written, and that it might even have the hand of Satan in it.

His speech and dress were clean. The clothes were the best of the Salvation Army and he loved suspenders with a good brogan, no cheap second-tier leather. Perhaps he wanted to be a bit old-timey or reminiscent of his own old wise uncle, who had been a barber and taught private guitar lessons. Peden was once a barber too. He played original interpretations of anything on amplified violin. The black fellow across the hollow who was his monitor wished he would not do this. Peden's amplifier was powerful. It had been abandoned on Highway 20, almost in Peden's lap, and it still had the name and logo of a heavy-metal outfit, its former owners, painted on it.

Peden drove a Comet, a thing out of the age of Sputnik. Low expectations. But he could fix it. He couldn't fix everything, but he could fix this weary orbiter. When he was drunk and driving it, he imagined he was riding a hydrogen bomb to Los Angeles. But when Peden was sober, he was apt to wonder if there was a god, or not simply a divine wind of oratory investing man, and this divine wind was blind and deaf and cared not in whom or at what time it manifested itself.

Peden had not meant to either be a lay preacher or play electrified fiddle. But look here, he couldn't help himself, and he had no models for these behaviors. He could not name one electrified violinist. He knew no other preachers but Byron Egan, whom he had met recently in their common run back and forth from ruin. And what of those pastors who were always Christian and wore new three-piece suits and had the ears of large congregations? Byron Egan said they were lucky but soft, for even Christ was not a Christian until the day he needed to be and knew it.

Cars were pulled up near the shack at the portals, wide-open storm-wire panels with the chain lock hanging down. There were too many cars. Mortimer recognized some of them, he thought, and listened to a harangue of some sort in the shack proper. One of the first whose back he saw was Frank Booth. Then the back of Dee Allison herself, and Sponce, who seemed to be handing her off to some other young fool. The other young idiot held something interesting in his hands. The keys to the '48 coupe. Mortimer knew them well. Didn't even bother taking the rabbit's foot off, the thick thief. He looked around for the car but didn't see it. He knelt behind a shed and listened to Peden go on to this large group, and he saw many he knew, was in fact intimate with. They spoke back to Peden, young but creased in his large tweed suit and vest. When he became a Christian, the lay preacher took on the appearance of the actor Strother Martin. And he began wearing suits, also of the Salvation Army.

The furniture about him was nicked but pleasant enough. Mortimer set the plate for him. He owned him. Without rancor until the loss of this automobile. He'd even send over Lloyd, or Edie, to keep him from burning his furniture after a drunk, as he attempted. *Some days you wish you'd married an ugly woman and somebody in your world would stay grateful*, thought Mortimer. *And do their job and smile.*

"What we make with our hands, what we worship . . ." Peden was going on. The rest was long, spotty although sober, Mortimer noticed. Eavesdropping on his own property was making him angrier by the minute.

"I have been under airplanes, under cars," Peden said, the smoke from the chimney pipe rising upward with his voice in cold air. "God has given me the ends of cars where dead convicts, ladies, babies and little puppies were flung against dashboards. This is my vision, my garden, brothers and sisters and uncles. He has given me the Jaws of Life to pry the poor victim dead or alive from the bunched steel where a snake could barely crawl through. Like if a chicken truck hit a Volkswagen."

"Amen," said Byron Egan, standing toward the front of the room.

"People are forgotten as soon as they are slaughtered, except by a few loved ones, you know that?" Peden went on. "Forgotten in these stains of blood you will find on the seat covers and floorboards, and ceilings around this yard. Don't even take the little ones with you if you look."

Peden raised his arms in the big suit. He did not look funny, just thicker than one supposed. "The Lord has given me this junken place, freed me of drink and drug, and sent a friend, Byron Egan, all the priest a Christian American ever needed. And best, He has given us His Book, which every man and every woman can read."

Peden breathed long, for this was difficult, and Mortimer felt the sensation of another man standing up amazed inside his own body. Familiar shape, with its khaki sports jacket and its safari boots recently removed from the pelt of floor rugging in his great Lexus. "I announce that Dee Allison is Mrs. Harold Laird, and that Harold Laird is her husband. May the Lord bless this couple, I would say young couple, but a teenage separates them, as it were." Dee lowered her head and Harold was not amused, although he liked Peden, who could have gotten the law on him before his confession and seeking of mercy. Harold wished he knew where the boys had taken the car. "Her last husband, Cato, is present, I believe, to confirm the divorce has been finalized and that he approves this union and defies any who might stand against it. And Harold has vowed to be the loving father and mentor of her four children. I say Cato, you are Cato?"

A tall man of graceful carriage, hair still black and thick, in a nice wedding suit, gray, leaned forward, as if he had learned a courtesy faintly European, a roll of the hand and a bow in the affirmative, and a calm smile on his well-cut face.

"Cato is here in protection of the boys and of his other boy or man, Sponce, for a while. The agreement to his protection and his support has been amicably decided upon, and his custody of the young Emma for an agreeable while during the honeymoon period and other adjustments. He seems a fine man, Cato, and will be a father to this favored lass, who smiles every time she sees him enter a room, and this makes her mother happy too. And they will be father and daughter in Toronto, Canada, for as long as the mother assents. Except for the filth and low-mindedness, he would still reside in the U.S.A., he says. Well, the America I know could have kicked Canada's ass all the way back to Paris and London, but out of the generosity of its great high-minded cleanliness of spirit, it has refrained from that minor task. But why am I going on like this at a wedding? I would surmise I am now out of control and will hand the services off to Brother Byron Egan. I do hope I have married the right people here during this spell. I don't feel shipshape right now and I apologize. Remember the good words, if they happened. I'm going to go take a nap."

Egan stepped up and indicated a seat between Sponce and Emma. Cato looked discomfited but was trying to smile warmly. His smile grew thinner, then curved back with a will.

Mortimer could make out no more than a third of this matrimonium and was by no means certain whether anybody had been married, but he was amazed and baffled by the presence of Cato, Dee's husband, who sent checks from Toronto. He was a better-looking and better-preserved man than Mortimer expected. Otherwise, he was outraged *any* ceremony was transpiring on his property, and in a *junkyard*. Why not the church, and what was Egan? Here he seemed to be only a lackey.

Egan's face was three-quarters healed, and he looked the same but leaner, and his head was shaved. He had cut down severely on the number of rings he wore, and he now went with a woman named Lottie who sat in front of him admiringly. An ex-junkie, alumna of various mild lunatic communes, in which she was invariably the leading advocate and then the first to pack off. Now a nurse, mildly religious, wild for teas of all nations, a smoker, good legs and quite defined high rump, baby lips. She had recently become an advocate of sexual abstinence, which was killing Egan, and he preached to her as well as the flocks, wooing them both.

Mortimer knew Lottie too, although if asked, his memory would be hazy, tentative, as if she'd been confused with her cousin. He had collaborated with Lottie a few years before on a porn acupuncture video that went nowhere, exciting only Mortimer and Edie. They decided it was too educated and had no audience outside, oh, the Chinese-grocery dynasties in Vicksburg and upward through the Delta. Marketing to old Chinese grocers was too delicate. Besides, the plot was thin, and why were there so many white people hanging around in the background just looking incredulous? But Lottie had looked good as a Chinese woman.

Now Egan spoke. "Old Brother, sit down and strip off your burden. Good Peden has risked much when not in the best shape. All of us in this strange church on the border of a junk pyramid, in the very parlor of the man who has hurt many of us so badly and so permanently. Who has blackmailed us and cowed us and bullied us. Strip off your burdens, get lighter, unjunk yourselves. Peden has brought us into the halfway house of his life, is gainfully employed by the very wretch at the heart of our troubles. I think the wretch is attempting to play, to have friends."

Frank Booth suddenly turned around in his card-table chair and looked through the window directly at Man Mortimer without seeing him. Booth's face had been reconstructed too, but radically. He looked exactly like Conway Twitty, midcareer, but instead of the tall thick hair, he had his own nearly bald head with strings of gray-white. Healthy sideburns. Mortimer quivered and nearly lost his legs, weak, firing with nerves. He knew he had not been seen, but he had sure seen Booth. He almost left the yard on his belly, crawling. *His* face.

"We are expecting two more guests shortly," Egan continued, "and we owe them our attention even if we do not like them.

"There is the business of marrying Gene and Penny yet again, in renewal of their vows. The couple will soon be here with their best man, Malcolm, a new member of the lake community whose handicaps have not prevented his service to the children at the camp."

"Malcolm is coming here?" cried out Max Raymond. "Will he be armed?"

"Well who isn't?" Peden said from his chair. "I personally know a peaceful soul, a sculptor and motorcycle mechanic, in possession of over a hundred and fifty guns. He likes to hold the history."

"Malcolm is an ex-patient of mine who wants to harm me," Raymond said. "But let him come. Let him do what he has to do. I stand to pay, and if it's my time, I'm ready to die for my sin."

Mimi Suarez was seated next to her husband. On this outburst, she rose and slapped him very hard, then left the meeting. Mortimer hid himself entirely behind a tin outbuilding where spark-plug harnesses hung.

"Could I ask," called out Sidney from his perch near the door. He had not been invited, and few had known he was there. "Is this a town meeting, a church gathering, or are you just screwing the pooch here?"

"Or just a debating society," said Dr. Harvard angrily. "Led by two thugs who've exchanged one addiction for another and who want to rub our noses in junk. Your revenge on others who've tried to bring some beauty and light into the world."

"Fine words, Doc," Sidney sneered. "No noble rot about it."

"Not one mention has been made of the animals. For whom old Feeney died!" Ulrich began weeping. He was smoking a cigarette and soon was hacking out bottomless gut calls, knocking over his oxygen tank. But he would not be helped.

"We're going on our way," said Harold, the new husband. "We've got underage kids and an automobile to find." He picked up baby Emma, and Cato the Torontoan followed him, Sponce and Dee out the aisle between the chairs. Cato still with his suave readiness to fly toward northern sanity and newly claimed fatherhood.

It was a different audience who waited for the renewal of vows from Gene and Penny. They were getting remarried naked and had written their own nuptial poems, and so although the crowd was surlier, they were by no means less alert. Lewis, Wren and Harvard lingered only to get a full frontal on Penny, who, though insane, was still a fine looker with nail marks about her ankles. Gene had the hack marks on his thigh. Trim, he wouldn't make a bad nude either, though his red beard and freckles and wild woolly hair looked as if they were fleeing in a red-and-white-confetti protest. The altar empty, people looked forward, backwards, sideways. Malcolm was late. Max Raymond was still there, determined to look his nemesis in the face. Peden had risen and was clear to marry folks again. It was his nature to get suddenly clear.

They awaited Melanie and Facetto. What arrogance was detaining them? Or were they deliberately missing the nude wedding? Gene and Penny were eager.

Mortimer stayed in the plug-harness shed. He would wait until all had cleared out but Peden. Then Peden was his. He already was, but he had forgotten and needed the touch of his master.

Why do we keep as keepsakes the implements of our own destruction and hang them on the wall? Mortimer wondered. *As if they were not hung between our ears.* Near Mortimer's head, on the wall, was a kind of shillelagh wrapped with barbed wire that Peden had used in biker and mobile-home fights. There was either dried blood or shoe polish on it. It was three feet long, shaped like a narrow bowling pin, with all its weight in the head. Mortimer figured if Peden was so proud of this, the man should know what it felt like. He knew he did not have the strength of old, but this club should carry the day. He wondered about just a bash, repeated bashes, without the first softness, the *gee*, the little feathers at the base of his spine. Did Mortimer have it in him, or would his hand go to his rear pocket where the rug knife rested in joy?

He was wondering when the day would be that they would let him back into real life, which he had once thought possible, at age sixteen in southern Missouri, looking out back at the chicken yard. Little bit of rain coming down. Not lonesome. But the chickens looked happy and they were so dumb, scratching and lurching. Killed and ate them, but his mother was very tender with them. They had names for their short time. Mortimer began to cry. Just a little, and soon stopped. Then, through the smudged window, he saw Gene and Penny pulling off their clothes on the porch of the shotgun shack. They both had long gnarled feet, he noticed, as if these parts had married and grown alike in time. And Facetto and Melanie were about to walk right up on the disrobing couple before they realized it.

John Roman may have been the most uncomfortable at the nude wedding. The world wasn't meant to be buttnaked and smiling ear to ear, he reasoned, and here came the poems. Peden presided woozily over the entire thing. Here was a man who in his bad, bad days had almost blown Roman over on a gravel road riding his giant Harley next to Roman's little motorbike, loaded with fish. Now a Christian orator when he was not playing hooky from the Anonymous program.

Roman was there because it was a place to be out of the house with Bernice. He knew he could not shoot Mortimer if Bernice lived on and lived well, so he had deferred the head shot on Mortimer. Roman was the only trained killer on the lake. He could summon a chilliness beyond such huffers as Raymond, who had recently confessed to Roman his own wound at the hands of Mortimer. How could Mortimer risk all his whore world and his fleet of lust hearses, all his women and thugs, for a bit of fun like this?

Now in stumbled the best man. Clothed, thank the Lord for small favors, but dragging a leg and unable to make low sounds like, for instance, a whisper. But what protocol was appropriate when two fools rammed together in poetry to initiate some awful Eden all over again? Couldn't Gene have combed his hair? Or worn shoes?

"Uh seen this guy in the tin *hut!*" Malcolm was moaning to the back row.

He was ignored. Penny picked up a guitar and began strumming and hooting a song directed toward the higher obedience of everybody to the untenanted, unastronauted moon.

When Roman first heard of integration, he thought it was a movement about meeting and drinking with people like Chet Baker, and he was a partisan. But it was mostly the Pennys and the Genes and the Pedens and the split-in-two Raymonds who were at the table.

Peden began speaking, looking neither left nor right. "Thank you for your arrival, Malcolm. It is good a husband and wife freshen their vows. We lose sight of the face of God, which we must at least try to see every day, and we lose sight of each other. We become annoying mists to each other, let's face it. Egan said those words, I stole 'em."

"No, wait, I've got my poem!" said Sidney. This grainy man was in the doorway watching all worlds. "Women. You can't live with them and you can't fuck their ears."

Melanie alone was scandalized, but she had brought her own scandal with her and so she stayed quiet. The ceremony jerked on to its end, and Sidney, nervous as Judas, suddenly ran for his car. Mortimer saw this act, hoping the rest would leave shortly. He was not good at waiting.

Egan moved among the crowd, glad the wedding was quick. There was no reception. The sheriff began talking loudly.

"I wasn't quite done, Facetto," said Peden. "It's my house we're in." Peden didn't like cops.

"I'm sorry. Go ahead. I thought we were going to talk about *the man*."

"Sure we are. Now I'm through talking. Go ahead."

"We are needing testimony against Man Mortimer," said Facetto.

"This sounds like you on television. The new breed of high sheriff," taunted Peden. "What the hell is new about Mortimer?"

The sheriff was angry, red.

"You've gotten plenty of airtime, sir," Harvard broke in. "Much expatiation on criminology. Little actual arresting of it. There is not much you *have* done except," Harvard swept his hand toward Melanie, "dally with a woman twice your age."

"I am older than that. We are in love," said Melanie.

"In heat," spat Harvard. "I think Facetto should abdicate for the woman he loves. Or whatever negligent sheriffs do. Man, you can't serve."

Facetto was mad. He had been taunted by mail, the telephone, distant shouts, and now by this considerable old surgeon whose intelligence he could not deny.

"You've got an orphans' militia over there," said Lewis. "Somebody's going to be hurt."

"I've spoken to them," Facetto said. Many folks stood up and milled, just absorbing him. Nobody else was listening. They were talking on their own and leaving. He was very sorry he had come. There was no face to maintain here, no walk to walk. He felt himself melting and near tears. His gun hand trembled. He was beginning to join the hate for himself. Melanie saw all this. She could not rush to him, and in fact she despised him a little herself.

"You can't gang up and destroy this man. He's a good man. He works hard," Melanie was saying. This too was ignored, drowned out, mocked. They themselves left and Peden was alone.

Peden, with a coffee, fresh and hot French roast from his loyal Big Mart maker, was in agreeable shape finally. The last of the kicks of the lush, peaceful even during the last wedding. No longer threaded out and driven forward, he sat and reviewed the life he lived in the junkyard, and he found it good. These stacks and caverns of heavy metal around him. They had a quietness. A solid face. It was something, he was something that made it signify. He had the Lord, he had his time. Who suspected any would haul in this rotted rust and take the better version of the same '48 with them? Peden still hoped he would get over it, and that his old debt would be forgiven.

The debt was this. Peden had once gone in to Mortimer while very drunk and asked him for $13,000 to buy a new Harley Davidson Softtail. Everything depended on it, Peden thought, for his own esteem. His soul was already in the bike. It was only a matter of what he would do to get it. He had a woman named Bertha at that time, from up at Redwood. She had satellite television and they had a good time, she mainly sober. Bertha fell off his new machine on a curve out of Panther Burn on Highway 14. She had no medical plan, only Peden. Peden borrowed more, and Bertha began working for Mortimer at the car place in Vicksburg. SUV demos. Good deals. Now Peden was in big hock, and the interest was berserk, but he and Mortimer kept smiling, and Bertha's back and leg were okay.

Peden lit a Lucky, sat and stretched in front of the potbelly woodstove. Very nice to be out of the rain, very comfortable here. Didn't need the television on, even if it was a good big fat Phillips like Bertha's. He thought of Byron Egan, what a constant pal he was. How all was right when Egan cheered him. Peden had had another pal who died, Debord. Debord had simply gotten lung cancer and died, but Peden was certain his friend rode next to him still. Whenever he thought of Debord, and then Egan, he became spiritual. Perhaps he should not even read the newspaper, to keep it that way. The trio was all they needed. One happened to be gone and needing no coffee anymore. But riding with them, his white hair behind him like fleece in a legend.

Just then a man came in the window with a club, clambering over the windowsill from the shotgun porch. Peden couldn't believe it was Mortimer or that he was coming straight at him this way. Later he thought Mortimer expected he'd be watching television when he came in. The club was big, with wire around it. Peden didn't recognize it until Mortimer had limped away, with little effeminate screams. Mortimer hit him once on the shoulder, then Peden was all over him, picking up chairs and an old wooden Coke case. He thrashed on Mortimer very well, over and over. Saw he was going for the hip, where there was a knife, he well knew. Peden beat and beat on Mortimer until the man could take no more, found the door and dragged away. Without even a threat.

For a good long while, Peden rubbed his shoulder and thought about a trip to the hospital. Then he decided on it but grew cold when he thought of Mortimer. He doubted the man could stand and feared rooming with him in the emergency ward. This was not a problem. Mortimer was not in the building.

FOURTEEN

PEDEN WAS A STRONG MAN. HE WAS MUSCULAR IN total despite the years of hard living. His shoulder was bruised black but healed quickly.

Mortimer did not heal much at all. But he didn't languish long. He hurt in every pore, every tissue. Even his lips had been hit. He was not angry at Peden. He would kill him, he was quite sure, and perhaps with his own hands. But he could not blame him. He hated his attitude, hopeful in his stupid mistakes, the '48 and now fighting back. When he called up Peden, he told him to destroy the ruined '48, take it to bits, every cell. His voice was even, and Peden wondered if the fight had proved something.

Mortimer himself wondered whether he would have to use a gun, for which he had no affection. He hoped not, but things would be coming up. His tongue was getting more tied, he could not explain and mollify as he used to do. The wedding. *On my own property, Dee, and with a medium-size mechanic, a fool.*

Frank Booth, too, chilled him with his bald head and Twitty face. What tribute was this? Or was the man deranged and unaware of what he had become? Bald Conway Twitty, if he had lived longer. Booth's appearance was a bad thing of the shadows, and Mortimer was horrified he would come near with some other weapon.

Maybe he should call the sheriff. Mortimer smiled. Unbalance the man still more. He would say it was out of his jurisdiction, but Mortimer would keep after him. He dialed. He loved the whining answer, the trembling he heard, the remonstrations.

"Oh, it's special all right," Mortimer said. "Man mocking me like this. Got a whole new face to do it."

"Why did he need a new face?"

"Don't you even read the papers, man?"

"I read a lot of papers. You don't want to forget who you're talking to, sir. I don't have to stand for this."

"Yes, I'm sorry. Getting out of hand over here. It's just spooky. Thought you could speak to him."

"What would I say to the man about his chosen face?"

"Most of us don't have that option. I see your point."

"You don't just go up to a fellow and say, 'Fellow, I don't like your face.'"

"You don't? Well I do, all the time. Too much, I guess. Thanks for your time, anyway."

"Who is this again? Mort Durr?"

"Yes sir, Commander Facetto."

"They don't call me *commander*. Sheriff is fine."

"I'm sure it is. Bye now."

He had a vision of piling all his SUVs together some afternoon and burning them while the sheriff's department and other fools looked on.

Mortimer knew Sidney was his man when he wanted him, and he was able enough to drive to the bait store on a Thursday when he could also hold down some soft black-eyed peas and corn bread at the bad restaurant. Sidney's lackey Opal was minding the store, but this girl told him Sidney was down to the new boat in Farté Cove. When he drove by, he saw Sidney amid a great mix of men and advisers nearly working on the boat. It was another barge going up, all right, and now Mortimer wanted it, to sail it and make it smell good

and have something for his whores. He would be well known
on the lake and finally a pride of the region when he became
an elder, because you were colorful then and people liked
to see you prosper. Get nostalgic about when times were
colorful and wilder and better. Let go because of history and
what you'd done for it. A picture of him shaking hands with
the law. A giant three-deck riverboat with paddle wheel in
the background. Rest Home of Old Whores and Fishing.
This joke hurt his liver when he laughed.

Still, he liked Dr. Harvard and the suddenly plenti-
ful crowd. He didn't know a third of them, must be twelve,
fifteen down there. Sidney was off the deck but the center
somewhere at the end of the pier, jawing. The boat would
be his in the future. *I made Sidney famous,* thought Mortimer.

They heard the big stuff over at the camp on a Saturday
afternoon. It was dynamite. The Ten Hoors had decided to
make an island out of their camp, and nobody could stop
them after they got the explosives permit, which was fairly
easy. You can blow up your own place if you've room for it.
Harvard, Lewis and Wren, working on the barge, with Roman
and Raymond lifting heavy pieces for them, and Sidney looking on, heard the *whumps*.

They were blowing canals. They had hired this company, but the leader of the gang was a man who lived to
change the earth. He was seventy and loved his job. He had
not gotten enough of this in Korea with the marines, blowing away bridges and roads in the famous retreat from
Chosin Reservoir that cost the communists one million dead.
But this man had not veered, he was happier then than he
had ever been, except for right now. *Imagine making an island out of your place suddenly,* he said. *Imagine. Right here at
home.* It was going to take a lot of bomb here. Across the

lake the men and Melanie and Bernice could see the sky get humps of black along its horizon line. Perhaps whole trees and their dust. Sidney hoped for an enormous accident if this was not one already. Limbs and ash and bone-spray in the air. A real shame.

Ruthna, Harb, Alexander and Whit arrived that afternoon. They had decided they could no longer abide the suburbs, especially since they could not make the house payments. They were something on the order of a middle-age commune and quickly agreed that nature and the lake were just the thing. It was changing them even as they hauled in their luggage, in fact. They had rented a modern, beamed ski-lodge affair, which gave the tourist the rare sense of having fallen off an alp into a steaming bog. They were near the Roosevelt lodge where Ulrich and Egan lived. When the dynamiting started, they were horrified. Their tall white sycamores trembled. They were hungover and in hell. Ruthna fell flat on the ground. Whit held his ears while his luggage scattered.

"He is always talking about his mother and father and Christ," said Mimi once the scare had passed. Ruthna was becoming her confidante.

"Then he will be tired of talking, Mimi. All theological discussion will become shameful comedy. He has said people are snakes who love talking late at night about God. They don't know God, but they surround themselves with other pretenders. These are direct quotes, I think," said Ruthna, who knew Raymond too well.

"But what does Raymond have for acts? He has his saxophone, he doesn't even have much money left. He has the friendship of punks and old men."

"And you. Maybe he will do something for the orphans, like his mother did. He can't forget her."

"He tries, he speaks of his deaf absent father all the time, the gunner in the war against Japan. I think he was jealous of the orphans," said Mimi.

"I've got to go. We'll try to be sober next time we see you. Things have fallen apart and we've fallen here."

"You're at the right place, Ruthna. I don't know anybody much who's not decomposing. Even Max says people are hardly necessary anymore, and they have no acts. They tend to float away. It's frightening."

"If the Son of God has not visited us, Mimi, who are we? Am I just a lush and actress and tramp?"

"Well, he always said at least you were something, as long as you could stand it. I want to worship something bigger than me or I'm lost. It must be the music, but not always. Not at three in the afternoon. Only an idiot sings always."

"My acts are all bad, Mimi. What about that? I have no imagination for a good act. Am I dead? I guess I'm normally courteous. So are the dead."

"Max wants to see a chariot of fire or light one himself."

"These poets keep wanting to suck the water out of the ocean with a straw."

The boys were all driven out. It was hard to hide a car painted like this. But they did not want to see their new stepfather. They had seen their father for the first time since they were six and seven and wished he'd stayed longer. Though to them, Canada was just one of many places farther away than Sharkey County. He never heard about the car, and they knew nobody was in favor of small boys owning and driving such a machine. They imagined ogres of many types lost just behind them in their smoke, but nobody had gotten close. High speed over the gravel at the penultimate velocity, over rocks like low shoals of water. The amateurs are dead behind you. This is how the boys felt, and they had gone back to Benson & Hedges, long ones. They were also hidden in the last dry purchase of the swamp behind Raymond and Mimi's house.

They waited until evening to announce themselves. Looking for Mimi's titties through the window seemed beneath them now. They loved her singing too much. They sought her now because they were much growner. They had traded their mother for a car, and Harold was all the father they had left.

Lately Harold was picking up wheel rims and flexing with sledgehammers for his strength regimen. He ate two steaks and salads at a time, his acne went away, and he had found chemicals in the Big Mart pharmacy that cut and bulked you out. These were expensive, but the boys saw he did have a better body.

They did not take pity on their mother's private needs. Nor were they aware that she liked Harold in the least, which she did. He had even begun higher mechanics at the trade school. He brought down the swearing in the house. He threatened to play games with the boys. He was not proud of providing these children with such a garish rocket. His breakneck labor, his theft, which still had to be paid for. He cringed now when he thought he could get away with the switch. One *was* a car, the other a hulk of gummy decay.

Yet he was a husband and Dee was patient with him. Under other circumstances he would have been glad the boys were gone again.

Dee liked her boys more, but there was something smaller about her. She wondered if marriage to this stern young man would mean much to her living world, such as it was. She was always away in her visions now. She saw men burning, crying out, and now children, great filthy explosions, deep and shallow water in which there were corpses, all in the shell of Big Mart, bombed and half covered by water. Men cried for water and ran up to her and she spat fire at them. This was a vision, but it had a sleepiness to it, as if it were being carried on by her closed eyes into night dreams. She began watching the color television that Mortimer had given her long ago, asking that it imagine her, because she was afraid. She had great anxiety, and the sight of Harold in his school clothes, with loafers and sweaters, would send her into such a foreign mood, she could not imagine how to address this young stranger, the boy naked in the bed beside her.

The boys were good fishermen when they bothered. Their gear was at the lost lake. It was a tiny oxbow lake three hundred yards from the rear of the bad restaurant, whose food exhaust could be smelled still, even here. Nobody was home at the Raymonds', and they killed the time fishing, hardly saying a word.

The boys had spin-cast reels and a newish Shakespeare bait caster. Bless all the gambling failures and crack addicts, a man could really shop in the pawn. Were the laws not just a little too stiff, you'd probably have found used children there.

The boys kept the rods leaned to a tree at the little lake. They had discovered the place. Nobody else came. They cast with a single bait, never changing lures, the old Lucky Thirteen. If they could not hear the pop and see the strike of a big bass, they had no interest in catching one at all. They took five good bass in an hour. One of them was nine pounds. They did not eat much fish, and they released the others back into the black-green water. Then went back to their car, worn and with tight smiles. If they could see Mimi Suarez, it would be a fine day. They could go home soon.

"There must've been five orphans in that one tree watching us. Thinking we're the car desperadoes. Didn't think we'd even notice."

"They scared the devil out of me, but I just kept on throwing," said Isaac.

They were glad to be desperadoes, watched in secret by city children. The orphans were going outside the camp at will, several of them armed.

Harold and Sponce were hunkered down at the rim of the sinkhole, staring down at where the car had been. They watched and watched. As if the mother and son would come back to it, open the trunk in its mud and slip in again. So that their minds could get back to the moment and begin making order.

They were grave robbers, but who was it cared so much? Egan and Mortimer. Who cared so much that this '48 hulk was swapped with another decent '48? Mortimer. Who was after Jacob and Isaac in their custom-made red and gold teenage car? Mortimer.

Now they heard through Egan, who'd invited the newlyweds to church services, that Peden had whipped the hell out of Mortimer, who had come at him with a bat. But Hare was haunted by his own romance. In his serious college clothes, Hare was turning Christian under the influence of Egan. He and Dee attended church now.

About this time Harold lowered his head, and a high-grain bullet of less caliber than a .22, called a Bee, parted his hair and lifted it. They were not aware they were being shot at from an immense distance, and the pops seemed irrelevant to the tragic hole they now studied. There was no blood but a curious burn down the part of Harold's hair. He could not account for this. He had been mad with lust and plans. Now that he was preaching to Dee, he was wild with guilt. He trembled when he recalled the bones still with meat on them. The unreported dead. It took a sort of Jesus to remember them, with that sweet smell, the ligaments draped down from the sockets. He heard the child's screaming from his head wound once the wind started.

They sat on different pews.

Peden and Egan argued with Max Raymond about who owned a church. You couldn't just buy them, although this one, owned by Reformed Presbyterians, was very much for sale by its richer child in Vicksburg. Raymond was going to buy it. He had promises of money, and a CD with his wife and band that was going somewhere. The band was ebbing at the casino, but they were getting gigs as far as Biloxi and New Orleans now. He had found some old doctor money he had forgotten, from his old drug days when he feared the worst at every turn. It was quite a lot. The firm paid you even for being high and invested wisely for you. Funny, the way he didn't care for money and yet fell into it.

"You can buy a church. And you'd have to let me in if I bought it," said Raymond.

"We'd let you in anyway. The definition of a church is open, isn't it?" asked Byron Egan. He looked at Peden, because the junkman was nervous, his cheeks jumping.

"Nobody denies the wanderer," said Peden. This didn't seem quite on the mark. The three men shut up awhile.

"My emphasis would always be on acts, not chats," said Raymond. "I have turned around on this matter and gone against Luther and the rest, I know. I'm not sure there was ever even a sect of me. Offshot from *in fides sola*. You can have a church without firm belief, is all I'm saying. Most churchmen can't tell you what they believe anyway."

"All right," Egan said. "Christ himself said whoever is not against us is on our part, and he might know the church. Buy it. We stand. I and Peden have a church and the doors are wide open."

"For none of us knows who lives tomorrow, who may tarry yet come the sun dead on his pillow," Peden burst out. He rose from the pew as if delivering an involuntary oath and strode toward the trombonists gently tuning in the little chair gallery to the left of the pulpit. These five men were dark black and were cousins. They had no interest in recording or selling their music. Many said they blended like the best tea of heaven, and they could make you cry with their hymns. Only one read a note of music, and he was not the leader. The leader was James. He played the enormously belled bass trombone. Two others had valved trombones. So intense were these men in their harmonies that there seemed no other world for them.

Now the trombonists stopped and looked at Peden as if he were a goat wandering into their music.

"Say, men," asked Max Raymond, with his instrument case between his legs, "you think I could sit in with you a few tunes? James?"

"No."

The men, dropping the saliva out of their spit valves, looked at one another. "It ain't no place to make your entrance," said James. "Nor get out if you was in."

"It be in there like a piece of hair on a bar of soap," said another seriously. They were musicians but much like deacons too. They frightened Raymond a little. They began playing again, silvery, in trouble and then deliverance. One of them with the bell of his horn under the church light going gold to bronze to red.

Christ, we are your throat.

FIFTEEN

MORTIMER AND SIDNEY MET IN THE BAIT STORE AFTER-hours. Sidney's emporium was prosperous now. It needed both Opal and Iona, his new helper. A yellow Lexus sports wagon was parked behind the store. Sidney watched Mortimer with pleasure. Thin, bent, elderly in almost every movement. Pain on his face. The pretty boy home sick from school.

When all was clear, they went out and told the girls to exit the Lexus newly stolen from Sevierville, Tennessee. It was yellow with a cream white grille in front. It was a little girl's car, in fact.

Mortimer put on a CD in the jambox. The girls had done this before. The music was elvish dancing music that Mortimer had gotten at a bargain in the mall. Nobody had ever bought it. It was a junior college symphony from Kansas.

The orphans, Betsy and Irma, began by holding hands and skipping together in the aisles of the heavily stocked store, knocking over flashlight batteries, sardines, bananas. Since Sidney had restocked, you could see the equipment for much iniquity. Magazines about muscular naked girls.

The girls walked to the tunes and disrobed privately behind a far aisle. They were not certain how to carry on, but the elvish meadow dance music urged them onward, and they came out demurely in nothing. Mortimer cheered them to continue to dance. No hand touched them. It was an arrangement by the artist in his last creative fever.

He and Sidney watched from padded chairs. They shared a single-malt scotch bottle between them. Farté Bait

House glasses to drink from. They seemed to desire nothing else; they were not anxious but meditative. Once Sidney accidentally touched Mortimer's arm reaching for his drink, and Mortimer's knife hand flew to his back pocket. But there was nothing there, the movement was involuntary.

At the end they gave the girls money and said it was a very fine audition. This was the form of Mortimer's current sin. Sidney was the more lecherous of the two and had gotten tight enough to hold the shoulder of the child Betsy. But this act was so repellent to her that she almost fainted, so he left her alone to return to the yellow Lexus and home to Clinton, where they had pallets and a large television in a vacant room, with snacks and sodas and their own phone, in Mortimer's very teenage hangout.

Melanie, Bernice and John Roman ate at the rib house, Near 'Nuff Food. Its theme was medieval chaos, and people dumped buckets of ribs on a tablecloth of butcher paper, then tore off a length from the top and bagged the rib bones in preparation for the next arrivals. It was festive and harsh, and a success. Employees of the bad restaurant ate here.

The face of Frank Booth passed by a window, and Roman was shocked again by the surgeon's ability to bring a third Conway Twitty into the world. He reached for his big rib knife, a heavy steel thing, and awaited Booth's appearance at the door.

Booth came in the door, with Ruthna and the very drunk Whit and Alexander. Ruthna was not drinking and looked cleanly figured, getting some of her womanly curves back. Melanie admired her and thought she had seen her around the lake. Bernice was deeply affected by Melanie, who had stayed close to her through the illness even though Roman sometimes had doubts about the lady's curious goodness. His reservations were gone now. He saw she could not help being a good woman, and he was sorry for her pain as an old lover. He was a happier man now that Bernice was back among the living, but the Booth man hovered near him, and the women noticed him too.

"Is he that singer, or isn't he?" asked Melanie. "'A Bridge That Just Won't Burn'? He's bald now. Doesn't he wear a hairpiece when he comes here to eat?"

"That is not Conway Twitty. That is another man who looks like him. And it ain't right," said Roman.

"My word. With the woman and her poor drunken friends." The group of them sat down at a near table. Whit and Alexander had brought brown bags with liquor in them, allowed on dry Sunday evenings.

The bald man with Twitty's face was paying serious court to Ruthna. He was touching her face and being most solicitous about her hair and comfort as she combed away at a snarl. He seemed to be feeling just capital, but there was an appalling quality to this, seeing a dead singer making time with Ruthna, just back from the dead herself and nearly as pale as her drunkmates. These men had not turned into mean drunks yet, a miracle for the decades they had been lushes. They sweated and carped merrily, waiting on the fat ribs, the cowgirl wenches, the huge fruit-jar glasses with ice and lemon setups. Melanie saw that Ruthna was not as ardent as Booth, but she was not disinterested.

Roman snorted. "Skank."

"You ain't the total darling you once were," said Bernice. His healthy wife. He could hardly believe she was here. Maybe he suffered from Mortimer for her life. That night of the masks. Her pain had seemed to have had no reason, her waiting, his watching. He could not keep his eyes off Booth's face. He felt lifted from his seat, memory throbbing in his wrist. The thing, as if warned, turned and beheld him directly. *Help me*, the lips seemed to form.

Roman held his rib knife tensely, poised. The women were scared and jittery now, including Ruthna, who seemed at last to recognize the mask of her date.

Ulrich and Egan were visiting Peden in his house by the junkyard. Peden now had a gun he rested in different rooms. He had reports of Mortimer in good humor, but scrawny, aged. Lloyd drove for him almost always. Edie gave him rubdowns in Clinton and Rolling Fork. She was showing her age too. Maybe she was back on the Valium.

Sponce had only his stepfather Harold's connection to Peden when they stole the '48 together. They knew the call for the car was out and that Mortimer intended to hurt somebody about this matter. The boys had not come home at all since their mother's wedding weeks ago. They might be legal drivers before they were seen again. That or dead in the trunk of their '48.

Sponce could hardly stay at home with Dee and Harold. He did not understand his own position there anymore. There was no family left, only the marriage, a queer thing that seemed to make his mother weaker and Harold officious, strutting and lecturing Sponce about life, now that he was almost a graduate of the mechanics college.

Sponce became a wanderer with no home and barely a car, only Harold's old Chevrolet El Camino with its truck bed and car cab. It smelled like very lonely oil men. It looked like their wallets inside. A web of rusted veins ran all about. It had a good engine, but sleeping in it was hard when he quit playing like he was training for the air force. But where could he go?

He went into the orphans' woods and walked, knowing they were all around him from across the canal around their island fortress, and he held a rifle as if he were an idle hunter of deer, perhaps lost. He sought their company, but he did not know how to acknowledge them. He wanted a confrontation so he could shout out his innocence, but he fled when nobody pursued. He walked himself into a ragged hungry thing. By the time he made it to Peden's house, he was stunned, sleepy, a scarecrow driving a car from the era of eight-track tapes. But he stumbled onto the porch and held out his hand.

"I come to give myself up."

"Have a seat, boy."

"Could I have some of that coffee? I don't want to put you out."

"Come on in. We were all having some."

"I been everywhere. I'm wore out by three counties. But I'm telling what I know."

"What did you think we wanted to hear?" asked Egan. The boy worried him with his hungry look. "You been looking for your little brothers?"

"Partly, partly. Just stopping by, how you do. Ship in a storm. Winter is cold and wet and dull. On old Mortimer, he might not care about much. How the woman at the store said. He gambles some, but he don't care. He's like kind to animals."

"He *is*?" put in Ulrich. "Then we could be friends. We could be eagles together."

Egan and Peden looked at Ulrich, a benign affliction, standing plump in his suspenders in front of the woodstove. Sandals over big wool socks. Vast assless pants. He smiled at Sponce, and Sponce knew him for a father.

Peden relaxed from the news in this boy's narrative. He put his arm around the boy's neck, smelled the oil and sweat, drew back. Peden was from nowhere people in Pocahontas, and his formative years were much staring at kudzu, wondering how it could be faster than him or his uncle Ed and do whole school grades in just one summer. He knew this boy better than he knew himself.

He crossed the room and raised his pistol, only a .22 but a Buntline barrel on her, hollowpoints, long rifle. The illusion of self-defense. It looked like a gun.

"We've got a choice here. I'm not worried about that car, I'm worried about your brothers. But brother Sponce, can I have a gun and love Christ?"

"You asking me?" asked Sponce. "Yes. I do. Or have. Christ used a whip on the money men. Turning the temple into a money changer."

"Let me ask you this, then. Where is the temple?"

Sponce couldn't answer.

"You want to get a bath and clean clothes while I'm making you some tamales and you think about it?"

"Yes sir, I do."

"A man has to sleep with as many animals as possible," Ulrich blurted. "But not in the sexual way. By no means. An execration. No. Just get in the bed there with them, invite them on in, know their smell and their cold nose. You smell the good dirt in their fur. Fur is individual. No two alike, like a snowflake. It ought to be a state law."

The others listened, but he was through and at peace.

It occurred to Egan that every one of them in the room was old beyond his years except Ulrich, who looked like a stupid, lined boy. Harried and singed into senescence, red in the eyes, the rest. They were rushing to die.

★   ★   ★

She called him into the room to watch her die but then said she didn't want him to suffer and tried to send him out. The moment was vague, but the nurse told him she was gone. So Harvard's wife, Nita, died in their bedroom in their house, a large stone one, overlooking the lake and a front lawn full of century pine trees eighty feet tall.

Isaac and Jacob lived in Harvard's front room now. The '48 was parked behind the garage. That Mardi Gras car. These strange boys he had pulled off the roads with some order of new strength. How he loved them. They loved Nita, and she smiled at them the last week too.

Harvard did not have deep thoughts the two days her body was gone to prepare for the funeral. He would drive her in the pleasure barge to the church in the glen, where Egan would preach the funeral for a woman he had never seen and Harvard would ask himself, *Where the hell have I taken us when this man Egan stands at the gates facing either direction?*

He had useless thoughts and intense ones. Such as the storms that gathered then left, so you wondered were the same storms simply circling the lake. Such as nobody has ever left home. Nobody has brought news back from anywhere. Every awful scene rotates to somebody else, and they will not believe it either.

Nita, honey. Fifty-two years with you. Married in '48, so I had to have the car too, along with the boys. This may be a miracle, something meant beyond my plans. I hope so. It felt like it. Without the boys I'd now be dead, I think. He thought of Melanie. It sometimes happens that the wife outlives her husband by thirty years. But more often, two.

He hated God for putting Melanie Wooten there in the years of his wife's suffering. Melanie, to be looked upon, enjoyed in the abstract, comparing always too favorably with

Nita. *Even I can believe in God if I hate enough. Please, to spit in somebody's face.*

To the few who knew he had the boys, their mother, the sheriff, a couple of the inner circle of sane oldsters, he offered no apology. He had to have them, that was all. He found a pistol and some shells in their car. He was not certain who wanted to harm them or needed this car so much. They were cloudy on it themselves. He drove them to school, the pistol on the floor under his seat, handy. If the killer gave him time to get it out while he stood there like a sack of salt with a bull's-eye on it. They would stay there two months while the couple honeymooned and the stepfather got established, Harvard said. The car was stolen, and he wondered if anybody was seeking it. He helped them wash it, but he would not let them drive it.

Harvard and the boys talked, wearing suits and carrying Nita in the repewed common galley behind the wheel of the barge. Just them alone with the casket. The stained glass around it deep purple with greens and yellows. Harvard had done a magnificent job, as if it were all for Nita, bless her after the waiting and torture.

Way over across the lake, insectile mourners stood on the shore of the glen waiting for the boat, Harvard's hand-crafted tribute. Nita now in dignity denied her by the suffocation of her last months. Pain that will have it out with a good person until that person hates herself, loved ones trying even harder to love and deny the confusion. The tiny mourners stood in back of a church newly painted and air-conditioned. Plain, with little trim and a squared Georgian softness collected by its steeple. It was Raymond's church now, and the old cemetery next to it was clean and fenced and greenish.

Mortimer saw the barge pass below the bait store and wanted it all over again.

He loved the elegant and slow now. The machines that had never rushed him, the old carriages that had never harried him, the tender old verities, but what were they? Things like church, dogs. Football. Children wrestling in the glen. Those good people. Not a finer man in the county than your postman daddy, what's his name? And your mother the postlady, the chicken lover.

Mortimer had a club already. Pals. Women to look at or pet him. It was good to be off the cock farm in many ways. This cool point of view where beauty in women shriveled back to what it was actually worth. You stick with Edie, Bertha, Marcine. Good country people, trustworthy. You got a rich old fool in a handmade boat and had what? Mortimer wanted back the good past. The times that woman had taken from him, eight years back.

It was time to sit back and smell the room. Harvard. Never cared for him. Understated aristocrat, somebody said. His lake, his thin hands. His wife died on him anyway.

Mortimer knew he had graduated into old, which made him new blood, the youngest of the old. It was strangely good to know this. He could start having an overview, seeing he was always meant for the center. Neither the chills nor the fevers of before. *Maybe I cut because I want them to have no face too. Because if you've got somebody else's face, you never had one, there ain't no memory of you.*

Peden had taken his youth. He was given little choice. Mortimer had come in the window with a club. A mistake he would not have made earlier on. He imagined Peden was weak and easy because he'd seen him drinking just the day before.

Maybe I should burn Peden's house and him in it. He's got nowhere else. Even if it failed, it would flush him. He needs to be in my club. We can meet and talk about nothing but faces. A support group. Name it "What Am I, Chopped Liver?" Get on public-access or PBS. Shoot the show with the junkyard in the background. Close-up of scars and sharp metal edges. My people. Here, let's see your face and its problems. Would you get a light on that? Oh Lordy. Too bad they don't still have elevator jobs, or folks that live in belfries.

Booth entered his mind, and he turned on Pepper's old stool, where he lounged while Sidney was at the funeral. He suddenly thought Pepper stood behind him. He was shaken, all alone here in the store.

I give surgeons work, he thought. *I take the vanity out of my friends' lives. I make them face the music of their essential selves. Oh, it's hard to be sincere these days. All these things I have done, and yet my work seems never to be over. Because this lake is mine and I didn't realize it. I am expanding without panic or even plans. There's many a little girl to be friends with out there. The ones that won't rush you. My video work. A man that stays busy ain't ever in trouble.*

He looked about the store at all these expensive devices for pulling spiny, scaly meat out of the water. He didn't understand it. Never had. Even doctors and rocket scientists at it. He was limp with innocence. He was no longer planning. Just heard a voice in his ear, getting louder.

Booth, I'll cut your throat where you stand, and I don't never *have to ask why you look like this now. I could've done it before at the ball game. I let you go. You hearing me?*

But he had nothing on him to cut with, and the nearest pocketknife fifteen feet away on the wall. What he loved now was a Pakistani three-quarter machete with a brown, green and yellow handle and golden gills on the blade. But it was in the car and remained only an exquisite hypothesis even when it was in his hands.

His own pool, his houses, his spirit. When he was certain nobody was in the store, he said to himself, "Hardly anybody does anything by hand anymore."

It was a strange vacant bright day, this funeral day for Nita Harvard. Not a speck of a man or woman, not a single fishing boat out there on the water. The wind was out of the east and the fishermen knew it was hopeless.

"We come to begin a church and send away a neighbor to what this church and all love is about," began Byron Egan. The trombones had just quit, and unknown mourners were present just for them, the band without even a name. Brown, yellow, black faces, posing as friends of Nita and Harvard, or now of her corpse. Nita had never been a mingler even when healthy.

Egan had had a difficult time with this one, and he felt he was turning into liquid in front of Max Raymond, harsh witness, and his lot.

"She did not go to church," he said, "but Nita Harvard, what I hear about her, lived a life that deserves a cathedral. Her sense of humor, her fairness, made life more lovely and lively for those around her. What else can we demand of a neighbor? Flowers, tennis, a life graceful and generous. Even so, old fool cancer got in her and really tried to lay her low. But now where is she? High, high in a new church, launched toward heaven with its new friends and old."

At first Harvard thought it might be a sort of tag-team eulogy, with Peden stepping up, but this man only brought a tape of Nita's favorite tunes. "I'll Be Seeing You," "What's New?" These went across nicely on a big Sony jambox, and the funeral was over except for the churchyard cemetery with its small tent over her loamy slot. She had barely looked at the church while living. She practiced a distanced Episcopalianism and did not especially like people.

Mortimer could see the church, a white thimble across the bumpy water blown easterly from the bait house.

Somebody he was talking to and hustling years ago told Mortimer there was a town at the bottom of the lake. He thought of his own town in Missouri. He imagined it underwater. His parents' hair straining upward, circled by the corpses of suspended chickens. His parents were wearing their postal outfits. Stupid in this fixed image, they had a kind of hopeless love on their faces and no opinion at all. They neither cursed God nor acknowledged Him. In death, if they were in fact dead, they carried on, changing nothing, being nothing, walking their gray lives along the rut in the ground.

Mortimer could live on no middle ground. The fact that his last fight had reduced him nearly to ectoplasm terrified him. He had a nostalgia for himself. Now he toiled with the binoculars and cursed eagles who intervened between his eyes and the pleasure barge.

Harvard manned the boat, still alone with the boys on his way back to the cove dock. He did not want travelers. This was duly noted by half his friends, who had dressed less for the funeral than for the pontoon yacht ride and were ignored. Some had worked on the new craft and were angry. There can be no second maiden voyage, and having to wait on the shore struck them as rude and unfair. They watched these yard pups go solemnly with him in their new little-man suits; many groused.

Mortimer, with the big Pakistani blade, walked slowly, bently down to the cove. He saw the willow sticks budding where the snakes had lain. Where he had fallen and shrieked.

The pontoon boat chugged without hurry its three miles. The boys had never had this view and it made them children again, knowing where they lived from the water's point of view. They felt tiny and good. They were proud of themselves for holding out against this waving mass their long years.

"Hidey," said Mortimer from the winter willows. "You ain't trying to land on my side of this lake over here, are you?"

They saw the big blade and were only thirty feet from his face.

The head was floating toward them, the singer's tall waved gray hair and the smaller creased face. He might now be Earl Clyde, lounge hawker and crooner, sixty-five and still going, reaching deeper and deeper into his throat for a tune. They saw the blade but then only his shoes, a spangling black pair of opera slippers. Could they be? Only Harvard knew what they were and doubted his eyes.

Who could remember a gun in a launch amid boarding his wife's casket, the funeral, the suiting up of the boys, the pouts of old friends when they couldn't come aboard, the sermon and music by bike scum, one of them with a black tattooed cross on his cheek? Who could remember?

The boys had the pistol. They had never forgotten. Isaac raised it, the original bullets in it. Five of the eight went off, but the child was no shooter. So he got Mortimer only once through the earlobe on the left, which hurt a great deal. His hand went to his ear and he howled briefly, the blade spinning as he let it go, nicking him across the shin.

Harvard saw a great deal of smoke for such a small black gun. He could not believe any of the five shots had hit nearly what was meant by it. He wheeled the boat into the dock but was all over the place, like a semitrailer on ice, berthing it.

He recalled the head shrieking in the willow sticks and now the thin body beneath and the opera slippers dancing on the early spring grass. The thing went up the hill like a black goat. The boys were fascinated. Mortimer was so much littler, benter. He could not move very fast, but he loped now to his car, holding his ear.

Harvard docked the boat with their help on the lines. He was having a stupid dream in which the boys were not at fault. He wasn't over the shock of Isaac firing the weapon. He was no longer particularly sad or angry.

Melanie, outside her kitchen door, looked down to them with a hand over her eyes against the western sun. She waved.

She was dressed well, in black. He didn't know whether she had been to the funeral. But he had been conscious of her the entire day. Released to feel what he would.

SIXTEEN

IN THE BAIT STORE THE PARENTS OF MAN MORTIMER were waiting. Lloyd, Edie and little Marcine were in the store too, with the elder Mortimers, who had just shown up at the car agency. They had come in a long old Ford wagon with canaries caged in the back. The gang was fascinated.

Mortimer ignored the long car, which had wandered slowly and sadly but stubbornly down from Missouri. When he burst in all sick and bloody and woofing, his short gray parents quailed, anxious in their thick spectacles, leisure wear, hard shoes. They would have worn stilts had that been the style when they were thirty. The father spoke.

"We'd heard you were doing so well. We were going to ask you up to Branson to hear a concert with us. Before we die. The Oak Ridge Boys are back to doing gospel." Then the father saw the blood, the muddy patent-leather opera slippers. He saw Mortimer was not ripe for a concert right now and was not young.

Just a scratch, Mortimer insisted. He had shot himself hunting for snakes. He'd gotten bored and went down to get himself a few snakes. He guessed he was old enough to think about those nasty old guns now, but he'd forgotten how they could turn on you. He'd learned his lesson. Only got three small snakes anyhow. He felt a boy in front of these elders, sick and pouted out, puffy.

Big Lloyd came outside, where Harvard waited with the boys at the bottom of the steps. In their suits they seemed to have trailed Mortimer to be of service. And in fact they brought his great Pakistani knife to him, muddy at the golden gills.

"Is that your sword?" asked Lloyd of Harvard, who held it like a trowel.

"He dropped this knife-thing on the ground when he was hurt," said Jacob. They handed the gaudy medieval blade over to Lloyd. They seemed a crew of pleasant neighbors doing what they could. Lloyd huge and bald in a tan leather suit.

"You can go home, and I know Mr. Mortimer will thank you."

"He don't have to get anywhere nigh that close," said Jacob. "We ain't got a home anyway. He don't seem like he used to be when he was our mama's boyfriend and had all this money and a different car every week. He ain't old and ruint or anything, is he?"

"Don't you worry. He's the same. He's had some bad luck."

"Is he shot in the ear or the head?"

"Only the ear, son. We'll see you now."

"It was an accident."

"I know that. He told us."

Lloyd went in, closing the door. Marcine then came out on the steps. She was seventeen but looked twenty-one, pleasantly dressed like a secretary to a spangling car-agency showroom, which Bertha was training her to be. Her hair was naturally brown and full and French-cut. She thought she knew the boys and the grandfather guy.

"You boys live here?"

"No."

"What house?"

"We got many houses. Nature. Porches. Sleeping bags. On the water. Wherever."

"You dress in suits a lot?"

"There was a funeral. His wife."

"I express my regrets. I bet she was pretty and kind."

Marcine looked across the short valley and saw Melanie Wooten standing on her kitchen walk and holding her white hair with one hand in the breeze, still looking Harvard's way, concerned. But in her church-funeral outfit, black with white pearls at her neck. That woman didn't die. That's good, thought Marcine, stunned by this vision across the tops of the sycamores and giant willows. She loved Melanie even more for still living. The points of early spring greening around her.

Inside, Man Mortimer was mellower, gracious even. A fresh towel to his ear, he was expatiating on the foolishness of guns, their cowardice, their chicken distances to things, the modern cheap craven world. With adrenal glands open yet, flooding away, he asked his seated parents whose old Ford wagon that was out there.

"It's ours," said his mother. She was uneasy. There is no behavior for a woman in a bait store unless she fishes. The racks of prophylactics near Mother Mortimer were huge, next to brassy naked covers of magazines in plastic thermal seals. Vixen eyes of large destruction.

"Well, get your birds and bags out for Lloyd. He'll drive it in the lake tomorrow. I've got something else for you. Like new. I'm putting you up at the casino hotel, first-class, long as you want. All my houses are under construction, repairs. But we'll give a party. A fine band. We don't have to travel to Branson, Missouri, to any concert. Good as the Oaks are. They'll be by here soon, unless they find out you're here and too wild for 'em."

They did not pick up on this joke, but he was their boy all over again. Mortimer felt this too, and this time he liked it, wounded, hiding his fury.

"Son, you're badly hurt," said his father. His mother touched him. She had been cleaving to her husband. Edie, middle-aged but with long good legs, got Mortimer out the door and drove him to the clinic, then home to Rolling Fork.

"Man comes back soon, Mrs. Mortimer. Don't worry. His business is big. Big, big. It wears on him, but he's a blue-steel spring," said Lloyd.

When Sidney at last came in the store, half drunk and full of funeral gossip, Mortimer's parents and Lloyd and Marcine had gone. But he saw the blood on the floor and heard tales from Pete Wren, who knew little but shared it anyway. He did know that Mortimer was hurt and that his parents had come down for him.

"He's getting weaker. I could own it all," Sidney whispered.

In a black Ford Expedition, alone, was Bertha, dead now. The windows were smoked, nobody knew for a long while she was there. She had swallowed Valiums and barbiturates with a cold quart of Country Club. Saliva webbed down her chin. She just couldn't take it anymore. Her age, who she was, holding the smiles till her cheeks hurt. Leading Marcine into the life. Several hours would pass before any thought to find her, because she was like good old furniture to hand. She was cordial always, yet a quiet one too, and well dressed and combed to the end. Peden wanted her badly. He thought to save her and missed by one day. Their date would have been the day after Nita's funeral. Gone. Blood now to her belly and the rigor passing through the smile.

Harvard backed the barge away from the pier and the boys, ever quick, helped on the lines. They wanted to drive, but he was making them watch carefully. He was afraid of being close to Melanie, so they sailed downshore to his own lawn and berthed on the grass. Although the launch was mainly his project, there were several zealous pilots and many of them keen to impress their own friends who were gathered to this beauty. But Harvard did not care. He would have his grief and his boys.

They went first to the room where Nita had died and took the flowers to all parts of the house so they could see them while they ate and talked.

Another funeral at the church. Preached by Byron Egan. Peden, heart breaking, was not allowed in. Egan did not want him to see Lloyd, Edie, Marcine; the other whores and reivers, black and white; car thieves wearing white socks with suits and thick rubber-soled cross-trainers. Speed and grip. Peden sat outside in the bleak blue Nissan. He listened through a window and held his gun.

Many robins got in the church from the trees and roosted among the congregation. They were drunk from some berries and fallen persimmons. Come into the mead hall out of the chill. In Viking history, once a Christian described human life as the flight of a bird through the mead hall. The outerness afterward, eternity.

The relations of Bertha sat in one sullen and miserable huddle in the front pews. Ronny the body-shop man was among them, barely recognizing his old girlfriend Marcine. Man Mortimer and his parents sat right behind them, concerned and prim in black and white mourning clothes newly bought in town. This was not New Orleans, where they knew best how to mourn drug addicts, evening ladies and jazz mothers. This place had none of that city's archaeology of concentrated sin.

Bertha's casket was open because she was at peace and made lovely by the beautician's touch. The beautician was her weeping but fastidious cousin Elka, who wanted in the Mortimer business. She wanted to take Bertha's place and knew well what she did besides shift car papers. She knew she could be tough and loved to fornicate anyhow. Elka wore white and pink today and sat near a quartet with whom she was committing three-cornered adultery.

Elka used to run in a circle of lower-Delta party girls who performed on crop dusters while they were flying and poisoning, just for the memory. Under the telephone wires, up quick. Then down for the gin and Costume Ball of the Scots in Panther Burn. Or dynamiting with bachelors in Robinsonville, making new homes in old levees and Indian mounds, where whole old guys might come out, and their pots.

Sidney Farté was in attendance to pick up his rumors. Many thought Bertha had killed herself because Sidney had been with her, and Sidney spread this rumor around as fact.

Frank Booth sat beside Ruthna, motionless. She had told him she knew Bertha and really loved her. Had once roomed with her at the Olympics in Atlanta. Booth was there for Ruthna, and to confront Man Mortimer with what he was now, a Conway Twitty face fresher than Mortimer's own, unlined. Nobody knew what Booth had on his mind, although Edie, who always carried a North American .22 Magnum derringer, promised to blow his head off if he came near Mortimer in his feeble condition and new black ear. Especially with his parents visiting or maybe even come to live, and he was surviving by their ignorant ministrations as he brought them here and there to bits of his empire in the lower Delta and in Vicksburg. They were amazed the river was so wide, having never expended the energy to look at it directly in Missouri. They recalled only fearing it and now feared it more. They were eighty. They had retired in good financial condition, but it meant little to them with no son, no hobbies and the new small house. No chickens inside city limits anymore. They had been sad for thirty years and wondered how especially terrible they were that he had run away from them. They went to church often and desperately and watched *Help Me* on television, in case he called out or somebody found *them*.

Now they had found him, they dreamed separately that Man Mortimer was not a nice person, and they tried to force a good dream about him, but it would not come. Then they began to remember how selfish a child he had been. Yet their love loved this too. They recalled that he was vicious, calculating and secretive, and they could see right through his present act, yokels that they were, and parents, at this very funeral. His counterfeited sorrow for Bertha. Still they loved. It was too late not to love, and it did not matter anymore where they themselves were. It was having him close, that was what life was for in the end. It mattered not where they slept. They barely wrinkled the bedspreads in the Gold Bowl room he got for them, mermaids on the wallpaper. Mrs. Mortimer's canaries thrived. The maid found the Mortimers so lost she took them on as a project. And they must help him, their son.

It was very intimate here, at the Church of Open Doors, open for the lost and dead of all causes. Raymond sat next to Mimi, his temples gray now and growing hair behind, as if to take up the ponytail Egan had shaved. He was disconsolate near the man who had stabbed him. He had tried to forgive him, but not very hard. He wished to be taken into a different room of heaven with Mortimer's blood on his hands. He did not require whole salvation, just a little table with books and coffee, pens and paper, the saxophone. Now Mortimer was little and sick. The monster Lloyd was close to him. Raymond hid his murderous thoughts from Mimi, who had dressed up to hide her impatient body. Long dress, lapels. She had no allegiances here. She was weary of Raymond. Weary of the band. Of herself. Of the lake. Why were they still here?

Then she remembered. They had no money. Even nature palled when you had no money. Nature was without religion sometimes when you looked at it poor, and all the creatures seemed bedraggled and begging, hardly getting by. You saw a fat one and wondered. Where was she getting her orders? They had the church. Then there was other money coming, the CDs, but that had proved a more difficult game than Raymond thought. He would always find some money somewhere, she believed.

Mortimer seemed comfortable sitting by his parents, perhaps enjoying his slide to invalidism. Or coiling tighter. He did not know how to act at a funeral, so he looked tragic, but the effect was that of lurid grinning. Egan saw this and the face almost ruined his eulogy.

Which was that Bertha was quiet and unknown as in Gray's "Elegy in a Country Churchyard" and that she hurt even in her prosperity like "Richard Corey," the suicide who had it all, as others cursed their bad bread and envied him. Did God accept suicides? There was a case for His Own Son's hesitant suicide on this earth. And so much cloudiness here as to shut up the meaner of us who wanted to keep souls out of heaven. Heaven was many houses, very big and wide. Many mansions, many houses, as the savior promised us, or He would not have told us so in His words. Many and large. "May heaven rest her soul in a home she can decorate at leisure," Egan said. Some of the crowd laughed; most didn't care but loved a good send-off where you met others who were horny from close death like you, among food and drink afterward. Four were simply dying for a smoke and had no opinion right now of God or the century just passed or Bertha. Bertha's mother would weep later, with a Marlboro Light inhaled and going.

Max Raymond suddenly knew his vision would come at the end of his life and not a moment before. He was nearly blinded by the realization that he was a nuisance to both God and man. He repented. He would act. He felt expendable to a higher power and this was good. He was resigned but in no way sad. He thought of Bertha as she went now, and he prayed to her in that black paradise.

Elsewhere Ulrich watched Melanie's greyhound. He couldn't get over it. He loved the face of this gentle beast, hunched as if alarmed by its own aerodynamics, its eyes sliding away, seeking affection as if its whole soul were poised on ice and betrayal lurked beneath each footfall. Of course Ulrich wept, but not too much.

"Where do you live, son?" Mortimer's mother asked. They were seated at a restaurant under the bluffs in Vicksburg. Beneath its foundation, it was said, were many who had received fire from Federal gunboats, who were losing to the rebel artillery very badly in 1863. Hundreds of bombs and cannonballs fired from the gunboats, many of them on fire or in other distress. Attack from the water was impossible, and even running the water was deathly. The river lit at night with all kinds of barrel flares and wrecks, perfect for gunners who could knock the heads off chickens at a mile. Lord God, war was fun for a while, till it crept up on you.

Now the riverbed's mass grave held a high-beamed, wide-planked bar and grill, that served oysters, fish and pizzas, and fresh salads from gardens nearby, fine French bread twists. Mortimer liked the lassitude here in the ferns and shadowed glass, as if the dead boys dancing with death had built it just for him 135 years later in a flush Vicksburg, very paved and rolling. Thinking of those good boys and their wails really widened the head for thought.

Mortimer looked benevolently at his mother, but this look was another unnatural one for him and he wound up grinning like a coon. He didn't like to be alone with them because they were getting heavier on him with questions, since they knew nothing beyond their county. They had no life except breathe the old air and sleep again. Mortimer thought, *I don't know anybody even nearly this old except the fools at the pier and Sidney,* who was growing younger, curiously.

"I have several homes. The construction has been slowed by the rains."

"Why do you lie, son? It ain't rained," said his father. "We don't care if you live in a palace or a doghouse."

"It has rained where they are. They're in other counties, spread out. I haven't got them ready for guest occupation. Can't you wait? The Gold Bowl too racy for you? You're afraid of gamblers and performers getting under the door?"

"No. We don't even want to go to your house except to be closer to you. That doesn't matter. We only want to know more about you and your life and friends. You know we have money. We have nothing but patience. We try to not even be here. I know that to you we are plants and hardly animals, son." Mortimer glanced up at his father in shock. Not a finer man in the county than whatshisname, your postman dad.

His mother came in. "Yes. Why do you get shot?"

"I don't get shot. I shot myself hunting snakes."

"We never saw no gun. We saw that weird chopping dagger."

"Don't lie again. We're old enough to smell out these stories, they don't save us anything painful. They're hard on us, they hurt. There's no cause for lies here. Even if you were a gangster, a car thief or married to several women at once. We came to love and have you. Our right."

"I'm a lot too old myself to have to tell everything to my folks." Mortimer spoke to the side of his parents' ready faces.

"I guess you always were. Old that way," answered his mother. They saw him now after long staring, and he didn't like it one bit. But on the other hand, he liked being the suspicious boy, charged with secrets, staring out at the rain and the chickens with tears in his eyes.

Sheriff Facetto and Melanie walked in along with Harold and Dee Allison. The married woman was using the last name Laird now, neither happy nor unhappy about the new echo of herself. *Dee A. Laird.* They sat very close to Mortimer and his parents before they knew who was there, at booth two over near an aquarium of riverine life and the oyster bar. The parents remained unfazed when Dee and the others saw them. Bland mysteries, aged, to the arrivals. They seemed too soft for him even now when he was ill and hurt. Perhaps they were his angels, his salt of the earth, as all men have somewhere. Or perhaps they were midwestern corn money, that very serious corn money you heard about, come down to blow some at the casinos.

The sheriff stared at Mortimer, and Mortimer knew he would do something merry and humiliating to this boy soon. He looked Dee over slowly as if he were a total devoted stranger. Recalling their nights. Dee was looking no-where, then suddenly directly at him.

Harold had gained weight in his shoulders, his fore-arms were muscular, his brow and spectacles, new, were intent. Serious mechanic, his own business, his own solid woman.

The sheriff wondered how Mortimer was hustling these old people of the Corn Belt. They dressed in checks and hard shoes. They might be Creationists gambling for their church fund. He had encountered this oddness a few times. They won too. Seemed to have a system or better prayers. What changes the man had, even looking now like that lounge comic with the enormous head and hair, Brother Dave Gardner. Weird interpretations of the Bible, impres-sions of crashing yokels who couldn't handle technology.

Harold was into a long declamation on mechanics, and it gave the sheriff time to think. His woman was drunk, and he was deeply in love with her. Her white hair was in some disorder, and he did not know what to do. He was adoring the world more and yet losing in the eyes of men, and this was plain in the sad look he gave himself in the mirror each morning as he combed his short hair. He wanted a smart marine look. Acting, acting, he was a ham and never denied it. Several still loved him for it, especially women he did not respond to at all. The only one who moved him was Melanie Wooten. Maybe he was making up for his failure to save his mother from his father, who had them both cowed. He didn't care. He was at the end of his sheriff's term and opposed by a very tough dumb man with a history of penal administration. Hoover "Who" Hooks put his post-ers up quick. "Who" despised Facetto.

Crime was not particularly rampant, in fact it was calm, but Hoover insisted Facetto was lax. He wanted pawn-

shop spies, vigilante groups against whores parked in neigh-
borhoods, did Hooks. He derided Facetto as a schoolmarmy
dramatist whose body was in too good a shape for him to be
doing his job.

"Who" accused him of wearing Man Tan and shining his haircut.

The subject of Melanie Wooten also had floated to
"Who," and a campaign of rumor began, to the effect that
Facetto was deeply odd. Melanie was aware of her bad name,
and she drank.

Dee did not get around much anymore. She was a
bit softer if not heavier. Inside she suffered high winds, terrible lightning and hail. She saw pictures that would not stop,
the dead and wrecked, children, guns, high explosives, felt
hellish thunder. She stared as if down a string of blocks
through a town flattened by a tornado. She saw Mortimer
holding an oyster on a tine, dipping it in Tabasco, hunting
her with glances.

Facetto could hardly believe this man had come toward him a few months before on a Norton Commando
motorcycle like his own, in Mountie boots, laughing like a
twin. The man who had wanted to join the nonexistent
launch club after he fell shrieking into the snakes.

"Dee?" Melanie asked brightly, "how's your thing?
I mean, when you really get down to it, we old things want
to keep up."

Dee smiled for the first time in the evening. Mortimer's table had heard.

"Is she a harlot?" whispered his father.

"She's my woman," whispered Mortimer. "The
younger one. The old lady's just drunk and lively. She can't
stay away, Dee Allison. Married now, but we belong
together."

They were relieved, truly, that he had at last confessed to something clandestine. They had made way. They were loving him.

"Is there a tragedy in this situation?" asked his mother. She looked like an old pie somebody had drawn in, he thought.

Mortimer's empire was collapsing. Reduced to a showroom of fairly new SUVs, with some older models stolen from the coasts and Chicago. Some women, twenty-nine actually, roaming three counties. A junkyard, prosperous for junkyards. He wandered to his houses and they did not comfort him. The large-screen television in his bare Clinton home.

I got to get Peden where he lives, he vowed. *I see him letting his debt to me go, as if it was canceled when he whipped me.*

Who will I be serving in my older years? he thought suddenly. *Where will I be? Still home, counting my money and wondering what to give it to? Maybe the orphans. I could go straight and healthy after all this, I could make it. Just thinking of it makes me feel better. Using my talents, growing toward a light. I'm old history around here, and history itself must feel uncomfortable a right good part of the time. It's been good brooding here at the table, staring at Dee and hearing that old lady drunk. The world turning new for you.*

The world's a little thing, he concluded as his cognac came. *Peden owes me and he lost my car. He lost my history, worse, and he should learn how to suffer now.*

They're going to catch me one day, or I'm just going to walk in and give them my story, calm as a bard of old. Then it'll be over when I say it is. Maybe old sheriff boy could play the sheriff in the movie. I'd let him, I'd smile. Another way of his being mine.

A local college-age boy walked right up to the table where Mortimer sat with his parents, who were almost asleep from the unusual big dinner. "I know who you look like, but you'd have to be dead. Brother Dave Gardner. My dad played all his albums. Thought he was the funniest man in the world. Are you related?"

"Get out of here with that. I don't like you this close to my face. You understand me?"

His parents awoke to this talk and were frightened.

Ulrich had lost the dogs, or the dogs had lost him. The late-spring air was too thick for him and he worked, shouted, then stumbled toward the cool shade and ferned banks of Green Trout Creek. Then he was a bit lost himself. His compass became stars as his lungs fought for air, and he blacked out before he could turn up the oxygen on the bottle at his waist. What was left of his lungs after the cigarettes smoked since the days of German jet airplanes? When he revived, he wisely followed the creek toward the highway, but he wound up a mile west of the Raymonds' house. He tried to call the dogs again but could make no sound. It was his intention that morning to give them a good forest run, then wash his favorite dog and give it to Mortimer. All his plans went bust now. The dogs never ran away from him of a sudden like this.

Ulrich was very sick, staggering. He was terrified that ruthless deer hunters would kidnap his dogs for deer season next fall, then either shoot or abandon them, as they had done many times before. He knew all the dogs' names. He sent telepathy to them. Prayers, really. He knew he could not remain horrified much longer and live. He must get cool, take off clothes, get in the water maybe, strike his fist against his chest. They were smart dogs. He was the dummy. He had petted them too much.

Then he thought he saw a woman in a flowery dress in an alley of tall grass. Almost a flag, and foreign.

All his years came to right here. He began breathing again.

"Old man, who are you?" asked the woman's voice, unafraid, only curious. His sight was blurring. But he knew she would be a pleasant woman. Her hair would be black like the dress with flowers. She would be foreign to America but at ease.

"We smokers must be helpful to each other," she said coming up. She held a long, lit Winston.

"I'm a pitiful lost man. Lost my dogs. Maybe my life, running after them." He could not recall a personality for himself before the blackout. "I need help, I think."

It was Mimi Suarez. She was serene in her black flowered dress on a hot spring day, even in this vale of mosquitoes. Ulrich knew he was alive when her shoulders gave him pause. Spilling ringlets to her clavicle.

"I think I might be dying," whispered Ulrich. As fatigue and repetition prepare men for death until they seek it, Ulrich felt a final tiredness. No pressing on, no other place. He sat down and all of his failures went past in a brief caravan beyond him.

The woman rested with him on a stump where he sat with his oxygen bottle. He thought of the dogs again. He thought he heard them whimpering not far off.

"You decide," she suggested. "Either go ahead or stay behind for others. My grandmother in Cuba, and still there, told me this once when I was a little girl with an awful disease, a high fever. Only a few pictures in my young head, and them already mixed with dreams of my future in the U.S.A. I didn't know what they were, but here I am having them. The fever left, here I am."

They both smelled something very sweet and bad, and they heard the dogs running and whining below an old pecan farm, which had once had a mansion to go with it. Fever and then the Depression finished it off. The pecans themselves were enormous. Up to the grove was beige wheat. They saw the dogs now, and Ulrich pulled himself up with Mimi's help, grasped his bottle. Got a bigger blast into his lungs. They made their way.

This was where they found the little girl's T-shirt, cut to shreds, thrown over human dung, lying on an anthill a foot high. Ants were all over it. The dogs were circling and very concerned, but they had not torn the shirt. They were circling, and it was plain they were in the deepest grief over the child's shirt.

It is this place where Ulrich died.

Little Irma.

Who had recently, during her flight, talked to the boys on Harvard's lawn. She knew she was pursued by Malcolm, but he was crippled and she did not think he would kill her once he caught her. She was starved, skinny and alone. Malcolm would not let her have her own suicide like Bertha's. She was on the way to becoming Bertha, she had come to the orphans' camp with suicidal urges, which she had acted on twice in Indianapolis when she had living parents.

She stumbled upon the Allison boys in Harvard's driveway busting up a long-dead pecan limb for the simple reason that it was whole. She did not know where she was, but the house was so wide and nice, with its pine-needled lawn, that she thought it might be a church or a fort, and she dreamed of it as if it were in a book right before her. She had had friends who lived in such homes, but it seemed two eras ago. She was playing Ping-Pong in a garage of one in Indianapolis and an old man came out of the house and said, "I see it now, child. You will become a medical missionary somewhere and be a great woman." He was the grandfather of the house, and she took him for mad and giggled along with her playmate, but now it seemed a deep saying and a future waiting on her, if she could walk out of here now, away from Malcolm, who claimed to love her, him an old hairy man.

He loved Irma, but it was Mimi Suarez he wanted and her husband he wanted to exterminate. He was lost in waves of passion. Driving him down a gray wall. Like those motorcyclists in the velodromes at the state fair.

The boys looked like they belonged here, and she was encouraged, even in her weakness. They were her age, native to this boondockery. The pines, the briars. She felt like a ruined hibiscus, the most exotic plant she knew. Stomped, gums bleeding, perhaps white around the mouth.

"You an orphan?" Jacob asked her.

"Yeah, I'm an orphan, a real orphan, on the move. Nobody stops me," Irma said. She almost fainted but smiled.

"Are they after you?"

"One man. I think I'm on my way to being a medical missionary."

"You real skinny and pale. We'll get you a cola."

"All right."

Jacob went off to the house and Harvard came out on the porch, but it was not clear he could make her out at this distance. A big old smooth yard.

She sat on the lawn in a sweaty Big Mart T-shirt with a little cartoon girl and an enormous flower on it. This cartoon girl had big eyes. *I will work with tiny orphans like her on my shirt,* thought Irma. *There's so much I could tell her.* Jacob returned with a cold wet towel and she pressed it to her face and arms, then stomach. They watched her belly button with no apology. It was pretty, a deep tunneled shadow. She also had the buds of breasts in the cartoon shirt. It unsettled the boys, the idea of her, their age. They weren't ready to be like her. In fact, they were closer to infants.

"You couldn't live here like us, but you could stay and play with the boats Doc Harvard made us for a while till they came got you. Eat some popcorn and get ice from the machine on the refrigerator," said Jacob.

"No. I have to walk on." She was in a dream and taking care of foreign children in it.

When she walked away, she had only enough energy to last for the mission. She believed health would rise in her as it had many times before. *I could begin with those boys. I will tell them about Jesus and Mary. How they are better than parents.*

Irma suddenly heard something after a mile in the woods. She wondered if there were great apes left in these thick woods, with its little alleys of sawgrass. Then she knew it was Malcolm thrashing toward her. A thing fighting its own sweat, tall pink stumbling, hair streaming.

Irma knew he was coming from her dream mission in the foreign lands. She said to the thing, "Go ahead and eat me."

"You notice anything new about me?" asked Malcolm.

She took off.

"You ran and made me mad, now," panted Malcolm, covered in burrs and scratches. "You ain't got nothing but me now. You want to see my new moves." She ran as he was beset by an attack of diarrhea over an ant mound.

Mortimer, all he did was look. Betsy had a book about Conway Twitty. This man had changed his name from something like Vernon to Conway Twitty, from the names of two ugly towns in Arkansas and Texas. Or because he had a sense of humor, but by his eyes she did not think so, if photographs told the truth. He was a family man, upright, embarrassed by lewdness or even rumor, although he was sexy with his tunes, the writer wrote. Mortimer sat across the room watching the gigantic Japanese television while Betsy read. She tried to find Twitty in his bone structure.

She did not think of this, but it was a strictly adolescent house they occupied, nothing but a few sticks of furniture and thick throw rugs and the giant-screen television, sloppy at the base with mixed videos. Not a plant or even salt. Loaded with snacks and sodas. Otherwise a clean kitchen, no odor except the smell of manufacture.

"I will tell your mother and father what you do with me," she said once.

"You're not even going to see them. Don't be an idiot. You're not here against your will."

"Some of it. I'm thirteen."

"Get back in the book. Nobody's hurt you."

"You and me, old man, are orphans from normal. Remember? But I can change."

"Stay quiet and you can be anything you want."

"We'll see."

A curious pause on the front porch of the bait store. Mortimer's yellow Lexus parked, no others. Dark clouds but not a speck of rain, only this deep shadow. Raymond and Roman could see Mortimer and Sidney at the counter inside peering into a glass-lidded case full of knives on velvet. They seemed at church. Not yet touching these treasures.

See this little man, the high wavy bush of hair, the thin ankles in tasseled and buckled moccasins that seemed trimmed with actual coral snakeskin. Raymond and Roman had meant to buy supplies for crappie fishing on Harvard's launch, then have some talk of cancer, music, the history of Roman's Indian tribe, Jesus Christ as a man of the whip, taking time to make it right there in the temple. Raymond had not known a black man since the days of southern apartheid, although he called their names.

The fifties. In Raymond's small town, there was a tiny college campus on which the faculty and students lived in three-storied Edwardian brick houses. The snow and then vicious ice had been on three days, a storm of the century for where they lived, in southern Mississippi near the capital city. A professor's house caught fire. He was a veteran and had brought back live German rounds and weaponry in glass cases. It was not clear whether he just taught Nazis or taught them because he loved them, their flags, their helmets. Much of this ambiguity in the early fifties.

The water pipes were frozen. Nothing to do but throw snowballs into the fire engulfing the professor's house. Then they saw the glass cases, and the bullets began exploding. Two men were scraped, the crowd widened. A hopeless single fire truck, officious yokels wringing their hands but having fun too. Germany rearing up on three stories and blowing its flak around. Raymond had no better memory. That evening of the fire and the booms and the thrilled citizens, a bullet of the Reich could touch anybody. The professor might be in there, on fire and lecturing.

What I am, thought Max Raymond suddenly, *is an overprepared man. Here I am back at the burning place, where I keep returning ever since I was eleven. Shiloh. Where man meets God, but the man has come too early and wearing the wrong things. I have suffered.* If you are able to explain suffering, a man once told him, you weren't really there.

Raymond stood ashamed before Mortimer. A bootlicker to a phantom.

John Roman was also humiliated to meet his attacker. Getting shot was nothing like this. This little man had his number.

"Hello, Man," Roman said, surprising himself. He and Raymond watched Mortimer climbing down from the stool. A head with his wig, exempted from blame, by a shape totally shifted into sickness. He might as well be a little girl, almost unbalanced by his large hair. Maybe he didn't remember Roman.

Raymond and Roman moved off as Mortimer and Sidney laid hands on the glass. Eloquent hilts. Arcs and stilettos, a near sickle, smaller but heavy in the blade like a bolo. A sickness sat in the room, which they each seemed to have agreed not to discuss. Their faces blank, the men acted as though they had never met.

Mortimer said something had to be done, these evil children were all over the place. Uptown, other towns. Some had been making nude movies, was the rumor. Nobody had much shame left. Mortimer smiled ear to ear.

"I picked you up this tonic. Brings up the immune system, said the old boy at the herb store. I'm feeling better for it myself. Feistier. Heart's back in my projects," Man said.

"You ain't looking it. You poorly."

"We ain't old yet."

"I am, and sick as a dog," Sidney lied. He awoke nowadays with a fine mean on.

But Sidney knew sickness. The way you could sink inside yourself and worship it. Shock them by your dilapidation yet refuse to fall.

Mortimer's people had changed too. They were not as stupid as he thought. They had their own righteousness. They were no longer amazed by the excesses of his career. The SUVs, the strange empty homes, the small film production concern in Clinton. He knew they expected sin close to him. When he left for business, he saw pain in their looks.

His old man was interested most in the junkyard, where he played quarter poker with Peden. His man Peden, in the shotgun house, whom Mortimer was allowing to live unmaimed. Peden and Mr. Mortimer played cards and talked fifties automobiles.

Mortimer tried to find his mother a hobby, but her eyesight was not good and she preferred silence. It bathed her, she said. She loved telling clean, pointless stories in which her struggles were the only memorable thing. Changing a tire on her own and finding a neighborhood dog nestled in with a family of coyotes. The old woman had insight too. When he brought little Irma past his folks at his SUV agency and told them she was the granddaughter of a client, Mrs. Mortimer's face went red.

Still, she said they loved him and owed him for being stupid about his needs in Missouri. She agreed how a chicken yard in back could humiliate a boy who needed cars and girlfriends. How they went to church too much, expecting the pastor to correct all troubles straight from the pulpit, and how some of these pastors were fools who had barely entered life before they began announcing on it. She hugged Mortimer over and over now, commenting on his new white hair.

He felt something for her and his father. It was intense, this feeling, a fresh one for him. Made him nervous and awkward around them. He gave aid needlessly, as out of a tube of charity inside his heart. He sat with them, saying nothing, three porch-bound elders watching for cars at the four-way stop.

At the house Mortimer finally had finished for them in Rolling Fork, they sat for three hours without a peep. Mortimer's new shoes the only true expression hereabouts. Penny loafers, black, the leather stamped with leaping trout.

The house was plush leather furniture, gold and bright copper hardware set next to black for kitchen and bathroom fixtures. Stinking of fiberglass and new wool on the floors.

After the silence, while he was leaving, he said, "I'm happy we got all that cleared up."

They laughed their first laugh together.

Mortimer drove to Big Mart to buy his mother flowers for her sitting room where she actually sat as if friends might arrive any second. He pulled up behind a man loading topsoil. Mortimer thought he recognized him, Bertha's nephew Ronny, whose body shop he had used. The man did not know who Mortimer was, now in a Rolls Land Rover stolen in San Francisco. The man kept loading the topsoil in front of Mortimer's windshield, with his car door out in the passing lane. Mortimer could not move, yet he was practicing patience, thought, depth. Then he put his face out the window and asked, "Would you shut the door so I can get by, please?"

A look of disgust crossed the man's face. Mortimer reached to his ashtray, put on his new ring. He had lately been interested in the concept of *irony*. How on the face of others it meant insult, such as Pepper had shown him before his beheading. The man had figured Mortimer to be a small irrelevance. This man closed the car door with that irony on his face. He was, after all, a busy foreman at the body shop now. Who was this skinny sissy with big hair in his tank of a car? Mortimer saw all this. Then stopped his car in front of the man's. "Excuse me, sir. Would that be a look of *irony* on your face? Would you be giving me irony right now?"

"Tire iron, you say? No, I don't lend out."

At this Mortimer's right hand flew up and a ring-mounted razor swiped across the man's chin and lip so there was an awful amount of blood. The man squalled through a dark mustache of it dripping over his hands, at his chin, his jowls. "It's the rudeness, man. Everywhere. And you worked for me, forgot me, let your real self loose on me out here."

The man recognized him then. He was astounded by his thinness and wild high hair. Puny Italian sandals and no suitable beach sand for hundreds of miles.

Ronny watched for Mortimer's return and other strokes. Waited on the story of Mortimer's fury. He could not believe his own lips bore the tale, pouring down his shirtfront. He did not know why it had angered the man to find him ungiving about the tire iron.

Mortimer walked in on Peden and his father. They were paging through Peden's file box of calendar art. Motorcycles or cars with women. Lazing across a car hood, handlebars, a fender. On one a man's great tongue against thighs, scrawled there by a jokester. Worship of moving parts, combustion, bodies these two could covet. More than a spaceship or a moon landing, this local steel mesmerized them. No destination but the thing itself.

They barely recognized Mortimer.

"I need meth to tide me over. To end the blues and the nasty world out there. You know how it is, getting well," he began straight off.

"You at the wrong place. No meth for three years," Peden told Mortimer. He looked at Mr. Mortimer's face. "Even when I sold, you wouldn't find me at home doing it."

"Pawn guy said you holding."

"That man is dead, the holding man," said Peden.

"Peden is now a Christian minister. He won't even touch a beer," said Mr. Mortimer.

"Man, you got to help me past this day. I might kill myself. *Myself.*"

"Which pawnbroker?"

"The guy, man. Tattoos. Civil War sabers, metal detectors."

"Who are you?" asked Peden.

"C'mon. You know me."

"No I don't," said Peden.

"Everybody knows me."

"So?"

"I exist, man."

Mr. Mortimer gathered himself to Peden's side. "You could be a demon to be dealt with by the Lord."

"He would know me. He would."

"But I don't. You'll have to forgive me."

"I don't."

"I believe I killed somebody but it was in another country."

"God help you, you haven't gone anywhere," said Peden.

"I exist, man," said Mortimer.

"I took you for somebody you're nothing like. Now I can't remember *that* person. You're the demon itself. I've seen them before and you too," said Peden.

Peden looked at Mr. Mortimer, the father, who had made a noise. He was actually squirming, lost in humiliation. It had been thirty years since he had reckoned on the fact his son might be an absence, or all things present at once. Against the chickens in the back window, he had watched the profile of the boy and comprehended him as a dangerous nullity, although he could not have voiced this. He knew only that he had been frightened and should be dying of shame.

Egan approached the orphans' camp slowly. He had the dogs in the car. Ulrich's death had nearly broken him, and he thought what he would find at the camp might do the rest of the job. The camp was strangely silent and marks of destruction were everywhere. Two dead orphans were floating near the bridge to the northern entrance, shot at close range in the head.

Trembling Egan left the dogs in the car and crossed the bridge. Exploring the grounds, he saw no one, though he thought some orphans might be hiding in one of the buildings. Finally old Pete Wren waved to him and came out of the assembly hall. He was living at the camp lately as a counselor emeritus, had worn a bathrobe during the whole catastrophe. He told Egan everything had started because of some new arrivals: two big black inmates from Norfolk, Virginia, and Paterson, New Jersey, and a white boy from South Mississippi who had made himself an orphan, who had killed his own father after watching his mother die of alcoholism, but was exonerated. Wren seemed curiously calm but wouldn't stop the irrelevancies, Egan thought.

"I came over because I was inspired by the church services held by you and Peden that woke up a thing in me, to act, to do some good in my old age, because I stole my cousin's good name. It felt good to drive here and be taken right in. I slept the best sleeps I had slept in years on my hard simple cot.

"There weren't many rules. Before long, I began to find out there might not be *any* rules. Gene or Penny were always talking about love and trust at the center of the universe and how vigilant we should be against the Old World, as they called it, but the children didn't seem to listen. They also seemed to have sex a lot, and about where they wanted it, fairly loudly and known to the children, and I could not, for the life of me, decide the lesson in this because it did not appear purely natural man-and-wife devotion but a sort of scheduled thing like a cup of coffee. They said they had been instructed by the Ultimate Pain of the bad life they'd had before now.

"Then the orphans gathered and all moved into the main building one night. They said they weren't Oasis anymore. They were Ataxes, which spelled attack and from an axis of high consciousness about children or something like that. A new bad spirit was into them, little and big, led by those black boys and the boy who'd killed his father. Somebody took a random shot at Gene and Penny trying to start a sing-along. I thought the shot was a firecracker at first. The big boys said they had learned things about who was the enemy and they were getting down serious to it. Everybody on the other side of the lake was bad. They had been using the girls and enslaving them, then turning them away when they were hurt and no good to them anymore. Gene and Penny had to know about this and didn't tell them.

"One of the black boys, the one from Paterson, put a pistol right in Malcolm's face and kept it there. The smaller rough boy told him to sit in the chair. True, I have had my lifetime of trouble with black boys and men. They were rude, sassy, out-of-the-way tricky when a straight yes or no would do. Had all the tricks especially for old white men because I guess they want up on the old colonel of the plantation. Rheumy-eyed, can't take care of himself, looking for somebody to open the door for him. But a cigarette, is that too much to ask when they have a box in their pocket? Then you say you don't have a light, and they push out a dead lighter to you so you're lighting your cigarette but it's dead. These guys are rigged for whites like that when they're fifteen. Do they learn this at the knee of somebody, or at church, or special power groups? They'll go to prison and they come out with more cigarette tricks and are losing the war every day. Minister Farrakhan, can't he do something? They need love even with old bigots like me."

"Wren, you old fool, shut up," Egan said. "What happened here?"

"I'm saying it was them and Leopold, the white boy who killed his father. He was a Mississippi Irish criminal. You'll see a strain of that pop out in the best families who've been mild and rich for three generations. Then the guns come, the screams, murder and suicide. Anyway, Leopold was quiet but in command because he had the blood on him. What most in the world he hated was adults messing with children. He was some rough animal who had been passing for mild. You'd think only an inner city could breed that coldness and that easy killing. No manners, a hiss for a voice, and big dead eyes greener than green. Became his daddy's monster, a stroke of revenge, no mercy. He and the black boys twinned up in some awful memories together. They would say the war was coming, and in a war there was no guilt. Nobody would ever find out who did what in a war. You had freedom to kill and hurt your slave masters. Nobody looked at me, and I'm glad they didn't.

"They kept Gene and Penny on the movie stage and accused them of being depraved. Penny began weeping, then told how much they had sacrificed, her and Gene. 'You are the child we lost, come back to us in many souls.

"'You done tore each other up getting your piece, which is slobbering on each other in front of children,' said the white father-killer. Then they nailed Gene and Penny in their room and began starving them.

"Then the three boys walked up on poor Malcolm. They hanged him on a tree right in the horse yard, but they were sloppy and Malcolm pulled up and hung on the limb before he choked. But hanging there was bad enough. They let him crawl down and live like it was what they meant. But he better never make a whimper. And he wouldn't."

"What were you doing while all this was going on?" Egan asked.

"I would say I was a mascot, too old for them to blame for anything. All I can brag to is I was around, in a corner or under a stage or in the projector room or the broom closet, and sometimes I held the scareder little ones on my lap.

"I don't believe the orphans are the ones who cut Penny's head nearly off. I was in the building where her and Gene's room was. I think it was Man Mortimer."

"Mortimer?" Egan shouted. "He was here?"

Wren said, "He was here, walked right through everything like a floating head of hair protected against gun lead and explosives. The orphans saw the pleasure boat approaching and opened fire, and the white father-killer had taught them how to shoot. Dr. Harvard was driving the boat with Mortimer and his mother in it, but he didn't seem a willing pilot. Large Lloyd and Edie were aboard too, Edie holding a derringer on Harvard. Harvard had an old shotgun with him and a few shells, and there was a snake pistol and flares in the survival locker. When the shooting started, Mortimer and Lloyd and Edie hit the deck and returned fire as Harvard tried to turn the boat around again, but Mortimer jumped off the boat and waded to shore. He didn't turn back as his mother fell dead on the bow.

"The older girls, that first pair in trouble with the video lesbian girls thing, were snapping those guns, one with a telescope on it. They wanted to hurt Mortimer personally, owed him. But he walked right ashore, and I can't imagine them not having a clean shot.

"It got to where I was making peace, I was a peace-maker. I brought back peace and trust in adult humans, kept them from setting the pleasure boat on fire a second time. I helped them out when it started settling down a little, waiting for the law, gathering ammunition, food and explosives, gasoline, moving barbed-wire fences. Even setting the moat on fire at one point because they'd seen it in the movies right there. You're the first person to come."

Egan took Wren back over the bridge and drove for Sheriff Facetto.

EPILOGUE

TWO MONTHS LATER FACETTO PULLED OUT THE ELECTION over "Who" Hooks, mainly because even the slow caught on to Hooks' own private hysteria toward the end, wherein he fired off a Glock automatic during a rally for crime-fighting. This was too ardent, and Facetto began looking sane.

Melanie was not in love with the man anymore and considered him an inept coward. She was annoyed by his breathy dramatic pauses and rises when he told her about arresting Mortimer and taking a deposition from Wren. This community's nightmare treated as if it were some trivial dramatic work that had floated past a theater workshop he was in. She told him he was childish and she did not want a child in the house anymore.

Sheriff Facetto was more than disconsolate. He ceased being.

On the complaint of the body-shop man Ronny, Facetto's deputy Bernard arrested Man Mortimer at his junkyard. Mortimer was looking for something among the wrecked cars. He told Bernard this arrest was impossible, since the whole county worked for him. Yet he was led away in cuffs as his father and Peden looked on.

Mortimer began telling his whole story then and would not be quiet.

Facetto would not look at his face during his confessions at the station. Looking at the ceiling, the sheriff at last told him to please be quiet, please.

"Nobody is listening to you anymore," said Facetto.

"But I am, sir," said Bernard.

"We've got plenty. Make him quit talking."

Facetto soon left town for a far, far state.

Mortimer would not stop talking in Parchman Prison, either. Nobody wanted him near them. The thing that was hardly anything but a big head with a mass of white hair on it kept reciting his misdeeds. And further, the discourtesy and irony you found so widely practiced. In all his years at the prison, he never got up to the death of his mother or walking through all that lead until he freed Gene and Penny. Nor Penny's death. The new sheriff was willing to accept the town's certainty that Mortimer was the killer and left it at that.

John Roman and Max Raymond drew closer together, but Roman did not want anybody talking with him while he fished, and he did not like talking God at all. His wife Bernice was well. He loved God cautiously. He did not know how long this love would last.

Harvard and Melanie were married by Peden on the pleasure barge. Their marriage was that of pals after a fight and long silence. It had become too late in time for fights, and often even memories. They clung.